HELSINKI GOLD

HELSINKI GOLD

. . .

Nathan Hebel

Helsinki Gold is a work of historical fiction. Apart from the well-known actual people, events, and locales that figure into the narrative, all names, characters, places, and incidents are products of the author's imagination or are used fictitiously.

Copyright © 2024 by Nathan Hebel
All rights reserved.
ISBN 979-8-3268-4877-2

For Dad

CHAPTER 1	Initiator	1
Interlude	*Sol*	13
CHAPTER 2	The Gadget	15
Interlude	*Mongolia*	36
CHAPTER 3	Alarm Clock	40
CHAPTER 4	The Sausage	43
Interlude	*Indiana*	49
CHAPTER 5	Staging	52
CHAPTER 6	Absorption	58
Interlude	*Kentucky*	68
CHAPTER 7	Ivy	71
CHAPTER 8	Saturation	81
Interlude	*West Virginia*	86
CHAPTER 9	The Shrimp	89
CHAPTER 10	Layer Cake	98
CHAPTER 11	Mass Defect	110
Interlude	*Atlantic*	128
CHAPTER 12	Radiate	130
CHAPTER 13	Tamper	142
CHAPTER 14	Strong Force	152
Interlude	*Belgium*	164
CHAPTER 15	The Super	167
Interlude	*Finland*	188
CHAPTER 16	Accretion	193
EPILOGUE	Winsome Cripps	205

Chapter 1 – Initiator

July 19, 1952 - Helsinki

KALLE STOOD AT the base of the concrete tower, apart from the rest of the detail. His gaze alternated between the ground in front of him and the clump of dignitaries surrounding the President. Men in pressed wool suits smiled with boredom.

Old Papi was in a foul mood. Kalle knew it without even looking at the man. The other faces on the security detail were enough. Hell, just looking up was enough. The sky had followed through on the threats of rain, dousing and muting the parade ground, the track, and well, everything. 70 flags ringed the stands, limp and heavy with water. The mismatched nylon rectangles clung to the poles despite a brisk wind, resulting in a meaningless jumble of colors. Surface tension on the steel had the upper hand for now.

Well into his eighties, President Paasikivi told anyone who would listen that he only had these Olympic Games on which to focus his waning energy and attention. These opening ceremonies in particular. Germany had ruined Finland's first chance at an Olympics in 1940 and now this lead plate overhead was darkening the do-over twelve years later.

Finland's grand welcome to the world was to open in just hours, and stewards stood by with air blowers and brooms, hoping to dry off the track at the first opportunity. No one deserved to walk through puddles in the opening parade after long travels from Greece, Antilles, Argentina, Australia, …

"You'll want to snap into focus pretty soon, Kalle." Henrik strode up with a casual air. "Just kidding, I don't give a shit. But as a suggestion, you don't want to leave a bad impression on your first time out with us. Old Papi doesn't want daydreaming on this day of all days." Rangy with meticulously unkempt black hair, Henrik wore the glinting expression of a schoolboy who thought he was the first to come up with the idea of pulling legs off of insects and tying tails of mice together.

Kalle squinted in response.

"Oh, I'm sure in the office you boys never call him that out loud. Think it, but never say it. Out here it's our game. The louder you say it the better, until he hears you of course. Then you're dead."

The rain shifted with the wind. The spatter encroached the space underneath the concrete awning. Everything else was wet here at Olympiastadion, and the VIP terrace overlooking the bowl of the fourteen-year-old structure was next on the list. A table loaded with refreshments stood just on the edge of this new line of rainfall. A young steward came over and hesitated. He grabbed an end as if to move the table further in but abandoned the idea and walked away. Kalle's squint completed to a full blink.

"Well, not dead dead. Worse. My old colleague Jarvon is still on Lapland patrol, chasing bears and talking to rabbits as far as I know."

Kalle resigned himself to the small talk that came with this new assignment. "Can you imagine the years of work Presi… Old Papi … put into this day only for Mother Nature to ruin it? I actually feel bad for him. It's embarrassing."

"What's to be embarrassed about?" laughed Henrik "This is standard procedure for Finland on the world stage. We find the most inconvenient way to screw up everything."

Kalle changed tack. "True. We shut down one of the tent villages already. 200 tents deployed for all the expected continental visitors, and how many showed up? Four. The OC screwed up the television broadcast contract, so the world will have read about it instead of seeing it. This whole thing has been a farce from the start. The rain is just the cherry on top."

Henrik nodded. "Well, all is not lost yet. I'd bet the old man will force the clouds to turn off the spigot in time by the sheer force of his willpower. You watch."

On cue, the rain intensified and the continuum of wet slaps on walls, floor, and boot-tops muffled the end of Henrik's prediction. The accumulating friends of the President and assorted staff milled about looking for something to do, waiting for action to be taken. For most, they just wanted to get the Games over with.

The open conversation gave Kalle a little space to vent. "Any particular reason I'm here today? I'm sure you know I don't have any protection duty experience. Of course everyone is being pressed into extra volunteer duties, but I was thinking of something more like taking tickets. In a booth. Out of the rain, you know. For example."

"Well, you're not here for your muscles, obviously. The word around the ministry is that your English is perfect, is that right?" asked Henrik.

"Well…"

"I'll just take that as a yes. I want you to protect the President from all the English-speaking assholes who are going to try to corner him for the next twelve hours. You hear as much as one "*howdy doody*" or "*Marshall Plan extension*" and you jump in. Throw your body in the middle of it if you have to. Even if it's Zeke. Especially if it's Zeke. Otherwise, just stay out of the way. Frankly, you're the only one that might get to do something today. Who would want to attack Old Papi?"

"Who's Zeke?" Of course Kalle knew, but Henrik seemed to be on a roll…

"Jesus Christ, it's true. You office boys really do have shit for brains. You'll know him when you see him. Well, you'll probably hear him first."

Henrik watched with amusement as a couple track stewards tested out their air blowers to predictable results. "Actually, the rain is perfect. Our Soviet comrades love to be miserable. Old Paavo will like it too. He'd light the flame in a blizzard with a smile on his face. Maybe we'll be able to run out the clock on this day after all. Well shit, I better take a leak before all the fun begins."

·

Doddering white-haired dignitaries dragged their humid clothes along the plaza at the base of the tower. Their flat expressions were offset over the rail by the growing buzz of the class IV crowd in the bowels of the stadium. Finns had descended on the standing room only section, complete with rubbers, calfskins, and the occasional transparent umbrella. It was a dense packing of individuals, strangers chattering with anticipation through the shower. Only 450 markka to get a peek of the best athletes in the world hosted by the best people in the world. Advance ticket sales abroad had been a complete failure, but word spread to the locals. A coming together of the world through sport? More like a coming together of Finns out of curiosity, pride, and good-spirited Midsummer tradition.

Henrik's prediction was not looking too good. The rain weakened but persisted. Dampness on the track coalesced in a smattering of small pockmark puddles, highlighting every minute imperfection of the supposedly smooth surface. A civil engineer's nightmare. The air blower corps was fully engaged but clearly outmatched. The stewards paced their nozzles through shorter and faster arcs, but their tense body language signaled the conclusion Kalle already knew from a quarter mile away: the puddles would stay.

"Henrik? Henrik! There's my man! I almost thought you were avoiding me. We've got to work on your English today. '*How are you? What is your name? Those shoes look very fashionable, but still practical.*' Whew, what a lovely Finnish summer day gents. I personally feel this is all a ruse to knock out us Americans with colds on day one – we're not used to this dampness. Two hours on a wet parade ground? No thank you. The spoils of old age? A roof, Henrik. A roof. Ha!" It seemed likely that Zeke had arrived.

Walking at a snap toward Zeke, Henrik called Kalle over with a glance. "Mr. Ambassador, it has been too long. You are right we have much English to catch up on. Never to be as good as your Finnish naturally." Henrik reached out for an enthusiastic handshake. "You will be pleased to know I have it on good authority that the sun will be poking out shortly. That should save your boys the trouble of an embarrassing trip to the infirmary. But, sick or no, I expect that you Americans will take home more than your share of gold here, just as in London."

A small group had clustered near this conversation, which seemed to happen quite often with the American ambassador. More so today with his tall companion.

"Mr. Ambassador, I would like to introduce you to the newest member of the President's field team, Kalle Paasilainno. He's a bright young man who will actually stand a chance at understanding all of your American witticisms. Kalle, this is Ambassador Ezekiel Williamson." Henrik ushered Kalle front and center.

"Zeke. Please just call me Zeke. Pleasure to meet you, Kal!" The enthusiastic hand came out again. "And this tall fella here with me is Robert Silverton, also a relatively new addition. We plucked Robbie out of some dreary university drudgery a month or two back to live the good life up here in Helsinki. Of course, we get the new recruits here in the summer before they realize the mistake they've made."

"Have you been to Berkeley, Zeke?" Robert laughed, "It's not exactly drudgery. But yes, it is true I needed a change of scenery and I have enjoyed my posting here to the fullest." Robert looked down upon the assembled group from his considerable vantage point. He looked more likely to be walking with other athletes through the puddles today than toiling away at the political glad-handing. It was impossible to ignore his wide grin and sturdy frame, much in the same way that it was impossible to avoid Zeke's upper decibel running chatter. Even the sour-faced brown suits in the corner had taken quick glances over, and up, to Robert.

Henrik's spirits seemed much improved. The ceremonies were about to begin and Old Papi would shortly be ushered safely down into the rainy pit of the stadium.

There was a beat, and Kalle took the initiative. "Let's grab something to drink. I hear Henrik's English is much more entertaining that way."

A mechanical laugh from Henrik. "Yes yes, unfortunately I cannot join you just now. The President has a schedule to keep today, as you can imagine. But please enjoy yourselves. I'll join up with you later." Henrik didn't wait for goodbyes. With two quick steps, he was beyond the surrounding cluster and out of sight.

Kalle steeled himself for the task ahead. He would much rather be at the office with supply plans and shipping schedules. It was busier now than ever, and this side-assignment would only compound the problem. Why was he pressed into this duty anyway? Some misinformed idea of a reward for all the good work, I suppose. Everyone would be conscripted into the Olympics over the next two weeks anyways. So sipping sima and baby-sitting some Americans should be a light tour of duty all things considered. But Kalle had not yet fully understood Zeke's prodigious capability to talk and drink. And talk.

Without Henrik to share the load, Kalle came under broad attack. Waves of questions came, with barely time to respond before the next. "No, I moved here when I was young. Up north, a village called Malu. My father owned a small mill there – still does. No. Well, I'm very busy and… Yes, someday I suppose." An interview without warning.

"Timber export control and promotion? Ha, well you managed to find the easiest job in the world, am I right? Well done, Kal! They pay you to fall out of bed in the morning," Zeke bared all of his teeth with this observation. Kalle flushed in protest as Zeke continued. "As long as the war lasts, I suppose, it's full speed ahead. Export control. Ha, fantastic! I swear you Finns think of everything. A toast to Kal, who took time off from his control to drink with some simple westerners."

The loose congregation near the trio had dissipated in some natural Brownian progression without any obvious trigger. Attention of the group at large slowly came to focus on the field below. Flags were on the move and officials were walking with purpose in all directions on the track. Muted fanfare had begun filtering up through the crowd. The ceremonies had begun, but Zeke was looking skyward. "Kal, this tower here is quite impressive even by today's standards. It was built with the rest of the stadium for the 1940 games, is that right?"

Kalle nodded. "Yes sir, ready and waiting for this day. It's 72 meters tall, which is the distance of Matti Jarvinen's gold medal javelin throw back in 1932. We swept all three medals in Los Angeles." Happy to be discussing anything but the validity of his office work, Kalle pressed on. "Finland is only competitive in two summer sports, distance running and javelin. In particular, the javelin is ours. We have more gold medals than any other country. More than Sweden."

Zeke looked over to Robert. "Did you know about this? For a lay-about like myself 72 meters seems incredibly far. How far did you throw? 60, 65?" To Kalle he continued, "you see Robbie here was a standout athlete at university. In the javelin so he tells us."

"I threw the stick a bit, yeah. But 'standout' is an outright lie, boss. I had the strength, but never the technique. I am excited to watch the experts this week. The men out there, they have a way of coordinating their limbs. It's just…"

"Well maybe you can pick up some tips from the pros here. Get yourself back into the game? Imagine. A diplomat-athlete." Zeke trailed off. The topic had lost its steam.

Their drinks empty, Zeke cast about for a refill, another line of questioning, something to fill the void. "Well, what is the use of a beautiful 72-meter tower if we aren't going to check out the view from the top? I prefer the big picture anyway. What do you say?" Clearly not a question, Zeke made for the stairs, with a brief detour to chat with a bartender. Vodka supplies procured, Zeke, Robert, and Kalle began the 23-flight journey. In the spirit of good sportsmanship, the elevator was out of the question.

The crowd and the trumpet preamble were muffled by the concrete of the stairwell. The growing humidity of the day had accumulated in this isolated column. Kalle's face was set in grim determination by the tenth floor, thinking ahead to the embarrassing sweat and heaving he would present by the summit. He trudged step-by-step up through the haze to watch a parade of athletes in sports he didn't care for in the least. They weren't even doing the sports part today – just the parade part. All of this in the name of international cooperation that Kalle was tasked with circumventing today. This duplicity circled Kalle's mind – a spirit of brotherhood in Helsinki while a war raged in Korea. Everyone decried the war out loud but was privately enriched by it. It would be a farce if it wasn't so depressing.

Robert graciously took a measured pace in the lead, obviously not winded. Zeke seemed more than capable of the journey for a man of his age, but at least his chatter was paused for the duration. Damn Americans impose themselves on everything and then smother you with their unrelenting capability.

At a minimum, Kalle was putting an additional 72 meters of separation between the Ambassador and the President, vastly improving the odds of a successful first assignment. The cross-section of the two colliding today was closing in on zero.

The stairwell was the one place not dressed in bunting for the day. Approaching the top flight of stairs, Kalle had given up any pretense of control. He yanked on the railing every other step for some semblance of momentum and lifted his feet the bare minimum. Not even a millimeter higher than necessary. His white shirt was a shade darker underneath the ill-fitting wool jacket.

Opening up to the top level, light and breeze welcomed the trio. Two teenagers with Olympic ring pins on their lapels stood up from the bench next to the elevator. Clearly volunteers for the day, they approached uncertainly. "Mr. Järvinen?"

Kalle drew in a ragged breath to respond no, only to hear Zeke pipe up first "Yes this is him, of course." Gesturing to Kalle with a flash in his eyes. "Mr. Järvinen is starving, can you please have lunch brought up? We'll take it on the balcony."

The pair of youngsters mumbled something, looked down and shuffled back to the elevator to await a ride down to search for a kitchen or kiosk of some kind.

Robert gave an easy laugh as they strode out to the balcony. "Who on earth is Mr. Järvinen?"

"One unlucky jerk who will wonder where the bill for sandwiches came from, I suppose," replied Zeke in a cheery dismissive tone as he had already moved on to other things. "Now this was the view I was looking for."

During their journey up the stairwell, the parade of nations had begun. Platoons of athletes had half-filled the swampy infield of the track with their smattering of colors. The balcony was a tighter fit than the promenade at the base of the tower. A large metal cone of some sort slanted up above them. It crowded the space but at least granted some cover from the remnants of the passing showers. Zeke produced a bottle of vodka and glasses from his coat, and they drank to the generosity of the mysterious Mr. Järvinen. Conversation ambled around to Zeke's colorful history, including missing out on all the great battles of the Pacific. Kalle was warmed by the vodka and took interest in the stories as they tumbled out of the Ambassador with occasional self-effacing barks of laughter at his own predicaments. Robert smiled easily as he looked down at the stadium below. He had heard these stories before, but never tired of them. He enjoyed noting the slight changes in each iteration.

"Excuse me, is this the right spot? Should I wait here?" A timid Finnish accented voice broke in behind them. Another man dressed in Olympic attire shifted his feet. He seemed rather unsure for an official, but this pattern was emerging with staff at the top of the tower. He was older than the other two who had taken their lunch order, probably about Kalle's age. He did not have a tray of sandwiches with him.

Affable as always, the Ambassador greeted the newcomer warmly. The newcomer received no answers to his questions but didn't press the matter since he was happy to be in the company of those who appeared to be in complete control of the situation. However, the space on the balcony proved too tight for four, and an awkward shift into the adjacent hallway commenced. The newcomer did not introduce himself and only smiled meekly in response to questions in English. The conversation ground to a halt and Kalle busied himself with small sips from his glass. The speeches from below came in clearly and the group patiently listened in instead of reinventing another round of halting small talk.

The newcomer excused himself in search of the restroom. Zeke raised his eyebrows to Robert, who moments later also headed into the service section of the top floor, grabbing a wooden folding chair propped against the wall along the way.

Kalle and Zeke moved back to the railing under the metal cone. Down below a tiny, hunched figure approached the podium, Old Papi. It was his chance to show off his abilities in Finnish, French, and English. But the words went largely unheard – the crowd murmured in anticipation of Paavo Nurmi's entrance. The bearer of the torch into the stadium was a secret in theory, but there could be no other choice for Finland. The only man to eclipse the nation's javelin exploits. The dominant middle-distance runner of his generation. Olympic gold medalist nine times over. From the tone of his voice, even in French, it was clear that President Paasikivi was wrapping up and the crowd turned to the stadium entrance tunnel.

Robert had returned alone, mentioning that their new friend was going to be detained in the bathroom for quite a while. A faint pounding issued from inside and Robert flashed a grin. *Thud… thud*

thud. Kalle's mind raced back to the freedom of his schoolboy days. It occurred to him that these Americans remained schoolboys to the end: optimistic, full of vigor, and foolhardy. It was admirable and he was jealous for a moment.

A streak of light. Nurmi had entered the stadium at full speed. This was no lazy ceremonial lap of the track for the Flying Finn. The stadium came alive as his familiar strides struck a note of remembrance in the older attending Finns who had watched newsreels of Nurmi. Afternoon matinees leading with updates from Antwerp, Paris, Amsterdam. Always the same composure at the front from start to finish. Efficient and confident, he was the Finn who led the world. For the crowd below and Kalle above, Nurmi had sealed the connection: this was our Olympics. This is our time, and the world will know us.

A band played as Nurmi lit the cauldron on the infield. A large metal cone flashed to light. The announcer cut through the cheers to narrate, "The flame's journey has come through Finland's history. Now the torch will make its way to our future."

With the focus on the cauldron below, the trio on the balcony had lost sight of the torch which was now being hustled by Olympic staff into the base of the tower. The announcer continued in Finnish, "In a few moments, ladies and gentlemen, a second flame will be lit by the future of Finland. Representing the voice of a new Finland, the voice of the future, award-winning author and national poet laureate Aanders Järvinen. 70,000 heads turned up to the tower balcony. Robert and Zeke turned to Kalle.

"Oh shit."

The elevator opened and an enthusiastic official strode through the hallway, fiery torch in hand. He glanced uncertainly between the three men waiting for him.

With an elbow from Zeke, Kalle stepped forward. "It's an honor, Mr. Järvinen," gushed the official in Finnish. "I must admit I haven't read any of your books, but my wife says that they are wonderful. As we discussed on the phone, can you wave to the crowd with the torch for a moment? I'll start the gas line then you can just shove the torch over the top of the cauldron."

"And then what?"

The official furrowed his eyebrows. "Well, and then… boom, off we go, yes?"

Kalle nodded blankly and took the torch. It was lighter than expected and reeked of kerosene. It had been thoroughly doused beforehand to be sure the flame survived any amount of wind – generated by Paavo Nurmi or otherwise. The acrid smoke that curled off must have been disgusting in the cramped elevator ride, but the official's beaming face registered no ill effects.

The imposter poet turned, walked to the edge of the balcony, and held up the torch. A javelin's throw below, shouts rang out. Fishermen, trappers, loggers, displaced Karelian farmers, grandmothers, lay-abouts, liars, thieves, dreamers, and export planners all waved and cheered the voice of a new Finland. Kalle waved back as he looked down at his people with moist eyes. After lingering at the railing a beat longer than was necessary, he turned away and lifted the torch up and over the lip of the metal cone. Boom, off we go.

Thud thud… thud thud thud.

Interlude – Sol

~65,000 BCE – Sol

THE WEAKEST OF forces reached out to infinity, its pull a persistent whisper. A sole hydrogen atom careened through the vast near vacuum. An ion, actually. Solar winds had blasted away the electron partner long ago, leaving only the up, up, and down quarks hugging each other for the wild ride to come. A slow arc developed, bringing the big bang's virgin proton into the grasp of the fiery miasma of the star.

The interior was all heat and pressure, building up as the ion sunk deeper and deeper into the soup. Finally, the scorching temperature yielded a transformation. The ion tied to a neighbor to become a deuteron then another for helium. The released energy rushed away from the new element only to be swallowed up moments later. This quantum of energy skittered around – absorbed and re-emitted countless times in every direction.

Tens of thousands of years passed with the same cycle; the same energy perfectly preserved. The only thing that changed was the escape angle of the emission. True escape was to come shortly, as the pinging gamma ray edged closer and closer to the surface of the sun. Finally, due to a series of unlikely consecutive bounces away from the core, the singular photon ejected itself from the giant gravity well. The wave shot off on a ramrod straight trajectory into empty space along the ecliptic, appearing to be on the path to leave this system once and for all.

The path forward for the photon was indeed empty for a while. However, 150 million kilometers downrange a small speck of insignificant spinning rock wandered into the way seven minutes later.

Chapter 2 – The Gadget

July 24, 1952

THE AFTERNOON SUN lingered high in the sky above the stadium, waiting with the eager crowd for The Race of the games. The 5000-meter final. The bleachers were filled to capacity and a low murmuring laid down a baseline of sound against the sharp crack of spikes hitting cinders.

The tall nervous-looking Herbert Schade paced quietly in the holding corral. Easy to pick out in the crowd with his bushy brown hair and glasses, the German Schade avoided eye contact he ran scenarios through his head. So many contingencies, so many excellent runners. All in their best shape, all targeting him. He was now the Olympic record holder after all, powering through the heats two days' prior. The 5000 should be a relatively straightforward race for him, lead out and dare anyone to match him for twelve and a half laps. The primary concern was the Belgian Reiff. The defending champion was known for a furious kick and might have an edge if it came down to a dead sprint at the end. That was exactly how Reiff beat Zatopek in London four years ago. Speaking of Zatopek, all else being equal the Czech would be a major concern too. But a blinding fast 10,000 earlier in the week took the edge off of both him and the Frenchman Mimoun. They had to be exhausted. Then there was the relatively unknown Chataway. He probably had breakaway speed too, being young, sitting out of the 10,000, and enjoying a slow qualifying heat for the 5000. But who really knew? He had never seen the 21-year-old Brit before in his life.

Reiff, Zatopek, Mimoun, Chataway… Schade had worked himself around in a circle and would rather just puke and get it over with. The crowd was buzzing, the sun was hot, and the wait was interminable. Field judges waddled slowly out to their designated points on the far side of the track. Take your time, boys.

Emil Zatopek sidled up, and Schade was thankful for the intrusion. "Fine day to put in a few laps together, eh Herbert?" Zatopek jumped into German as if they were best friends catching up for a weekly chat over coffee. In fact, they hadn't spoken since the European meets last year. 31 years old and rushing headlong toward baldness, Zatopek had an easy smile and friendly manner with everyone he met. Especially with competitors moments before a race. Despite being the chattiest Communist Army captain to be found, Zatopek was given some leeway by his minders. His gold medal in the 10,000 afforded him at least as much, and the Party was fully expecting another one today. Often misunderstood by outsiders as brash and overconfident, the track community knew his nature was simply to meet and shoot the shit with everyone. In America, he would have been called the mayor of the track, a true ambassador and asset. In Czechoslovakia, he was a liability that the Party went crazy trying to manage.

Conversation meandered from the weather to the city to the depth of the field. Schade tried to gauge Zatopek's energy levels and confidence from his answers, but it was impossible. Zatopek's smile and amiability was inscrutable. Even while talking about a race, he didn't appear to be thinking about the race.

For Zatopek, he felt a familiar ache in his hamstrings and calves, which gave him comfort. He had put in 15,000 meters of racing already this week along with dozens of 400-meter intervals on the path in Otaniemi, the Communist athlete's village. The ache was his comfort zone. Sore legs meant ready legs. Millions of Czechs and

Soviets were listening in on small transistor radios, hopes pinned to a Communist hero in the making. If Zatopek was aware of this, he didn't let on.

·

"So, let's talk turkey, who's it going to be: Schade or Reiff? It's Schade's to lose you have to reckon." Ambassador Williamson shifted his weight on the narrow bench along the homestretch railing.

"And lose he will," Robert responded immediately with the conviction of a teacher to a student. "Schade's in a bind. He likes to lead out, and he'll have to today. He'll want to beat out the sting of Reiff's kick."

"Exactly, he can play to his strength. And frankly, he looks to be the strongest out there." Zeke prepared to entrench his position of backing Schade simply for the entertainment value. It had been a long day in the sun.

"Oh, he is the strongest out there, but he's going come under attack from both sides. He has to thread the needle. Go out too weak and it will become a 400-meter sprint to the finish that Reiff wins hands-down, with maybe Chataway second right on his heels. On the flipside, go out too strong and the 10k boys tuck in behind and wait for the inevitable burn out. Hell, even Mimoun could win it in that case. But if you're asking who I like at the end of the day, it's Reiff."

Zeke glanced up at the sharp confident jaw next to him before returning to survey the judges settling into position along the curves of the track. There was a small twist of bemusement on his lips. "Reiff?"

"Yep, Schade has been refused entry to the big races before this week. He's inexperienced and he's too smart. He'll overthink it. He will fight the urge to bolt out of the gate. He will. He'll overcorrect by playing it too safe on the slow side. Therefore, Reiff first,

Chataway second, and Schade limping in a distant third. You heard it here first."

"You seem to have convinced yourself. And ordinarily I would defer to your experience. But not today. Today you have been the one that is too smart. Let's make it interesting, shall we? My Schade versus your Reiff. Say dinner, tomorrow night?"

"Boss, you have yourself a deal."

"I can't believe I just put myself in the position of rooting for a German."

.

The concrete walls of the dressing room dazzled with a fresh coat of white. The women's facilities were small but spotless. Dana Zatopkova sat staring into the corner. Even the corners were swept. She had the room to herself, as the other girls had not yet arrived. Not nervous, not bored, Dana was just staring, mind wandering. Anything could happen this afternoon: first to last, record to scratch. She recalled the effort made to get here today, not just her sacrifices but those around her and those whom she didn't even know. She was not a rookie to this, so now there were expectations. Expectations despite being outclassed by many in the field weeks ago in the test event.

A gunshot cracked through the hallways, severing the train of thought. The 5000 had started and everyone else was outside to catch a glimpse of the stars at work. She of all people should be along the railing too. Another check of the gear bag. There wasn't much to forget, spikes, a towel, and a brush to clear out cinders and clay between attempts. Her legs felt fine, her back too. There were no ready-made excuses today. If she was not good enough, she was not good enough. One way or another it would be obvious on the first throw.

The mechanics were drilled in by rote: run run run run lift run run reach cross-step hips arm-plant press follow-through don't look don't scratch. The javelin was notorious for being the event no one had asked for. The javelin required concentration, power, speed, and technical perfection. As if that wasn't enough, the result was all decided within a fraction of a second. The 5000-meter run was much more forgiving. 2500 individual strides spread out over thirteen minutes; one poorly executed stride could be papered over with the large sample size of better strides, better decisions. A mistake was just rounding error in an overflowing pool of repetition. The javelin had many opportunities for error. The twist too early, the plant foot off-center, the angle too shallow. So many points required perfect action without any fail-safes. Any singular error was fatal. It was the event no one asked for, but the event Dana was born for, nonetheless.

Crowd noise filtered in, layered over by the stadium announcer rolling along with a stream of incomprehensible Finnish punctuated by names she knew by heart. She really should be out there along the railing.

·

The race was twelve laps, with an extra half lap of jostling and stutter-steps at the start. Fifteen men crammed into the nine-lane track. An arc of feet, knees, and arms all aimed toward the focal point: the beginning of the turn. Something had to give. There was not enough space for everyone at the same place at the same time. Compression didn't serve anyone's purposes. Schade sprinted out to avoid traffic and establish the lead. The also-rans blinked and deferred to the pre-race favorites. An orderly bunch evolved in the opening 200 meters, with Schade in front followed closely by Reiff and Chataway. Zatopek trailed off to the very back of the pack.

In the opening laps, Schade heard the staccato click click of spikes behind him signifying the whole field had come along with his early pace. The speed was unsustainable for most if not all of them. World record pace through three laps. Millimols of lactic acid titrated into Schade's bloodstream. Poison accumulated at a rate imperceptible to anyone except the fifteen elite men circling the track today.

Three laps stretched to four then five. The square power began to impose order. Schade created his own wind on this cloudless day. Air pressed into his body at a quadruple load for double the pace. This was the down payment made for taking the lead, for dragging Reiff out of his comfort zone. The field stretched as each runner hunted for a slipstream, a lee to minimize their surface area exposure to the wind's attack.

Schade's broad shoulders and obvious strength were undercut by the peculiarity of his stride, a mincing prancing affair that gave off the appearance of hesitancy. But he was anything but hesitant with open lanes in front of him. The click click volume faded. For Schade, these dropping decibels were the signal that the plan was working. There were now only three of four pairs of feet in earshot instead of ten.

Heading into lap six, one pattern of footfalls increased cadence and volume. Schade glanced at the shadow on his right. "Herbert, take a break for a bit. Follow me for a few laps." Zatopek's friendly tone clashed with the grimace souring his face. The Czech didn't wait for an answer and popped ahead into the turn. The race had a new leader at the halfway mark.

·

With the unassuming procession of the first mile out of the way, the action at the front brought out murmurs of appreciation in the stands. By general assent, the fans stayed on their feet for the balance of the race. The burden of the narrow bench biting into Zeke's backside had been lifted. "Quick pace, Robbie. Your guy Reiff isn't getting the slow jog you were hoping for, is he? Tough break." Zeke glanced up and down the railing, checking for familiar faces. The front row was a mishmash of VIPs and frumpy track coaches,

European business executives and local boys sneaking in to fill the few tiny open spaces. All eyes were on Zatopek, who had moved steadily up from last place to take control of the race.

"Yeah, very quick. But your guy never got the separation he wanted either. Zatopek might rein in the pace, and Reiff would be right back in it. Don't order from tomorrow's menu just yet." Robert kept his focus on Reiff, searching his stride for signs of breakdown and willing him forward. It would simply not do to be wrong against the boss – especially about athletics. It didn't build confidence with the old man. Robert's profession valued trust above all else. With a Reiff loss here, at best he would become an anecdote. The ex-athlete bested by the old man. But there was nothing to be done at this point – no control over the situation. He had backed his horse and would have to live with it.

Zatopek was firmly in front in lane one, managing the pace. Schade, Mimoun, Reiff, and Chataway had all bunched up behind. The pace had to be slackening. They called Zatopek the Czech Locomotive, the embodiment of non-stop energy leading the train. However, by the look of him in person, there was no resemblance to a train's sleek efficiency. Zatopek was a flurry of flapping arms and legs. His gait was a comedy of bias accumulated over a lifetime of injury, favoring, and overwork. A swiveling head blurred the grimace on his face to all but the sharpest eyes and quick-shuttered cameras. A snapshot would give the impression of a hapless body struck by lightning. He was not The Locomotive, but The Gadget. A wind-up trinket bought for a nickel on the Atlantic City boardwalk. Intentionally off-center weights would give the metal toad, rabbit, or clown a hiccupping gait, tottering with fits of randomness. Uncontrollable in defiance of its metal stamped form. It was The Gadget leading this group for all the world to see.

The bouncing bubbling noise of the crowd wrapped around Robert and Zeke and began to take on a pulse, a form. Three rhythmic beats, like some kind of ancient chant. "What are they saying?" Robert asked.

Zeke shrugged as he glanced again down the railing to a vacancy in the standing masses. He turned back toward the track and cupped his hands. He shouted against the building volume of the crowd, "Come on you big hairy German. Pick up the pace!"

·

There was no pretense at this point that Dana was still in the dressing room to dress or prepare for her event. She had to be out by the track now, but she was not. The morning had been uncharacteristically tense. Usually, her husband was unabashedly relaxed and confident, but today was different. Dana too had a queasiness within her, as if something was not right. Some piece of the puzzle was not fitting together.

Killing time, Dana took in her surroundings. Antiseptic desolation surrounded her. She was in a nameless hospital ward with a mystery illness, alone. Her family unaware of her condition. Dana would have to face her fate by herself. Time alone allowed these thoughts to creep back in. Frantic short attempts to claw back the curtain just a little bit. Take a dismal peek into the future.

The clock read 4:37, just past halfway into the race. The cadence of the announcer's nonsense accelerated. Underpinning his staccato, a slow bass line was muddled by the refraction and reflection of the corridors, "shap-toh-mick, shap-toh-mick, shap-toh-mick." Dana's natural charming smile returned to her face. She shook her head and laughed. Emil was in charge.

·

The surprise of Zatopek's push to the lead lasted for only seconds in Schade's mind. He never had any intention of playing the follower today. But a 5000-meter final was a race of adjustments, and today would be no different. Any frustration of upset plans was offset by the welcoming Czech slipstream. His blistering pace for the first half had probably done the job in beating the sting out of Reiff's legs. Zatopek's enthusiasm was another problem, but one thing at a time. There was no reason to be a hero and immediately swing back out to lane two. Better to settle in for a bit.

A lap in second place felt very good. To Schade the comfort was a major concern. They were slowing down. It was impossible to hear splits from the timekeeper as they crossed the line after eight laps, but they were slowing down. He heard steps on his heels. Chataway? Reiff? Both? Another lap in purgatory.

Two miles in and Zatopek was fine with the current configuration. His strained eyes and neck belied a race going according to plan. Maintain three more laps like this then put away one quick 400 just like all the hot laps out in the woods. Just one quick lap would be enough. The click click sound behind him veered suddenly to the right. Sprinter incoming.

.

A sharp elbow caught Robert just under the ribs. "There goes your guy." Zeke nodded out to the head of the race. Reiff had burst out from fourth into the lead in the span of 50 meters. Robert arranged his face as if he had been expecting this all along. In truth, the sudden intensity of the attack had caught the whole stadium off guard, Schade and Zatopek included. The gap that formed was closed nearly as quickly by Zatopek in response. Coming out of the turn the Czech pulled back in front of Reiff. The Belgian countered, running even faster. Given there was still a mile left to race, the speed was alarming. Tactically, it made no sense whatsoever. A duel at this point was a recipe for disaster. The crowd cheered their approval with blood lust in their throats. The prospect of bodies soon littering the track fed into the festive mood. Good value for money today.

Robert had no calculated dry response for his boss. The race had become electric in an instant and his focus was out front to enjoy seeing what would happen next. The back-and-forth sprint between

Reiff and Zatopek was suited for a bell lap, not three laps prior to the bell. Neither man would cede the lead through the turn into the home stretch, inducing all manner of shoulder-brushing, glances askance, and additional flapping from The Gadget. "Shap-toh-mick, shap-toh-mick" was heard over the din, with the Finnish majority firmly backing their adopted champion Zatopek into the start of the tenth lap. Robert had just leaned into Zeke's ear to shout that this couldn't go on much longer, when his impending prediction was proven correct. Reiff flinched first and backed off so abruptly that he seemed to be headed backwards into the peloton of Schade and crew. More applause from the crowd along the rail, for Zatopek's win of the battle and for fair play appreciation of the Belgian's sortie.

.

Zatopek had paid full tariff for the unplanned gap lead. He had burnt a match or two on lap nine and didn't know for sure how many were left in the book. There was a fine line between being leader of the pack and being prey. As lap ten wore on, Zatopek appeared more of the latter. Schade corralled Chataway and Mimoun into a tight wedge that ate into the lead. The temporary alliance generated its own energy. Schade was gathering confidence despite his burning lungs. By lap eleven, Zatopek was caught and the faltering Reiff dropped out of the race altogether. The Battle of Lap Nine appeared to have brought casualties to both sides.

The bell lap. The bell. Nothing in athletics was more predictable than the Pavlovian response of runners to the ringing of the bell with 400 meters to go. The roar of the crowd muffled the pounding steps, the ragged breathing, everything. Everything but the bell. Whether cast in bronze on special order, packed with the starter's pistol in an official's worn-down travel bag, or borrowed at last minute from a neighboring schoolyard, the bell waked runners from whatever trance they had fallen into and called on them to throw themselves into the turn. The peal was a sharp shout over the din that the pain was almost over and there was no point holding back. This is why you are here, be a man about it already. Go!

After enduring a couple laps with a target on his back, Zatopek had his answer prepared for the bell. One hot lap, just like in the woods at home. He accelerated immediately at the finish line, prepared to reestablish a gap lead that he would hold for good. He pressed ahead with full effort and grimaced with pleasure at the feel of wind in his teeth. But only a few seconds later Schade charged past in lane two, followed by Chataway, followed by Mimoun. A nightmare procession at the worst possible moment. Under a full sprint, Zatopek saw himself fall to fourth. The 4700-meter mark is a terrible time to gather some composure. All he could do was try to maintain contact with a trio that suddenly seemed invincible.

.

Robert rested his meaty forearms on the railing and leaned over the void. With Reiff laying exhausted on the infield, Robert had reconciled to his fate of hearing about Schade's skill and determination (not to mention Zeke's superior horse picking) for weeks to come. The crowd around him was quieter now. There was no chanting of Zatopek, no screaming remonstrations for someone, anyone, to go faster. There was no such thing as faster on this backstretch. Schade held the lead on the inside, but Chataway was hounding right on his shoulder with Mimoun next to him.

Robert had no idea what would happen. He couldn't even hazard a guess. The three leaders and the straggling Zatopek were at the furthest point of the track from the home stretch stands and the menagerie of VIPs. The smudges of singlets moved at surprising speed, and which of the three smudges would bounce forward next seemed as random as bubbles in a beaker, or cells in the petri. Despite the seriousness of his work and the tremendous amount of stress he imposed on himself, Robert was grateful for this moment.

He was grateful to witness this event in person. Regardless of what random event would come next, he would not forget this thrill.

•

Chataway was the smudge to bounce ahead. Freed from the bounds of strategy in the last 200, the young Briton's legs pumped him forward in a dash heading into the final turn. Schade pumped his arms with more effort yet decelerated. Mimoun kept his head down as if not wanting to experience any of this. Zatopek was still The Gadget, but maybe cranked a half-turn too far: arms legs ears heels elbows.

Into the final turn, vision was sharpened into the narrow field of a painted curve demarking lanes one and two. Individual, white-flaked cinders had been kicked into the black on a prior lap. A whiff of pipe smoke was carried across by some weak breeze that no one felt, being overrun by the athletes' pace. There was pain, but it was an abstraction. Movements took forever. Will that left arm ever pull back, in time to pull forward again? Plans gave way to confusion. Sounds were generic and ignored. There was no bell call to attention.

In this final semi-circle, every meter outside was three more meters to run. Chataway's youth was spent, and his legs failed him in the same way they failed everyone else. Schade and the others joined up at the apex, four men abreast at full sprint.

Chataway's body overrode the brain it was carrying. One misstep, two. There was no energy left to correct the imbalance. Inertia slapped his body to the earth. Limbs sprawled out across lane one as the race thundered ahead without him.

Schade inherited the inside track, still attempting to accelerate. There was no response in his legs as the group of three reached the homestretch. It was all he could muster to keep his body upright. No more prancing, slogging would have to do. Schade faded. The group was winnowed down to just a pair with 80 meters left, Mimoun and Zatopek.

Mimoun had not been in the top three at any point in the race until now. Only his close friend stood between him and the gold. Algerian by birth but French for life, Alain Mimoun had prepared for these Olympics with more miles than anyone in his adopted country thought was wise. How else could you expect to race the 10,000 and the 5000 in the same week? He was thoroughly bested by Zatopek in the 10,000, but now he was presented with an 80-meter footrace to even the score. A limp had developed somewhere along the course for Mimoun. It wasn't clear when or how, but it didn't really matter. He gave 20% more force in each right leg push-off to account for the deficient left. But it was not enough; the math was never going to work regardless of the effort.

Zatopek breathed giant gulps of air on the homestretch. His body was the only one to respond to the call. Faster and faster he propelled himself down the stretch. The realization that the line was his for the taking poured fuel on the fire and his speed increased beyond anything seen so far in this race.

The dumb-struck crowd returned to full volume as Shap-toh-mick gave a resounding conclusion to the Race of the Games.

.

Robert enthusiastically joined in the chant as Zatopek had ensured a draw no bet. Zeke for his part beamed at the chaos surrounding him in the stands. The power of the performance was undeniable. He redirected his gaze onto the infield, where Zatopek walked casually arm-in-arm with his friend Mimoun. Chatting as if they were simply killing time on a weekend afternoon. "Zatopek arrived late to the city, did I hear that right?" Zeke questioned Robert without moving his head.

"Yep. Tonsillitis they say."

Zeke barked out his laugh. "Uh-huh. You know a lot of guys who can run like that with tonsillitis? It's curious, the country's star athlete misses the chartered flight to the Games and the best excuse they can come up with is tonsillitis."

"You know those eastern bloc doctors. Maybe he just had a sore throat, but the docs wanted to cover their asses and claimed he was green something awful at first." Robert fell into the devil's advocate role in the way his boss had come to expect.

"Nah, no no. Someone's been a bad boy." The easygoing smile in the Ambassador's eyes had retreated to something more focused and curious. Down on the field, the victor and his runner-up friend had been surrounded by shuffling/running officials and coaches, all adjusting their ill-fitting uniforms reaching out to attempt awkward congratulations. A group of suits had begun escorting the loose aggregation toward the stadium bowels.

·

Her duffel slung over her left shoulder, javelin perched on her right, Dana was ready for war. The feverish chanting had broadcasted the result back to her. The anxiety of the day ebbed out to reveal the core of the task at hand – to launch her weapon her way. Ignoring the other girls who had filtered in, Dana strode through the broad hallway toward the light. A loud mixed group stumbled in fits and starts from the opening in her direction. She knew there was a thinning head of hair in the middle of the scrum somewhere. Emil was probably being ushered to a press conference before even having a chance to grab a glass of water. He was the better of the two at brushing off these annoyances. Despite his demonstrative personality, Dana knew his natural disposition was clear-headed focus. He could dismiss noise out of hand. To Dana, sometimes the noise filled every nook and cranny.

She wanted to leap in and embrace her husband for what must have been the most excruciating and thrilling race of his life. It would have required making a scene and forcing her way through a thick layer of fleshy coating – she did have a large pointy stick after all.

The stabbing would have to wait for another time. Instead, Dana Zatopkova walked straight past the pathetic agglomeration of pretend coaches and sweating bureaucrats into the blinding light of her arena.

.

The stadium had started thinning out, with the sounds of satisfied chatter along the aisles feeding the exits. Zeke and Robert kept to their uncomfortable perch. Zeke would have been happy to follow the action out onto the streets toward the pubs in Kamppi, but the javelin was Robert's keen interest, even if it was just the women competing today. The process of bringing a young staffer under your wing was an enjoyable burden for Zeke. Usually, it was an easy trade to put up with the naïve questions and blunders in order to be in proximity to the youthful energy. Robert was as naïve and energetic as they came. He was eager to please, too eager really. There was something unsettling about his charming open face offset by his readiness to jump into action. He had a friendly impulsiveness that could invite trouble. It wasn't clear how he would respond when put to the test, but Zeke would find out soon enough.

Zeke looked over at his right-hand man, on the edge of his front-row seat watching women's javelin warmups with the rapt attention of a schoolboy. Zeke smiled to himself and shook his head. Kamppi can wait. After all, he could oblige another hour at the track watching young women run back and forth arching their backs and throwing things.

"The crowd was funny in that race, eh?" Zeke leaned into Robert. "All the Finns were for Zatopek from the start. Why's that?"

Robert responded with a minimal shrug as he kept his eyes on the warmups.

"What we need is the inside scoop. After all my time here, I don't seem to understand the Finns any more than I did on day one. All this surface. Quiet deflecting surface in every meeting and every event. Thousands of Finns here today were chanting for a man from a country almost none of them could spell correctly or point out on a map. Baffling. We need someone to explain the common Finn to us. But not the usual state department guys. We should find an innocent bystander. But now I'm rambling because I'm bored and my colleague here is entranced by something or someone on the field. Isn't that right Robbie?"

"Hmm?"

.

There was a clear risk of a Soviet sweep of the podium for the women's javelin. They took three of the top four spots in qualifying and had posted the best marks all year. Dana was an outside shot for crashing the parade. A personal best could put in for a bronze.

Aleksandra Tshudina stood out immediately to the casual observer. Tall and muscular with a shock of short blonde hair, she simultaneously looked like a Paris model and one of the guys down at the pub. Word had it that she used go out drinking with the men's team until she tired of them. They probably couldn't keep up with her. Years of smoking had added to her naturally husky voice. There was no hope but to be intimidated by her on the field. The gold was hers to lose. Her 46-meter throw in qualifying was the best and she had made it appear effortless.

Dana had learned enough Russian through work at the ministry to carry a conversation, but no one was chatting today. Six attempts laid before the finalists. Dana replayed her mantra to help focus. Step step step step lift step step reach cross-step hips arm plant press follow-through don't look don't scratch. She visualized the inclined tunnel through which she would send the javelin. 40 degrees, the highest angle possible before her form would break down and she would lose traction from her oblique muscles. She wasn't as strong as the Soviet girls were, but she was just as fast, and she launched through a tunnel a couple degrees higher.

Late into the afternoon, the midsummer sun was slowly meandering north. The glowing fireball had loomed all day without cover of clouds, washing out color from the stadium. The weathered stands encircled the women, white on light gray. The javelin runway was a tacky well-baked clay pressed hard from the thumping of the men yesterday. Dana pulled back her starting point a few meters, as her strides in warmup were particularly lively. The metal-pointed wooden javelin rested lightly in her hand as Dana rocked back and forth slightly. She bursted from her line-designate and felt the wind at the same reassuring pressure as thousands of times before. TACK tack tack tack, TACK tack tack tack, the rhythm of her spikes into the earth rung out at a measured pace, with the frequency ratcheted up on every fourth step. Nothing was rushed but everything was fast. The javelin launched into the empty sky on a line as gravity hesitated to act. Dana glanced at the ground, no scratch.

A sharp intake of breath from an attentive Aleksandra told Dana everything. She bounced back to her paltry bag to grab a towel, even though there wasn't any sweat to wipe away. She knew it was a cracker of a throw and didn't want to hear the report on distance. Without a number, it was wide open. Dana jammed the towel over her beaming face and screamed.

.

"Whoa!" Zeke was no expert, but he had eyes. The first throw from the smallish Czech girl floated out beyond the 50-meter placard. He raised his eyes to a confused Robert, who was at loss to improve upon Zeke's astute evaluation. Put simply, Robert was distracted by the blonde tall drink of water watching from the side of the approach until the last second when the missile launched. He didn't know anything about Dana, other than she was married to Emil Zatopek and finished maybe in the top ten in London four years ago. She wasn't supposed to be a contender today. But now she was. That certainly was the leading throw for the first round. Aleksandra and her compatriots would have to scramble to respond to this.

As the rounds rolled on, a procession of 46-meter throws made it clear that Dana had caught lightning in a bottle with that first attempt. Aleksandra for her part was honing in her form without appearing to press full effort, each toss a handful of centimeters closer. Zeke stared down at his hands, smooth and petite looking in comparison to his bench-mate. Hands that appeared to have never been used in a fight. Appeared, at least. All this sitting did not comport with his philosophy. For a restless man like Zeke, there was nothing more depressing than watching elite athletes move powerfully while remaining perfectly still.

The last round of attempts began with a string of weak efforts. Sun and time had sapped the energy from most competitors. Fourth to last in order, Dana poured everything into her last run-up and throw. The consequence was a rushed and tight posture and another middling result to toss into the boneyard. All that remained for her to do was watch the Russian trio.

Robert leaned into the handrail. Aleksandra was last to throw, sitting in the bronze position with Dana and compatriot Elena ahead. Her classical strides toward the fault line set up a long, languid stretch backward to maximize her wingspan. The javelin fired ahead at speed while heads swiveled to track this final volley.

Fifty even. Silver.

Dana's first effort of 50.49 had survived all comers.

The remaining crowd broke into applause, appreciative of another well-fought contest. Zeke called to Robert, "Let's go," and without hesitation heaved himself over the railing onto the track. With less effort and more grace, Robert followed and asked in his casual manner, "What are we doing boss?"

"I thought we'd like to congratulate the charming winner before she gets ushered off to god-knows-where. A nice chance for a chat, right?"

"Yeah, sure," Robert replied as he scanned the infield ahead of him, expecting some sort of official pushback to their self-invitation to the grounds. But there was no real security presence at this point, since the men's events had concluded, and the stars had made their way out into the city.

Zeke was in his element, accosting strangers with his insistent charm. Warm handshakes, congratulations, and introductions were made to Dana. A bemused event page quietly turned away and found something else to look after.

Zeke launched into a characteristically wordy praise of her efforts, but Dana cut him off. "I'm sorry, my English…" Dana laughed and grimaced with her tongue out.

"Russian?" Robert asked. Dana responded with a nodding shrug. *"Great, maybe between us we can patch together two halves of the language then."* Robert continued in Russian.

The Ambassador took a quiet half step back and found interest in a nearby wheelbarrow holding bags of chalk, athletic tape, leather straps of unknown design and utility, and other tools of the trade. The false Russian duo bumbled along with energy to his side talking about what he could only imagine was javelin jock inside baseball. After a decent interval, he stepped back to reform the triangle. Robert narrated, "Dana was explaining to me that she designs all her own workouts and begs to get a videographer out to run film on her form since she doesn't have feedback from a coach she can trust. Truly impressive. *I'm saying you were truly impressive today, but I hope that you already know that.*" Dana smiled in response and looked down at her shoes.

With the path softened, the Ambassador led in "Yes, we were both quite impressed with the way you handled yourself today, especially considering all the surrounding pressures of this event." He paused to check if any gaps needed filling in Russian, but Dana's eyes seemed clear enough. "In fact, my wife and I are hosting a dinner tomorrow night at the American embassy, and we would very much wish for you to attend. Robbie will be there as well, as he rarely misses a chance for a decent meal. Of course, your husband is welcome to join if he is available. But to be quite frank with you, we would do just fine without him!"

Polite laughter all around.

"That is very kind of you." Dana hesitated and switched to Russian, *"but as you can imagine, our schedule is kept quite busy here."*

"Yes, but your events are complete, so I insist some celebrating is in order. Lani truly throws the best dinner parties in Helsinki."

"Yes, well Emil still might give the marathon a go. And besides, our Socialist athletes' village is… how do I put it… tightly administered." Dana spoke plainly without any furtive glancing around or lowering of her voice.

"You mean administered with barbed wire and guards? Yes, I've heard about this. What a crazy business." Zeke replied after the translation. With a casual and equally un-lowered voice, he continued, "although I bet a smart girl like you and an energetic guy like your husband could probably find a way around such … *administration.*"

Robert continued carrying the torch in favor of this dinner party that had just been born into existence in a rapid-fire Russian that one could only imagine was filled with a host of grammatical errors and outright fabricated words. However, at a minimum his gesticulations got across the main point that the dinner would simply not be the same without her. She would really be doing them a favor.

By this point the territory on the infield had thinned of the other competitors, while a contingent of less athletic-looking gentlemen lingered near the track, waiting with diminishing patience. Zeke and Robert sensed that they had pressed their luck on time far enough and rushed to give general directions to the embassy. With a final handshake, Zeke left with, "Drinks start at 7:00, we'll see you then!"

The men walked back on the uneven grass, managing as best as they could in dress shoes.

"Lani and I missed you at the thing last night. It was a great time," Zeke said.

"It was?" Robert smiled.

"No of course not. A hideous affair with blowhards and their lackeys with wet fish handshakes."

"Shame I missed it, then. I had something else come up," Robert offered, scanning the infield wall for an easy spot to hop up.

"Something else… Was she cute at least?"

Robert looked askance at his boss.

"Of course she was. Why do I even bother asking these questions?" Zeke muttered to himself.

The men clambered over the railing and headed to the exit. It was still early enough to head out for Kammpi.

Sitting alone high up in the empty stands, a man turned a program over in his hands and inspected the fine print once again.

Interlude – Mongolia

Spring, 1946 – Arkhangai Aimag

NARANTSETSEG SHIFTED ON the mat. By this point, there was no position comfortable enough for sleeping more than an hour at a time. The smell of dull smoke and sharp dung lingered even though spring had returned, and the yurt was opened and aired during the day. The men talked last night of moving with the herd soon. Nara just shook her head. Moving now was so stupid. Small fry would run on the Chuluut with the melt runoff any day now. One day's catch would last them a week at least. Plus, she was in no condition to walk for hours at a time. There was no sense thinking about it in the dark anyhow. What did any of it matter? She listened to the muffled river and the walls warping in the wind for a while then closed her eyes.

The shock sprang through her body in an instant, but the pain remained as if it was trapped and looking for a way out. Nara's eyes shot around the empty yurt. She groaned and waited for it to pass, in the way Bayarmaa had counseled. Through the morning the intervals shortened like clockwork, leading Nara to finally cry out for help. Bayarmaa and the other elder women came in prepared with rags and water. Tears escaped the corners of her eyes. The women consoled her that the pain would be over soon enough. Nara shrugged off the pain. The pain had nothing to do with it. She knew but refused to tell anyone. She just knew. Her belly had been still for days. The task at hand would be no easier or harder, it was simply another thing to endure.

The following period was a haze filled with grunts, gasping, tears, pain, water, and blood. Nara would not clearly recollect any of it. Finally, the child emerged in silence. Nara wanted to see and hold it, and the women obliged, avoiding eye contact. A girl, beautiful and tiny, was laid on her chest. The women busied themselves collecting the afterbirth with soiled rags. They carried the mess outside for the beasts without another word. The yurt was still. The baby did not move, cry, or breathe. Nara thought she had mourned the loss already, but this certainty on her breast brought the emptiness back. A quiet emptiness filled the world.

The sunlight through the smoke opening crawled diagonally down the northern curve of the wall. Sounds of the day filtered in: hooves scratching and pounding, men declaring the truth, and the occasional sharp laughter of the few children in the extended family. Nara was in no hurry to move. The baby had her father's brow, but her mother's rounded chin. And so much dark hair – it was a wonder that such a thing could not be alive.

By afternoon, Nara could sense restlessness outside the yurt. No one dared come in. She would have to go out to bury her daughter, allowing dinner to be prepared and life to continue. She swaddled the baby, dressed herself, and walked gingerly to open the blinding flap. Nara paused for a moment at the threshold to let her eyes adjust, then set off toward the slope. Bayarmaa joined her on the walk away from camp. Nara protested, but eventually shrugged and accepted the company. Bayarmaa conveniently had a spade in hand. Nara picked a spot sufficiently high above the flood plain and they quickly dug the small hole. Bayarmaa left discreetly to fetch water from the river.

The men were preparing to break camp tomorrow and were working late into the day consolidating loads. Toqto'ader scanned and found the small silhouette of Nara on the hill. He stood near the horse-ties and watched, frozen in place.

Nara took a last peek inside the blanket and placed the body down. Nara gently covered her with the brown clods adorned with fuzzy patches of green grass. Bayarmaa had returned with a bowl of water. Nara only then noticed she was covered in dirt, sweat, and blood. She plunged her hands into the icy cold water and splashed her face and arms quickly. Unsure what else to do, she poured out the bowl over the mound – leaving behind small traces of herself. This was all she could do. They would never return to this spot. Chasing meadows, hormones, smells, or who-knows-what, the herd would move on and lead them elsewhere. Always elsewhere.

The low rise faced toward long stretches of grassy plains, cut only by the speedy clear Chuluut. It would slow and turn brown with silt later in the year. No trees or shrubs existed to break the eye line from here. Distant mountains framed the edge of the earth, but nearly everything else looked the same as every other grazing spot. No clouds or birds were in the sky on a dry day like this. Only wind and sun.

Nara whispered a name to the mound, turned, and walked slowly down the gentle hill.

The afternoon heat hung in the dry spring air. The sun took on a position orthogonal to the southwest Arkhangai slope. Photons rushed through the cloudless sky ending their journey abruptly in the new dark soil patch. A precipitously warm drop of water took on one quantum of additional energy, crossing the barrier to vapor. A puff of air blew the gas up and away from the hill. The freed molecule dallied over the ground, a Brownian jig with a drunkard's walk. Night passed and another day, and another. Low pressure crept in nearby, and the rush was on to fill the void. Streams of air came in behind and the gas rose aloft. Up, up, near the stratosphere where there was less jostling and banging. The journey then began in earnest. Giant worms of air shot toward the east. Invisible molecules ushered each other along by some other invisible force. Days and weeks passed at ice-cold altitude. The black void beyond the curvature was achingly close. Eventually the jet stream slowed and dove down. The individual molecule was obliged to follow.

Chapter 3 – Alarm Clock

July 25, 1952

THE FAMILIAR THROBBING came with the alarm as Zeke rolled to slam the switch home. Headaches were common enough at this point that they barely rated notice. The pain was the price of admission for nights of chatter, jokes, and new friendships. Lani was up already. As usual. He chose to wait for the dizziness to wane. Imagining an old man like himself creeping his way to the bathroom with hands reaching out for support was ridiculous and depressing. He needed a fixed point in space to stare at until the room stopped spinning. The black curtains were thick and intricately embroidered, designed to guard against the early morning summer sun here in the northern latitudes. Gaps next to the curtain rod pulled Vs of sunlight into the room. There was no such thing as a full blackout in this house.

Zeke had become accustomed to the well-appointed rooms at the embassy over the past few years. It would be quite a change returning stateside next year after Ike won. Unlike most ambassadors, he was neither well connected nor a rich donor to the Democratic machine. They called him Harry's war buddy. Must have owed him something fierce for this appointment. Maybe back in 1917 he pulled future-President Truman into a ditch in the Argonnes just before a blast? Yeah right.

His diplomatic skills were limited mostly to his gift for gab. He certainly didn't finish in the top half at West Point. Making Colonel by the second war was the only thing close to an achievement. A Colonel who stayed in Hawaii for three years to manage supply and logistics as others shipped out into the fire.

The posting had been easy to justify to friends and family. The engineers needed support in the fleet reconstruction. The Marines needed training and resources prior to Guadalcanal. The volume of materiel flowing outbound required management and firm leadership. And on and on. But it was easier to play it off for a laugh. The officer's club in Honolulu was better stocked than in Okinawa, ha ha. There were fond memories from those days. The sun, the breeze, the pointless bickering with non-com analysts, and Lani. A time when he was experienced but not old. A time before the patronizing nods from an embassy staff who were probably just trying to wait him out.

Zeke didn't have dramatic Second World War stories to tell from personal experience – the closest thing to violence he witnessed was a group of sailors demonstrating the uselessness of MPs with a length of rope and an empty oil drum. But Zeke absorbed the tales of a million marines and infantry stopping off on the return leg. He listened to them all and was honor-bound to believe every word. Many of the men avoided or glossed over the worst of the horrors, but he heard enough about the death, mutilation, humiliation, mud, outrage, and paranoia to identify with his own experiences decades earlier. He remembered each terrifying story but precipitated out the worst of it for safekeeping to himself. The mixture of courageous, melancholy, and funny anecdotes that remained was rebroadcast by the Ambassador.

Retelling the bravery and stupidity on those atolls here in Helsinki was all he could think to do to tighten the world by a stitch. His staff tired of it and surely made fun of him behind his back. But who gives a shit. He was responsible for improving American relations a stone's throw from the Russian border. Anything to color the States as a friend was fair game.

As far as he could tell through this tour of duty in Finland, the objective was simply to keep your eyes open and not appear menacing in any way. It was no coincidence that a Pacific theater officer ended up on the other side of the world. There was power in the clear separation. Harry had the sense to avoid sowing any seed that could germinate into conflict just by bad luck.

And so, there were nights of stories, nights of jokes, and nights of new friendships. Three years of staying under the radar. Longer really, a lifetime. In a blink all the energy of youth had relented to a career lazily stuffed with moments adhering to the Williamson credo: enjoying the passage of time by taking the fewest number of chances possible. Maybe at some point he wanted to be great, maybe not. No matter, he never acted.

He thought back to a childhood spent with his brother. The two of them tramping through the forest, further away than their parents knew. That day when they stumbled onto that abandoned shack filled with dry waste wood. They did what any other pair of boys would have done. They lit it up. He remembered the intense heat, how quickly the uncontrollable blaze grew. Flames grew two, three times higher than the shack itself, licking nearby branches. For a while they thought the whole forest would ignite. It didn't of course, but the event spooked them enough that they never bragged about it to friends or even mentioned it again amongst themselves. He couldn't recall acting recklessly like that ever since.

The dizziness was gone, and Zeke shuffled over to the bathroom mirror. He made a cursory inspection of the deepening lines around his eyes and cheeks. Nothing would be under the radar today. A smile broadened on his face. It was time to start a fire.

Chapter 4 – The Sausage

THE NEW HELSINKI export and trade office sat prominently in Jätkäsaari, midway between the active port and the railroad terminus. The refurbished warehouse held a lingering smell of paint and lacquer which was ignored by the murmuring analysts inside. Kalle's office boasted a window with a direct view to the market on Santakatu, but he intentionally positioned his desk to face the opposite direction.

Kalle arrayed the morning's puzzle across the desk: the lumber manifest summary. The weekly decrease in outbound volume was getting worse despite the extension of June's incentive program. A quick glance through made it clear that supply-side wasn't the source of the problem. Transport was just not there. *Birmingham* didn't call again this week, same with *Saint-Nazaire* and *Drammenskammar*. The best guess was these ships were running to Oulu for loads of raw timber. The office didn't receive any data on those products, so Kalle made a note to ask his father about any scuttlebutt. It didn't make any sense, though. Who would buy raw when the capacity for the lumber was sitting right there? The sum of the parts had to exceed the whole by a factor of two or three. Band saws, edgers, gang saws, conical debarkers. The stock of new electric-powered equipment was able to separate and process volume well above current rates. Some must be sitting idle. The only other possibilities were that the ships found other work or that the war was over, and they forgot to mention it to anyone up north. All options were illogical, which was good. Illogic meant opportunity.

Kalle sat back and thought again of Zeke's remark 'they pay you to fall out of bed in the morning.' He has no idea the problems we have to solve around here. His mind flitted back to the moment he had replayed countless times in the past week. The lighting of the torch and the ensuing getaway down the stairwell, laughing like schoolkids the whole way down. Whatever came of the real Aanders Järvinen, last seen stuck in the bathroom with a chair wedged under the knob? Who knows and who cares. No rumors had surfaced from the event at all. As far as the public and the ministry were concerned, everything went according to plan. For his part, Kalle had not mentioned it to anyone. After parting company with his American partners in crime, he was left to his own recollection, sweetened with additional drama each time.

He knew the office found him dry and quiet. The secretaries teased him about it, even Annika. Especially Annika. But he was capable of hijinks. International hijinks at that! He knew it, and that was enough. He didn't need to blather on about it.

"The voice of the new Finland!" Kalle jerked his head up to find Henrik leaning casually against the doorframe at the threshold of the office. "I have no idea what that means, but the Ambassador told me to say that when I saw you next. Strange, when I think about you office boys, I picture mad scribbling on chalkboards and teams huddled over maps with lots of coffee. But here you are sitting alone staring at a blank wall." Without waiting for an invitation, Henrik took a seat opposite and continued, "I had a curious call with Ambassador Williamson this morning. You seemed to have made quite an impression on him last weekend. Congratulations on a job well done, I guess. Don't worry; I didn't report back to anyone that you actually did a good job. Your secret's safe with me! Sorry I didn't have a chance to meet up with you afterwards. Old Papi dragged us all around town afterwards."

Kalle shrugged and offered, "Well, I can't say I did anything special to keep the Ambassador away from the President. He did all the work himself. It was an interesting assignment."

"The voice of the new Finland? What's that about?"

Kalle leaned forward in conspiracy and took Henrik through the afternoon on the tower, burnishing some of the aspects to push his role more into the center of the action.

This was the kind of story Henrik liked best. Absurdity tinted with anti-establishment themes; he was already thinking about the version he would retell. Seeing the wide eyes and the smile on Henrik's unbelieving face, Kalle knew he had done enough to make a friend and relaxed a bit. Laughter poured out from the office, raising eyebrows in the typing pool.

"God, your office is depressing. Let's get out of here and grab some lunch."

It was barely 11:00 and Kalle had a sandwich tucked into his desk drawer. He stood up and answered "Yes, great idea."

·

The Santakatu market pulled in a stream of business all day, with wholesalers in the morning making way for the business lunch crowd by noon, with the locals covering the afternoon. 11:00 was about as quiet as you could expect on a sunny Friday in the summer. The Olympics had raised expectations around most of the town, with kiosks dueling to provide the most authentic Finnish whatever for the tourists. Santakatu was sufficiently removed from the lodgings and stadia that an air of the normal day-to-day reigned.

Kalle and Henrik walked in the direction of the shore. Henrik broke the silence, "I hope that you don't have plans this evening." Kalle shook his head. "As I was saying earlier, I spoke with the Ambassador today. He apologizes for the short notice, but you are invited to dinner at the American Embassy. Tonight." Henrik looked over to gauge the level of surprise on Kalle's face. "You'll have to tell me your secret to winning over these important political types. The best I get is a tip of the hat or pat on the back. The princess of San Marino winked at me once… I think. But she was ugly anyway."

With all the walking and talking, Henrik had seemed to forget about lunch, which was fine by Kalle. "Wait, so you're not going as well?"

"Nope, you are on your own Mr. smooth talker. He didn't go into detail about the occasion, other than to say it was no big deal. Just a casual get-together."

"So it probably is a big deal then…" Kalle offered.

"My thoughts exactly. If you ask me, there might be some Russians coming. That would explain why he is so short on the details. God, we could really use some spies of our own so we can sort all this out. Instead, we just have you. No offense. I guess you could serve as a neutral element to the party, you know, make sure everyone keeps their gloves on so to speak. As far as I know, you're the only Finn invited. Well, I'm sure you can bring a date if you want. It could be fun, actually. Unless it's a bunch of Americans and Brits making speeches to each other, which would be less fun and more torture. Either way, maybe a date is a good idea."

The two speculated for a bit, but they were both out of their depth and the theories spun away into thin air quickly.

"The embassy is the old Swedish Summerhouse, right?" Kalle opened a new line of thought.

"Yep, the Tollefsson Estate." Henrik turned and spat. "Well, I guess there's only so much damage you can do on your own there. So, while you're inside maybe you can peek around for…" Henrik faltered.

"For what?" Kalle asked.

"You know."

"I don't." Kalle lied.

"Yes, you do."

Kalle stared blankly back at his new friend.

"You're going to make me say it aren't you?"

"Yes, I believe I am."

"So, while you're inside maybe you can peek around for the hidden Nazi gold." Henrik gritted his teeth and metered out the phrase in precise enunciation, in an attempt to mask the ridiculousness of the suggestion.

"Jesus Christ, it's true. You field boys really do have shit for brains. You don't really believe those stories, do you?" Kalle jabbed, but he had been thinking the same thing. The American Embassy had only moved into the stately gray building abutting the Kaivopuisto Park just a few years ago. The previous German occupants of the building had left in a hurry in late 1944 thanks to the end of the Continuation War. Those around at the time had expected an informal and slow process of the German retreat from the otherwise calm Helsinki. But Uncle Joe was not interested in informal or slow. Germans, troops and ministers alike, were shown the door quickly and efficiently. The retreat across the Baltic was faster than anyone had anticipated.

Kalle had heard the stories of processions of trucks coming into the Tollefsson Manor just months earlier following the Normandy invasion but didn't have time to return later during the frenetic escape. Of course, they were just stories. Stories of Nazi trucks filled with gold on a one-way trip into the compound. Good for a laugh and a raised eyebrow over a beer with the boys.

"Seriously though, you hope that the stories are true just as much as I do. So, here's what you do. When everyone is seated and deep into the meal, just excuse yourself to the restroom. You'll want as much time as possible, so, I don't know; say your stomach is off today. It must have been the sausage from lunch."

"The sausage from lunch," Kalle repeated slowly and grinned to emphasize the ridiculousness of the plan.

"Yeah, well if you go off to just piss you can't very well peek down into the cellar for ten minutes, can you? Ask for a private bathroom, you know, delicately." Henrik read the dubious look on Kalle's face. "I'm just saying, not many of us get into that fortress of

American soil. How many chances do we have to wander around for a bit of treasure hunting? The voice of the new Finland is up for adventure, right? It will make for good material in your next poem."

"Ha ha. Well, you might as well treat me to a sausage now. For authenticity of course." The prospect of adding another feather of international hijinks to his cap roused an appetite. The invitation was confounding. The odds were high that this would be a boring dinner of political chatter to which Kalle was ill suited. Had the Ambassador misread him this badly? Did the Ambassador have bigger plans for him? No matter. He was a man in demand. Kalle picked up the pace through Santakatu. He was a man walking with purpose as his associate struggled to keep up.

Interlude – Indiana

Summer, 1946 – Paynesville

RON WALKED THE rows in the midday sun, again. It was hot and muggy work stooping down over and over to pull weeds, but it was better than the alternative. By this time-of-day Dorothy would either be on the porch chatting with Carol, or worse, inspecting the house for projects to take up Ron's afternoon. His daily inspection of the corn was timed to elude both of these encumbrances on his sanity. Ron never wanted to be a farmer. It had never occurred to him that he would become one. However, he married into the business. More like married into the lifestyle, truth be told. Calling it a business would imply that profit was involved at some point. From what he'd seen, farming was more like lurching from one calamity to another year after year. To be fair, he hadn't shown a burning desire or aptitude for anything else, and the open air suited him just fine all things considered.

The difficulty at the moment was the puny look of the stalklings. It was their first year planting corn since before the war, and by all accounts, the plants should be much higher than this by now. It was a constant source of friction and debate at the dinner table. Dot had become enamored with talk at church of all the tractors available this year. Those machines could triple the area planted, or even more. This year was the year to get back to corn. The demand should be good, but Dot's brother across the line in Shelbyville would take everything they harvested, if it came to it. She was right that getting a loaner tractor wasn't a problem. The problem was that blasted sun. Every day, that stupid ball baked the ground to a crisp while Ron hunched along. The gentle downward slope ahead was more grayish-brown than green.

It wasn't clear if any corn would mature at this rate. Somehow the weeds were still thriving in this drought though, stealing away what little moisture was laid down as dew every morning. Their haphazard leaves reminded him of the alfalfa he had hand-sown each of the past five years. The Wilsons' cows always needed the silage, and it always came up regardless of the weather. He should have planted alfalfa.

He reached the dry creek bed that marked the end of their property. Across the gulch was the Hoerner's. This part of their field was rotated out this year, which was just as well. One boy mangled and the other killed somewhere in the Pacific last year. They never got the full story, but the word was it was some kind of accident or friendly fire deal. Gil and Betty had not yet recovered from that devastation. At least according to Dot. Thank God they just had the girls.

Ron realized he had been picking stones and tossing them into the gulch. Who knew for how long. A breeze had picked up, bringing a frisson to the back of his clammy sunburned neck. He turned around to face down the next row back up toward the house and was greeted to a welcoming darkness in the skies. Clouds had built up out of nowhere and they sat towering in judgement over the gently rolling land below. The verdict was coming. Ron smiled grimly at the sight. He still should have planted alfalfa.

The warm humid air had careened from the southeast for a thousand miles before being stalled out by higher pressure in Jefferson County. A water vapor molecule jolted higher, cooling rapidly at altitude. Finally, the P-T barrier was crossed and a drop formed. The effect of the density was immediate. Free fall began and the drop hit terminal velocity in an instant. The path back down to earth was not nearly as torturous as it had been on the way up. The drop splashed oblique to a stunted stalk, sliding down to the tilled clay and soil mixture. A vanguard of other drops had saturated the ground just enough to prevent an immediate turnabout of re-evaporation. This drop worked downward to the root system and was incorporated into the plant, meager but alive.

Chapter 5 – Staging

CORNERED BY OVERWHELMING masses of pine and spruce, the few deciduous trees in the area resorted to hugging the coastline, gorging themselves on sunlight while they could. Dana sat on the lee side of a grassy berm, listening to the wind rustling the dwarf diamond leaves behind her. Thousands of tiny flakes connected by narrow stems were independently oscillating in rapid figure eights. The overlaying effect gave a smooth sheen to the chaos. The thin aspens and birches carried the whisper an octave higher than back home in the sprawling oaks of Czechoslovakia.

A natural respite from the city, Otaniemi was hemmed in by the sea to the south and east as well as the deep forest to the west. The brand new "Tech Town" university residential hall served as a self-contained athlete's village for Soviet, Chinese, Bulgarian, Polish, and Czech competitors. The village setting was idyllic but disconnected from the energy of the city. An academic's ivory tower paradise converted to an athlete waystation.

Still flushed with yesterday's excitement, Dana was unapproachable by the other athletes residing in the People's Village. Many had given their heart-felt congratulations last night of course at an impromptu party at Emil and Dana's Spartan double room in the residential hall. Now without the smuggled gin to fire them, hesitation separated them from the gold medal winner. So, she was alone with just her thoughts and the faint clicking of Emil's spikes on the track below. Others shook their heads at Emil putting in an hour of repeat 400s the day after his exhausting gold medal. But head shaking was for Others. Dana and Emil had long grown accustomed to being misunderstood for their methods and dedication. There was nothing more to discuss about the matter. Neither of them was coachable in the traditional sense. An uneasy truce had developed with the sports ministry, a situation that was for the best for everyone, all things considered. The results spoke for themselves, fortunately...

Lost in the whirlwind celebration last night was Dana's odd meeting with the American ambassador and the dinner invitation. Dana raised the subject with Emil in the morning, and he responded with characteristic enthusiasm. It was likely that he was more interested in the prospect of sneaking out of the campus than any dinner party. Dana couldn't have agreed more. After clearing 50 meters, she was capable of anything. At a minimum this would be good for a laugh with her best friend and partner in crime. Even if the dinner was a dud, they could cut out and join some of their western track friends by surprise.

The only real question was the escape plan, to the extent that you could really call it an escape. Emil was an Army captain and outranked the idle functionaries serving as guards, be they Czech or Russian. In theory he could just order them to stand down as the two of them waltzed out the front gate. But the indiscreet agents who would inevitably follow them would be annoying to the extreme. Therefore, an escape plan. The true impediment was their fame. Their location at any time was common knowledge on the campus, especially after yesterday's star double gold performance.

The situation called for some old-fashioned misdirection. Emil had let slip to staff at the cafeteria that he and Dana were planning a private picnic off in the forest trails, and a couple of simple sandwiches would be lovely if they didn't mind helping out a comrade. Over the week so far, the couple had made full use of the forest to get in walks and runs away from the stifling campus. They knew the trails well, including the southern branch that curled back to the water's edge. Not far from this shoreline, a small university boathouse held a couple dusty two-place rowboats. A marine escape seemed most appropriate here in Finland, and Emil was eager to show himself seaworthy to his lovely accomplice.

Unwilling to risk sitting by herself for too long, Dana got up and brushed down her pants. Emil could run in as many circles as he wanted to without her. She assigned herself the task of staging a boat in the brush near the shore for quick access later in the afternoon. She felt like loosening up her limbs and it would be better now in comfortable shoes when a little noise wouldn't register to any nosy wanderers.

The boathouse was not far from the main campus, but it was secluded enough to have been forgotten in all of the improvements to the rest of the university. The needle-carpeted trail petered out as she approached alone. The never-locked doors creaked slowly apart with a little effort. Dana selected the tippy-looking skiff over the fishing dinghy. She supposed it would be lighter and faster, but who really knew about these things anyways? It looked more fun, if nothing else. She glanced under at the hull, not sure exactly what she was looking for. There were no obvious holes at least, which would have to do. One stiff tug set the skiff in grinding motion and Dana kept the momentum out the door, trying to avoid resetting the standing friction of a full stop.

Tilting alone on the beach, the skiff looked rather less seaworthy than it did inside supported by the other clunky boat. A constant wall of air flowed to fill the low pressure somewhere onshore hours away. Choppy waves angled into the shore and caught Dana's attention with their crashing fits on the rocks. She grinned at the chaos and turned back toward campus to prepare for an entertaining evening away from here.

The duo cleaned up and put on the closest thing to formal wear they had brought along with them. A fine evening for a quiet walk in the woods, alibi sandwiches in hand. "They appeared, just like that. On the track?" Emil asked as they entered the shade of the first path into the woods, eyes on their backs.

Dana checked quickly and didn't notice any trace of jealousy in his eyes. "Yeah, I don't know if they had been there all the time or what. I was watching Sandra's last throw and turned around and there they were. I thought they were our 'coaches' or something until they spoke in English."

"Who else is coming, do you know? Maybe Dean or Lindy will be there. Boy they were lightning this week, I haven't even had a chance to say hello." Emil was never one to hide his enthusiasm.

"I have no idea. They only wanted to be sure I was there. They were very insistent on that. They even said something like it didn't matter either way if you came. How about that, big shot?"

"Well, I'm sure you'll dazzle them tonight my dear. I'll of course be very happy to just sit back in the shadows tonight." Emil flashed his confident smile which was either winning or ingratiating depending on the day. Today it was winning.

"Uh-huh." Dana dismissed his comment and motioned at the skiff which lay ahead ready and waiting. "Alright Captain, let's see how you fare in the navy today."

"Yeah, a one-man Czech navy. Domination of the seas for a land-locked country!" Emil launched the newly requisitioned vessel into the bay and put in an honest dozen strokes to gain clearance from the rocks before relaxing into an efficient cadence. He moved as if he had been doing this all his life.

The ride was too windy and undulating to be considered pleasant, but the simple concept of being out was invigorating for its own sake. There was no specific plan other than to put distance on to the south before heading east across the bay, hoping to be a small enough speck that no one would notice who was aboard. Emil moved the boat well through the water, but the distances were deceivingly far. The whole process was taking longer than expected.

They would probably be a little late, but the pair were not ones to concern themselves over timeliness.

The bay was scattered with islands which hid the line of sight to the old downtown peninsula and the American embassy. The wind and waves broke up as Dana navigated a backward Emil through the maze. The main shoreline to the north held a new connecting bridge which saw a fair share of traffic: trucks, buses, bicycles, and one slow-crawling sedan.

Emil was still smiling but had worked himself up to a point where his trademark grimace threatened to break out. Dana couldn't pass up the chance, "You should take it easy, darling. You still might have that marathon to deal with. Leave the rowing to someone with strong arms. C'mon, switch with me."

Emil nodded and flashed his eyes meaning "fat chance" and continued on, slightly faster.

Dana drew in a measured breath of the briny atmosphere before responding. "Have it your way, but I'll row us back tonight. You can count on that, Captain."

The city rose up before them, allowing an excuse to pause and take in the view. Selecting a berth on the busy shoreline proved difficult, as they needed easy access with a certain amount of anonymity. Dana spotted a small market with a couple fishing trawlers tied to a nearby dock. The couple proved themselves hopeless in the art of putting in, with a mixture of left, right, stop, oops, and god dammit called out in Czech to the bemused shoppers strolling on the outer edge of the market. If there had been any plan to blend in with the locals, it was gone now. In any case, the spectators remained completely unaware that this laughable display was put on by the owners of multiple gold medals.

While Emil cinched the ropes taut, Dana got her bearings and scanned the small crowd for a friendly face to ask for some general directions toward the embassy. A black sedan rolled slowly through the crushed gravel and came to a stop in front of Dana. Emil turned at the noise and came up the pier, wiping his hands on the sides of his best pair of pants.

The driver stepped out of the otherwise empty car. He raised his arms slowly from his sides. With a sober face and tired affect, he adjusted his hat. With a muddled accent, the stranger said in Czech, "Get in the car. Please."

Chapter 6 – Absorption

THE STREETCAR HEADING down into the southern district was slow and hesitant at this time of day. Beautiful summer afternoons meant congestion. Kalle gazed out the window as walkers were overtaking him on the sidewalk. It was nearly worth it to get off here and stretch his legs. It would be a nice break from sitting all day at the office and likely sitting at a stuffy dining table all evening. But his first priority was to prolong the onset of sweat underneath the newish jacket he had put on for the occasion. The stop just north of Kaivopuisto Park wasn't too far away so there wasn't any reason to switch horses mid-race in any case.

With Kalle leaning his head against the window, the other riders forgot about him and continued chattering away. Waves of idle talk bounced around the cabin, reflecting on steel, glass, and leather before finally settling in Kalle's ears. There was some regurgitation of the daily routine complete with predicable wrinkles, but more often Kalle found the phrases bending toward itemized complaints and opinionated soliloquies. Defeated 'but what she doesn't understand is's and exasperated 'that's why I'd never's. Kalle contented to keep his eyes focused outside, without rolling them once. If the ideas expressed were asinine or naïve by any objective measure, it didn't register on the face of the quiet man in the window seat.

Words. So many words expended every day. In person, on the radio, in letters. All around the world. Kalle could never fathom why so many words constantly streamed out. Nonetheless, he gathered as many as he could. Kalle valued words and ideas more than others, which explained the imbalance of trade. He took them in, absorption without reemission. Some days yielded nothing more interesting than the bad manners of an in-law, but other days were better. Kalle treated all these words and opinions at face value and with complete seriousness. It was a curious sort of blinders to put on oneself, carrying the default presumption that others adhered to the same code, gave the same import to every word spouted out into the ether.

With these blinders came the burden that hurtful throwaway comments were never thrown away. No one was to be waved off or ignored. To Kalle, people always meant what they said, even if it was a long time ago.

Kalle shook off the gloom as he approached his stop. A night of international hijinks was about to unfold after all. Over the course of the afternoon, he had concluded that any hunt for gold was impossible. It was more likely that the Ambassador would overwhelm him with so many questions that summoning up the courage to excuse himself seemed remote at best. But truth be told, he had no idea what to expect, given his complete lack of experience at large formal international parties. Regardless, *he* had been invited, not Henrik. He was perfectly capable of rubbing elbows with western upper society types. A few clever remarks and polite compliments would go a long way toward making an impression, and there was no reason to cock it all up snooping around on a fool's errand. The report back to Henrik would have to be just fabricated dead ends, that's all.

Exiting into the late afternoon sun, he worked his way south along the esplanade of the eastern harbor. He was early, so he could take his time. Ambling along, he formulated a few observations and questions he could try to shoehorn into the conversation at some point in the evening. General life and current events, but not Korea obviously. If spontaneous small talk wasn't your strong suit, you had to plan ahead.

Something hard jabbed into the small of his back. "Don't turn around! Keep walking slowly ahead and no one gets hurt," a gruff whisper jumped into his right ear. Kalle nearly stumbled at the suddenness and apparent randomness of the instruction but kept upright. He tried to appear composed while his heart pulsed in double-time. The walkway was packed with people, surely someone would notice and come to his aid? Kalle searched in panic, trying to make eye contact with anyone among the crowd. Passers-by passed. No help was coming. The jab in the back directed him toward an alley beside a small café with a tattered blue and yellow striped awning.

The voice behind him let out a strange coughing grunting sound. What kind of maniac was this? As Kalle approached the unknown of the alley, he turned slightly to catch a glimpse of the assailant. The grunting became full-throated laughter. Henrik.

"Aaah! You should see your face, my brother! Oh, that was good. So good. Did you piss yourself? Please say yes. It looks like you may have pissed yourself." Henrik couldn't continue his verbal onslaught for all the laughter.

Kalle chose relief over outrage, at least for the moment. "What on earth, man?" Kalle squeaked with a forced smile.

"Don't you desk guys get any training for situations like this? Close quarter hand to hand? Nothing? God, to think I had you on a detail to protect the President. It's a miracle no one has been assassinated on your watch… yet. Where's your date anyway? You're not taking anyone? Come on, you're way too early to head to dinner. Come grab a drink with me and my friend." Henrik was leading through the alley, which connected to a small terrace in back of the café.

Kalle regained composure heading into the bright terrace. Facing west, the open space welcomed in a full sun under blue skies. Whitewashed walls and a chipped yellow ceramic floor radiated the warmth and baked the patrons kitted out in relaxed summer attire. The fake attack had jump-started beads of sweat on Kalle's back. This oven of a terrace turned those beads into saltwater rivulets coursing underneath his jacket. Kalle searched for clouds in the distance but came away disappointed.

Henrik walked ahead and addressed the table hidden by his broad back, "I got 'em good. You should have seen his face. Ha!"

Kalle caught his breath as blood rushed to his face. Annika was alone at the table, grinning broadly at Kalle then flashing her eyes over to Henrik. Papering over his surprise, Kalle took a seat opposite his coworker and replied, "You didn't get me at all. You're going to have to sound a lot more menacing if you want to kidnap someone for real you know." Nodding to Annika, he continued, "I didn't realize the two of you knew each other."

"We ... used to know each other at gymnas. I nearly ran her over today in your office. The angles of your hallways are simply diabolical, but a pleasant collision nonetheless! You haven't changed at all Anni, by the way. Anyways, we were here having a drink and catching up. I knew you'd walk this way to your dinner, and I happened to see you through the alley. I thought a drink or two would help loosen you up." Henrik offered.

"You didn't do the finger gun thing did you?" Annika sighed and gave Henrik a playful shove. "I told you not to do that." Turning to Kalle, "So I've heard all about your big shot dinner plans, and your *secret mission*. Where's your date?"

Kalle hesitated.

"The biggest night of his very short professional life and he's giving it a go solo." Henrik explained, ordering beers for the table in the international sign language of the looping finger and eyebrow raise.

"I just got the invitation a few hours ago, and I didn't want to put anyone on the spot," Kalle added looking down at the table, warped from years of rain and spilled drinks. The excuse hung limply in the air and Kalle had no funny follow-up to fill the silence. Instead, he excused himself for the bathroom.

He took to a stall and unrolled a large wad of paper. His shirt was already sticking to his back, but he nonetheless angled his arm backward to wipe off the worst of the sweat. If the humidity relaxed a bit, there could be a chance to dry out later. One quick drink and a few nods of the head and he would be off to dinner. It was getting close to 7:00 already. The water from the sink was a welcome bracing cold on his face as he splashed more on for good measure. Checking the mirror on the way out, he noticed that the panic in his eyes when first entering the bathroom had evaporated.

On return to the table, Henrik and Annika seemed to be sitting closer together than before. "So, are you ready to go with Operation Gold Rush?" Annika jumped in as Kalle sat and reached for the waiting stein.

Kalle first took hold of the glass in front of him, a slippery sheen of condensation on the surface, and took a long drink. He smiled and responded with his own question, "We have a code name for it now?" Kalle played along with their enthusiasm for the hunt. It was fun, after all. But nothing changed his determination to bury the whole idea. He wouldn't jeopardize his time with the Ambassador. The only decision to make was how elaborate to make the story he reported back. With Annika part of the equation now, he decided to make it a doozy.

One beer became two and Kalle eased back in his chair, his disappointment on seeing Annika talking easily with Henrik having mellowed a bit. Henrik was pressing on about the likely areas of the manor to search: cellars and offices with unusual dimensions. Kalle's mind had wandered away a bit, his eyes settled on the back of an older man with worn overalls. He was standing facing away and slightly stooped. But his head was cocked as if in concentration. Kalle snapped back into the conversation with the word 'sausage.'

"Honestly, thinking about it more, the sausage excuse is pretty lousy. We need something better to give you more time," said Henrik.

"It was your idea. Plus, with a pretty large group no one will exactly be keeping track of all the guests. Once the Ambassador gets going, you know how all eyes will be on him anyway," Kalle said.

Henrik nodded and was about to respond when his eyes shifted left. A shadow cast over the table and a crackly voice gave a conspiratorial whisper, "so you're going for it, are ya?" The older bald man in overalls placed both hands on the table and leaned in with a smile. A smell followed directly after his question. It was a fishy smell reminiscent of a long day of work gutting the catch out in the sun. Annika shrank back in reflex, but Henrik laughed back in his typical welcoming way as if he had found a long-lost brother in arms.

"I'm sorry?" Kalle feigned ignorance as a first line of defense.

"Oh, you should be sorry, kid. Talking so loud that half the patio can hear every word you're saying. I came over to shut you up and help you out. I felt so bad thinking about you stumbling around all the places it might be, here there up down… bah!" The man projected the last of this out with such force that flecks of spittle launched across the table, landing in a barrage just short of Kalle's hand.

Henrik was immediately enamored with Vaino, as they came to know him. He pulled a chair over for himself and graciously accepted Henrik's offer of a drink, as he had appeared in front of them empty-handed. His overalls were in fact trimmed down summer waders, and the smell of gutted fish he exuded was in fact due to that exact work all afternoon down by the port. The staff of the café knew him as a regular, popping over for a drink and butting into conversations for his own amusement, to varying success. Opinions on Vaino from the servers ranged from "annoying" to "harmless I guess." Properly settled in, he begged them to continue, "So there will be a lot of guests? You can just slip away and explore?"

"Yes, I imagine I'll have ten minutes or more to myself to nose around. But to be completely honest, it could be anywhere, with the most likely place being nowhere. We're probably just talking steam," said Kalle.

"Oh, it's there," snorted Vaino. "And I might even know where you should spend your precious ten minutes searching."

"Oh, you *might*, huh?" asked Henrik.

"Yeah, I might. I mean, are we a team here or am I just a tool at your disposal? To use then toss back into the box?" Vaino countered. Annika watched on with amusement at these men rushing headlong in their never-ending circles.

"Fine, a team. Anything we find we split four ways. The Gold Rush Four, ok? Now, out with it old timer!" Henrik's tone was still jovial if a little more to the point.

Vaino nodded and took a quick look at the surrounding tables. He leaned in and began. "Back in the summer and fall of '44 I took to spending the night out on my trawler. There wasn't a cabin proper, mind you, but at least it had a low roof meant for shielding the catch from the sun on long trips out, you know. There had been a disagreement over my apartment lease… well the open air of the boat was best for everyone; you know what I mean. Never got any questions on my whereabouts out there. None of the krauts paid any mind to us … old timers as you say, after a while. Anyways, I woke up one night to some heavy waves. I thought a storm was blowing in or something, but it was just a wake. A large wake from a steamship reversing hard into the dock. Wartime deliveries, you know. We'd see these from time to time back then, but not at night. The horn didn't blow, and the seaman weren't barking for the halyards or any of the usual. All quiet-like. I had half a mind to think someone else was invading with all the speed and the hush-hush. Me being a curious man, I kipped my anchor and tried my luck paddling in closer."

"You saw the trucks?" Annika jumped in.

"I didn't see anything, girl. It was dark and I had a mind to keep my head down, snooping around as I was. But it was what I heard that mattered. As I was saying, it was all quiet-like. When they moored up, finally someone called out '*Wohin? Wo?*' Like, where to, boss? The response was pretty quiet, so I couldn't tell what they were saying." Vaino paused and took a sip, gathering energy from his small but game audience. "I couldn't tell what they were saying, but. But one word jumped out, and it was repeated a couple times with laughter. *Badezimm.*"

Vaino's audience of three stared back at him, their faces uncomprehending blanks.

"Crissakes, you don't even know a little bit of German, do you? Must have all been babies during the occupation. You know I'm beginning to think you're not taking this serious-like and are just having a laugh at me. I mean, I respect that. And I might do the same in your shoes. But anyway, if you don't want the key to the treasure chest, just say so and we can stop wasting time."

Henrik smiled and opened his arms, an offering for the storyteller to continue.

"*Badezimm*, like *badezimmer*. A water room. I dunno, probably a bathroom or utility closet. Maybe even a sauna." Vaino said. "And then I heard the trucks start up. Off they went up the hill. I didn't think much about it at the time, until the trucks came back a couple hours later. They rolled back on the ship and were gone before sunrise. I got thinking about what was so urgent and secret to bring up here of all places. All those rumors of gold you hear about? They all started not too long after that. And not by me either! I didn't say boo to anyone until now, more or less. Why anyone in his right mind would store gold in a bathroom is beyond me. But we aren't talking about people who were in their right mind now that I mention it…" Vaino was losing steam.

"I guess the bad sausage is back on the menu." Kalle shrugged. "It's perfect now. Like I said, the Ambassador will start holding forth with some story or another, and I can check one or two of the larger bathrooms for cracks in the wall. Maybe it leads to a secret compartment or door."

"Yeah yeah. But what if it isn't a large party, or what if you are the guest of honor? Don't get me wrong, I wouldn't have you as a guest of honor of course, but the Ambassador is unpredictable that way. If you are in the spotlight, a bad sausage alone won't buy you enough time. We need a diversion of some kind. I don't know, something interesting to absorb all the attention." Henrik was looking at Annika as he spoke.

She picked up the thread, turned to look straight at Kalle and cut through the crap. "I'm coming with you."

"What?" Kalle stopped short as their eyes met. Regarding his glass he ventured, "Well it's a bit last minute and I don't want to impose on your plans. And besides I really…"

No one was listening to him. Henrik spoke briefly to the waiter on the side. Annika excused herself to freshen up before heading out and Vaino watched her walk away. Kalle trailed off his conversation with no one and stared at the corner of the wall where shadows were finally gaining purchase. He exhaled slowly, conceding any say over how his evening would proceed. The hunt was back on. There would be no avoiding it under Annika's watch. While a *badezimmer* check sounded simple, he expected complications.

Annika and the waiter came back over together. "Salmiakki for four," the waiter announced with a slightly forced enthusiasm. Small vessels of the dark viina were arranged for the Gold Rush Four. Henrik beamed at the group around him. In the past few minutes, he had prepared something of a speech. "You two will do the heavy lifting from here on out. I know we joke about this being a dumb local rumor (no offense Vaino), but the gold is in there. I know it is. You heard the man, truckloads upon truckloads into the *badezimmer*. I wish I could be up there to help. Vaino and I will stay behind the park. If you run into trouble or need us to come up and help haul the prize away, bring a light to the pointless wall and flash it a few times. We can see the wall from this courtyard. We'll come up.

Between the four of us we can carry back down as much as possible and then hide the rest in the park to grab later when we can arrange better transport. This gold is our heritage. We hosted those German bastards for far too long, and only received pain in return. This is our responsibility to extract payment. No halfhearted peeking. No excuses." He raised his glass. "For Finland."

Kalle tipped back the astringent licorice spirit while exchanging a dubious look with Annika. They said their goodbyes to Henrik and Vaino who looked to be settling in for the long haul at the table, checking the menu. It was well past 7:00 by now. They were late. Whether that was an international *faux pas* or not, it didn't matter at this point. They were liable to make a few more material ones before the night was over.

The pair walked down the eastern shore promenade toward the large manor. "That Vaino. What an old curmudgeon. With his, 'I felt so bad for you. Let me tell you how it really is.' What a piece of work. I could feel his loutish eyes on me the whole time. Good thing he isn't sneaking around up at the manor, the fish stink would give him away in a heartbeat." Annika declared.

"Yeah, well…" Kalle nodded his head feigning half-agreement but withholding judgement on the man.

They walked in silence for a while around the southern bend of the peninsula toward the entrance. Each step closer strengthened Kalle's nerve. The Salmiakki helped too. "You look great tonight, by the way," Kalle said.

"It's just the same old outfit I had on all day at the office, you know."

"I know, but I wasn't talking about the outfit," Kalle returned so softly that only someone listening closely would have picked it up.

Interlude – Kentucky

Fall, 1946 – Shelbyville/Cooper's Hollow

THE LOADS WERE bad, somehow even worse than he had expected. Truck after truck of shriveled kernels from Dot's farm crawled past the gate without recourse. Periwinkle Sherman (just Sherman, please) waved off the last of the flies for the year and muttered to himself. Originally, the plan had been quality over quantity. And as far as the staff knew, that was still the case. But the bank… well… the bank was the bank. And family was family.

The sun was threatening to slide underneath the western hillock and drop temperatures at the estate by ten degrees in a heartbeat. Cooper's Hollow was a showcase for extremes: soaking up sunshine and humidity during the day only to outgas it all every night. The fog was the only saving grace, putting a floor on temperatures and pushing out the hard freeze date by a couple weeks for Mary's flowers. Sherman turned from the gate and followed the dust from the rumbling trucks back, puzzling out the best path forward with this latest monkey wrench in the plan.

Five years of making quick turnaround hooch, nearly paint thinner, for Uncle Sam had paid for the equipment and sheds around him. Sherman refused to label the army rations with his name. He was proud to send liquor to the thirsty boys over there, but not because of the quality. The whole enterprise had been practical from start to finish. With the war over, this year was supposed to be different. Thousands of freshly fired oaken barrels stood ready for use – ready for the full six-year hibernation called for in grandpa's recipe. Six years of waiting, and then Sherman Select Bourbon would be the name everyone ordered. No one else in Kentucky knew what the hell they were doing and the gobs over in Scotland wouldn't have mature batches at a similar quality for a decade at least. Even then, charred oak beat peat hands down, at least in the right hands.

First National wanted to double the output in order to make the loan worth their while. Six years is a long time to wait for repayment Mr. Sherman. As a businessman you understand... Equipment was never the problem, just feedstock. Meanwhile Dot kept calling and calling with her own troubles. Crossing state lines didn't stop his chatterbox of a sister from detailing the minutiae of her day to day, including the withering corn for which she and Ron couldn't find a home. The soil up her way was more clay than anything. Why his brother-in-law didn't just put his foot down and plant alfalfa, he'll never know. In any case, here Sherman was, trying to kill two ugly birds with one stone. The only way forward was mixing. Each batch of mash would have a portion of the family heritage corn. Not too much to spoil the stability, but enough to get rid of it. And First National would get their volume target. Twenty percent moisture... Blast it all!

If it was easy, then it wouldn't be fun. Sherman stood in the shaded cool of the boiler room, surrounded by pressure and temperature gauges, all pinned to the left. In a few short hours, this glorified horse stall would be anything but cool. The bourbon was made right here, today. The Sherman recipe wasn't written down – no ragged old parchment from Grandpappy Sherman locked in a safe. It was kept secure in Sherman's head, where no one else was invited. He trusted no one with the information, and he intended to keep it that way until he was old and gray. Any old recipe could call for a grain bill and any joker could run a still. The secret to the Sherman recipe was in the boil. Diacetyl rest timing and oxygenation pressure would drive the sugars out along with the grain's natural water content just the way he wanted it, unlike anywhere else. The rest would take care of itself. A proper process would overcome even substandard base ingredients. The pungent odor of the wort soon came in from the vats and Sherman was at home again. It already smelled like… before. Sherman Select was back. All that was left to do was wait until 1952.

Racked in the shed, barrel upon barrel of bourbon endured six Kentucky summers and six Kentucky winters. Being so far inland, Cooper's Hollow locals bragged that they had the worst of both worlds when it came to weather. Maybe poor weather for humans, but ideal for bourbon. The oaken walls contracted and expanded, again and again, imbuing color and taste to the semi-sweet alcohol and water mixture. The daily cycle was unrelenting, with no end in sight.

Chapter 7 – Ivy

THE VIEW SOUTH-WEST down the Kaivopuisto slope was breathtaking when the Tollefsson manor was constructed hundreds of years ago. A clear-cut all the way to the shore made sure of that. The building took the form of its Swedish first owner: imposing, over-sized for the job, equal parts impressive and ridiculous. Locals made a habit of deriding the ostentatious nature of it, but over time they nonetheless took pride in directing tourists to the best spots for viewing it amongst the now-mature trees ringing the park.

The manor was born as an enclave and remained so ever since. It came with thick skin suited to the job. The exterior granite walls were a least a foot thicker than had ever been necessary, certainly not for load bearing or even insulation purposes. The men and horse teams who dragged the blocks up the slope from the port knew this all too well. The blocks were shipped up from Germany and installed in the same rough-hewn shape in which they came from the quarry, with pits and crevices striated at oblique angles to the cut. Any piece requiring a trim or fitting was done via massive chisels. They were brought in specifically to maintain the appearance that the manor had risen directly out of the earth to adorn this small hill. Years of rain, wind, and frost heaves had not budged or smoothed the blocks. Some rounding and darkening on the edges were the only evidence that it was not erected yesterday.

Inside the walls, the manor had housed rotting food, spilled wine, piss, vomit, shit, and a few farm animals from time to time. Floorboards had been replaced from years of dancing and ornamentation had broken off in drunken rages about insults long forgotten. Pain and humiliation had been inflicted throughout the interior.

Worse than the abuse raining down from all directions were the years, decades, of neglect. In those lean times when summer visits from Sweden were too costly or an indifferent son came into possession, a vacuum settled over the place with only the padding of an elderly caretaker shuffling through from time to time. Regardless, each year the sun came back for the saplings to usher them toward trees.

The caretakers varied in ability and enthusiasm over time. At a minimum, most were keen to stave off the worst of the dust and mold on the interior, if only to make the area livable in their modest quarters and to minimize the damage if there was an unexpected visit from the family. The grounds, however, were subject to the caprices of nature. Thick pockets of needle-filled brambles blossomed on the lee side of the hill, inviting small creatures to burrow and thrive by seeking out discarded vegetable plots and narrow underground entrances to pantries and backyard storehouses.

At some point, for reasons passing any understanding of the locals, a low wall of stacked flagstones had been installed in back. It wasn't attractive and didn't deter the aforementioned pests. It wasn't large or obvious enough to be called an eyesore, more of just a baffling peculiarity to those looking from behind the hill up to the manor. The wall traced an irregular line, but broadly speaking it made a shallow V pointing away from the property down the hill like those cursed salients developed by overeager army captains for centuries. To make its function even less clear, it was built next to the cliff that was already demarking the northern end of the property. It didn't surround the grounds or adjoin to the shore. The ends just ended. It was a work of art built for no one. A pointless wall.

Eventually the Tollefsson estate said goodbye to the last Tollefsson and a series of hard-working Russian almost-aristocrats occupied the cavernous rooms. What the new tenants lacked in deep family connections they made up for with gumption. The estate was put to work, inside and out. Guest rooms housed a series of offices for regional business of trade and distribution in the name of the duke. The vegetable gardens returned to double size, with roots and tubers of all sorts being pulled and stored at volumes never seen before on site. The brambles were cut back to within an inch of their lives, but the flagstone V wall remained.

When Russia eventually left there was no clear use for the estate. Some of the older Russians had stayed with their Finnish wives and Finnish practices, knowing there was no place for them back east. Since no one really said otherwise, these families simply moved in. The squatting evolved into a series of internal reconfigurations. Walls were removed and erected with little notice or plan. Old offices subdivided and hallways detoured or dead-ended. The only constant was the increasing complexity. Entropy reigned over the estate. The patient over-sized blocks bottled up the gestation and shielded the chaos from view of the increasing foot traffic along the banks of a growing Helsinki.

The German granite shell welcomed a homecoming of sorts with a new occupation in the 1940s. But this lasted for just a blink of an eye and lead to nothing of consequence.

The manor as it stood in 1952 was not immediately visible from the shoreline, for all the mature trees scattered along the slope. The second-floor windows stared blankly out into the groomed lawn and newly paved driveway that wound back to connect to the autoroute. The black chimney was silent, enjoying the respite of summer. The garden was coming along well for this time of year, except for the ill-advised attempt at tomatoes. A new rectangle had been scored out of the turf nearby as plans for a greenhouse took shape. The new tenants were a lot of things, but quitters they were not. The tomatoes would come, one way or another.

Aside from the garden proper, the Americans had trailed along a variety of plants and shrubs. With the aid of the caretakers, an attempt was made to overcome the brambles once and for all through a smothering attack instead of the cutting frenzies that had tried and failed for centuries. Among the imported vegetation were some Canary ivy cuttings that had made their way over from who knows where, possibly a previous posting in Morocco by one of the staff. The ivy thrived along the base of the nearby trees, as other varieties had done before. Over the past few years, the creepers had advanced above the frost line to cling to the granite walls themselves in the sunny southeast side. The deep green offset to the gray stone was so stark as to appear as black shadow from the driveway approach in daytime.

Inside, new doors hung in the maze and thick braids of wiring pierced the walls to connect phones and lights in the name of progress. Otherwise, the manor appeared on the surface more or less the same as before. The abandoned enclosures, dead-ends, and weevil burrows remained in quiet isolation unknown and unexplored.

A warm breeze raced up the hill from the shore, ushering the smell of salt with a sour tinge of fish and seaweed. These were the summer smells all the locals were accustomed to and had embedded deep in their clothes well into autumn. Visitors needed a couple days in order to acclimatize. A new round of guests was arriving this evening… again. Just a few new pairs of eyes to ogle the photons recoiling from paint, stone, silver, and wood. Incessant rebounding and reception of light, firing fleeting electrical impulses to the fleeting brains of these walking bundles of words, half-formed ideas, and animal failures. The manor sighed in the wind as another cocktail hour approached.

.

A clattering of pots and pans caromed off the kitchen walls as Lani prepared a pork dish as close to her family's traditional style as could be expected at 60 degrees north. The fruits were so wrong it was laughable. But no one was around to share in the joke. Three years living half a world away from her family had beaten the joy out of making and eating fantastic meals. These days cooking resembled more of a catering job for Zeke's perpetual diplomatic get-togethers. There was a chef available on site of course, but Zeke had started asking for her to step in from time-to-time because he thought it gave a more personal and authentic touch at important dinners. Her Hawaiian style courses, no matter how bastardized, were always a smashing success. So successful that the time-to-time requests became constant, and all the dinners became important. She had married a man who lived to eat and talk. There was never a shortage of either up in this cold dark outrageous castle on the hill. Zeke's easygoing charm back home when they met during the war had worn thin up here in Finland. None of that was particularly unusual, but it seemed to happen relatively fast up here in this vacuum.

"Need any help in here?" Robert's smiling face popped around the edge of the door without warning. Keeping his momentum, he gave her a quick wink and scuttled away with a handful of lingonberries.

Lani kept her eyes down on the board, slicing vegetables.

"Seen Robbie anywhere?" Zeke walked in.

"Just missed him," Lani replied pointing her knife and giving a few thrusts. "And feel free to tell him the berries are for the meal, not for stuffing his mouth."

"Oooo, lingonberries? These are so good." Zeke grabbed a few on his way out, turning in the direction of the stabbing.

Lani grabbed another onion and continued slicing.

The Ambassador entered the dining room. It certainly wasn't a grand ballroom of any sort. It was functional for daily life while maintaining the minimum décor required for visitors. Like most of the smaller embassies, space was shared between official business and the residency. Many rooms needed to serve more than one function. That was fine by Zeke, as it jived with his down-to-earth practical sensibilities. Almost immediately on arrival three years ago, Zeke and Lani did away with the china, lace, and portraits of old dead people. The art choices were still muted in color, but more contemporary and abstract. New ideas trumped nostalgia.

The table had been compressed into its smallest form, set for only six tonight: Lani, Zeke, Robert, Kalle, Dana, and Emil. The Ambassador scanned the table quickly to determine that the staff did indeed set everything up as expected before leaving for the night. Satisfied, he continued to the drawing room in search of either a drink or Robert, preferably both. Sure enough, Robert's back was to the room as he busied himself at the high counter in the corner which served as a makeshift self-service bar. From the back, the curve of his muscles rounded through his jacket reminding Zeke of how formidable his new right-hand man could be in a pinch.

At the sound of footsteps, Robert turned holding an amber cocktail in each fist. "I'm going to get you good and drunk right now, so you'll finally tell me what we're doing here tonight."

"I have no idea what you are talking about, but I accept," Zeke replied.

"You did say that drinks start at 7:00, if I remember correctly. I'm just following orders, boss." Both men were silent for a bit, allowing for a chance to take a couple sips. It was already 7:20 and the two men who had worked in the building all day were staring at each other in an otherwise empty drawing room. "You think they'll show?" Robert finally asked the question in the air.

"Of course they will. Those two know how to get the job done. I'm sure they are dying to get out of that prison camp. God knows they could do for a little mischief this week. They probably just underestimated the distance out here to the peninsula. As for Kal, I swear all these Finns operate as if time doesn't even exist. Why on earth they even bother wearing watches I'll never know. I expect him to wander in any old time tonight. He seems like a reasonable sort, but in this way he's like all of his countrymen I'm afraid." Zeke continued, "of course if they don't make it, there's more kalua pork for us three. No harm in that. None at all, nope."

Robert smiled in agreement. The buzzer sounded and the guardhouse intercom crackled on. "Ambassador? Gibbons here. Some guests have arrived, but one isn't on the list." Ambassador Williamson cocked his head slightly at the box on the wall. He set down his drink and made for the front door with Robert close behind.

Kalle and Annika waited patiently at the gate. Charlie Gibbons, the young Marine who had never introduced himself except through the crossfire of the intercom, had already retired into the confines of the small shack of a guardhouse. Kalle's eyes fell onto the sign at the gate, reading:

> You are entering territory accorded immunity from claims by Finland to the United States of America. Please have your identification in hand. By crossing at this point, you consent to customs and search protocol. Your actions on these premises shall be governed by the laws of the United States. Welcome!
> U.S.C.§223(b)(4)(E)(iii)

"There he is!" Zeke was walking up the path at double-time. "I'm so glad you were able to come on such short notice. And who is this lovely lady gracing us this evening?"

"Good evening, Ambassador. I'm Annika Kuippo, a colleague of Kalle's. Very pleased to meet you. Kalle was telling me all about you earlier this evening."

"Well of course the pleasure is all mine. Kal, I didn't realize you were seeing someone – particularly someone so striking as Ms. Kuippo here."

Kalle drew breath to reply, but Zeke had already moved on to introduce Robert and usher the group back the pathway toward the manor.

The Ambassador turned while walking past the guardhouse "Thanks Charlie. We're all set here."

Whatever Kalle and Annika had been expecting on entering the manor, the foyer was a surprise. The weathered oak door gave way to a lush green entrance hall. Leaves and shoots of varying sizes dominated the space. Tall windows facing southwest allowed for tropical plants to thrive in the summer, perched on terraced shelves to either side of the passage into the house proper. The room was also crammed with ceramic Polynesian-inspired decorations, electric pump-fed fountains, and assorted vibrant tapestries. A large stone Tiki idol stood in the corner with a small waterfall cascading across his feet down into a pool filled with colorful fish. There was so much to see and smell that Kalle was momentarily disoriented. Annika took it all in with appreciation, absently touching a few of the plants on the way through the maze-like pathway. Zeke looked back to gauge his visitors' reactions, cataloging them in comparison to others who had come through before.

The pair was ushered into the drawing room, which reverted to the 18th century Swedish style of stone and timber. The room was light and airy compared to the humidity of the foyer, but it was also completely empty. It was clear they were the first to arrive.

Lani heard the commotion and joined the group. Kalle struck up a superficial but interesting conversation with Lani. How was life back in Hawaii, how did she come to meet Zeke, that sort of thing.

She was charming and engaging as she had ample practice at this sort of thing over the past few years.

Kalle asked, "The entrance hall. This is your doing?" Lani nodded. "It's unlike anything I've seen before. It's very impressive. I can't imagine how much work goes into maintaining so much life in that room. There is a simple aquarium here in Helsinki that I went to as a child, but it was covered with algae, and I don't remember seeing anything but green shadows of fish here and there."

"Oh, the room largely takes care of itself." Lani responded. "We have oysters and mussels who feed on the excess nutrients and plankton to keep the water clean."

"Well, that's convenient."

"Yeah, except that the parrotfish in there like to eat mussels, which was a problem at first."

"So how did you…"

"A refugium." Lani said. "We made a separate small pool for the filtering creatures. All the water is pumped through for cleaning, but the pipes have a fine mesh so the fish, especially the parrotfish, are kept out.

Kalle nodded in appreciation. He could tell from his peripheral that Annika was attracting the full attention of both Zeke and Robert. He smiled to himself hearing the teasing lilt in her voice. He had grown accustomed to it coming from outside his office this year, a sign that she was in a good mood and fully in her element. Tonight, she would serve perfectly as distraction in Operation Gold Rush.

Kalle was able to peek past Lani to the small table in the dining set with only a handful of places. Henrik had been right to think that it could be a small informal get-together after all. The hopes of making an impression on a broad range of international VIPs went down the drain. Kalle faced the reality of a full night of close-in small talk, and almost certainly no gold.

Lani made to excuse herself to finalize a few things for dinner. Glancing at the tight triangle of the other conversation, she added, "Would you mind giving me a hand?" Kalle diligently followed as

Lani set off through the kitchen, grabbing a couple rags, then onward further to the back door and the garden beyond.

The light was flatter now, approaching dusk finally. The breeze remained strong, coming around the manor to fill the vacuum in the garden facing northeast. Kalle presumed they were going to pick some vegetables or berries, but they continued on in the direction of the pointless wall. The sandy ground in front of them had been tilled up and gave off a charcoal odor. Coils of smoke ushered from the ground and raced haphazardly toward the west. The haze scraped tall grass along the way as the breeze withheld any chance to gain altitude.

"We're making kalua tonight. You know it?" Kalle shook his head. "Pork, in this case mixed with shrimp and rice and some spices. Ezekiel lit a fire down in the pit this morning. Then we dropped the meat on the hot coals and covered them with soil all day. It should be ready by now. Can you help me dig it up?"

Kalle found a spade leaning against the wall over a metal drainage grate and got to work. The going was easy as the ground was only loosely filled, and the meat was not buried deep. In fact, the dish and the coals were sitting on solid rock only a foot or two below the surface. There was no chance of extending the garden here, so the shallow kalua pit was perfect. Depending on how it tasted, he might suggest this to his mother since she also had a rocky section of yard that otherwise went to waste. Kalle took in a deep breath scented with earth, meat, and spice. Lani's eyes met his as he hoisted the smoking container up. They both grinned in satisfaction.

Walking back through the kitchen, Lani and Kalle met up with Annika, who was wandering the hallway on her own. "The Ambassador and Robert were called out to the front by someone on the intercom. It was probably that Charlie guy? He sounded pretty agitated."

Chapter 8 – Saturation

DANA SAT IN the back of the sedan while Emil rode shotgun next to the driver. They drove in silence on the narrow-cobbled roads along the shoreline of this older district of the city. She was lucky that she didn't have anything heavy or sharp in her possession at the moment, as the urge to pelt this stupid oaf in the back of his stupid head would have been difficult to overcome. Weird events like this were becoming more frequent and less weird. His accent while speaking Czech placed him squarely as Russian. Most likely a minder to watch over the Czech minders. A matryoshka of sharp eyes in ill-fitting jackets. Earlier, it had been easy to reminisce about Emil sneaking out of the men's dorm four years ago in London while they were first courting. Things were different now.

He was probably a minder, but one never really knew for sure unless someone did some probing. "Where are we going, comrade? If it's back to Otaniemi, you missed your turn." Dana finally broke the silence. From the back, she saw Emil's ears tighten against his skin. He was losing the battle to avoid breaking out in a grin.

More silence.

Dana looked out the window, watching the casually content working class Finns in the neighborhood go about their evening routines. She saw no hurry or anxiety on their faces. People were simply cleaning up for dinner or catching up with the neighbors. A Finnish idyll on the other side of the glass.

The car moved into heavier traffic. "Where do you want to go? We can head back to Otaniemi if you like. You can explain your little boat excursion. Perhaps you got lost, pushed away from shore by the wind. Or instead, I can give you a ride to your dinner engagement. I would accompany you for the evening naturally." The driver's manner was professional. Mocking words neutrally presented.

Dana crossed her arms and ignored the driver. No response was necessary anyway. The Lada puttered over the cobbles. Emil turned in his seat to face Dana, speaking as if in mid-conversation, "So I talked to Alain right after the race. I told him he should put in for the marathon at the end of the week. He's definitely in his best shape, and I suggested that we should have some fun just pacing it out for the first half. Then, well, we'd see what was left in our trashed legs."

"Have some fun? Has he ever run a marathon before?" Dana suspected the answer.

"Nope, just like me. We could figure it out though. Come on. It's still putting one foot in front of the other after all. But he laughed it off. For some reason he thought I was joking."

"For some reason, huh?" Dana trailed off as the car ground to a halt in the middle of the road. The driver leaned left then right, getting a view of all the gauges. The stop wasn't intentional. The Russian sedan had just died in traffic. The driver tried to restart, but only managed three brief *put put puts*. A second turn of the ignition gave no sound at all. He leaned to check the gauges again, muttering to himself. A line of cars was piling up behind them.

Emil offered, "Did you give a little gas when you turned it over? You have to give it a little gas, but not too much or you'll flood it. You know, a little pop and that's all she needs. Pop!" Emil clapped his hands to emphasize the importance of the pop in case it didn't come across in the driver's limited Czech vocabulary. Grunting, the driver bent down and twisted his head, examining underneath the steering column for some unknown reason. The two conferred with quiet but sharp gestures for a minute. Dana couldn't hear the exchange but could take a decent guess how it went.

The three looked at each other briefly and came to the silent conclusion that there was nothing to do other than get out and push. The driver asked Dana, "Do you know how to steer and turn the ignition and that sort of thing?" She nodded, and he continued, "Ok, why don't you sit up here and drive while we push. Maybe it will go with a rolling start."

If it had occurred to Dana or Emil that they could simply outrun their much older party-crashing semi-kidnapping Russian minder, it didn't show. The group of three set about the problem in front of them as a team. Emil's iron legs got to work, and the driver surprised the couple by lodging his shoulder behind the left taillight and moving with his own brutal efficiency. They soon gained an effective starting speed and Dana turned over the engine on the first try. With a couple quick pumps on the gas to make sure it was running, Dana motored ahead a bit and pulled to the side to wait for her two beasts of burden to catch up. She rolled the window down and draped her suntanned arm along the doorframe. The lowering sun felt good on her face with the cooling fresh air. Her hair was too short for a dramatic flip to the side, but she nonetheless deployed her winning smile and made her best attempt at an Ingrid Bergman impression in English *"Going my way, boys?"*

Flushed red with successful exertion, the driver finally cracked a smile. He introduced himself as Gregor Domozov, special assistant to the Soviet Olympic Committee. He opened the driver's side door and waited patiently for Dana to relinquish the reins of the Lada. The trio continued on their way to Tollefsson Manor with a crack in the ice.

.

Dana, Emil, and Gregor waited at the gate with buzz cut Charlie. He was formal to the point of being impolite. An uneasy truce settled in with the agreement that no one needed to talk until the Ambassador arrived at the gate. A Marine guard was not letting a Russian past the gate on his own discretion, no offense. Dana passed the short time glancing around at the grounds. There was a thick swath of healthy conifers giving off a friendly forest smell. Elevated from the city, the sounds of the evening bustle were muted. She heard the clop of shoes down the front stairs and turned just in time to see a cloud pass across Zeke's face to be replaced with a joyful bark of laughter. "Here they are. The conquering champions! Welcome welcome, we are so glad you were able to make it!"

Robert walked out behind his boss, keeping an eye on Gregor as they approached the gate.

Zeke turned to Gregor and introduced himself in his standard spiel of I don't believe we've met, we are always happy to have another guest, I hope you're hungry, and so on and so forth. He turned to the Marine and they walked into the guardhouse to confer briefly. With little input from Charlie, Zeke decided the best approach would be to avoid registering Gregor on the list of invitees or even on the entrance manifest at all. The Ambassador's protocol differed from the Marines from time to time.

The sun ticked along counterclockwise, casting acute shadows in the cooling air. "Well, the bar's inside so there's no use standing around out here. Let me introduce you to the rest of the gang." Zeke marched back up the path like a drum major leading his merry band. Robert brought up the rear and gave an eyebrow raise to Charlie as he passed by.

Inside, Lani busied herself adding two places to the table without attracting too much attention. The smallest form of the table was now a bit on the tight side and could have used an extra leaf. But it wasn't worth all the hassle. Tight quarters never hurt anyone.

Robert set to work behind the makeshift bar, lining up glasses for a round of old-fashioned cocktails. Zeke joined up to assist. In a casual but quiet voice he said, "funny having that old bear wander in here. This party could use a bit of spicing up, so maybe we give him a poke or two to see what happens." Robert snorted as he unscrewed the jar of bitters. Zeke continued, "but seriously, this could be good. I bet the two of you could find some common ground to cover. Maybe even off to the side for a bit." Robert paused his alchemy for a moment while Emil and Gregor approached the bar, appearing thirsty. Zeke shifted gears "I would take your orders, but I have to insist you give Robert's old fashioned a try. In his short time here, they have developed a bit of a reputation from the staff."

Robert took the handoff, "well it isn't all that complicated. Good bourbon helps of course, and that we have today. The secret is that you have to muddle the sugar and bitters completely at first. People get so anxious to pour in the bourbon too fast that the whole thing is a grainy nightmare. A few [twist] extra [twist] seconds [twist]... and *voila*." He handed the glass over to Emil, "maybe not worth its weight in gold, but it's the best we can do."

The clinking of glasses called the others to attention and Robert's services were in demand. Supplies distributed, the Ambassador cleared his throat. "Old drinks with new friends. Here's to a fun relaxing evening, and no contests – sprinting, throwing, or otherwise. *Kippis!*"

Glasses tipped to warm the assembled party. The Ambassador beamed and made friendly eye contact across the field: two more Americans, two Czechs, two Finns, and a Russian. The stage was not set exactly as planned, but Zeke was not a stranger to a dash of randomness. Embrace the chaos or be consumed by it. Robert was right; this bourbon really was quite good.

Interlude – West Virginia

Spring 1952 – Harpers Ferry

MALCOLM SAT IN the personnel-only cafeteria for lunch. Pay on the B&O rail line was not great, considering the hours and the expertise needed to operate these lumbering machines, but the meals and accommodations were second to none. This last loading station on the way to Baltimore would only take two hours at most, so he set to his goulash with dispatch.

A location at one time so important that it was razed to the ground a couple times during the Civil War, Harpers Ferry was a husk of a town now. The gloom of rain didn't help dress up matters at all. The bleak history of the failed armory raid and nearly as many floods as there were years had worn down even the most optimistic residents. The only people left were either too helpless to find prospects elsewhere or too old to care. Half of the rail staff wouldn't even disembark at all here, waiting instead to get into Baltimore. Malcolm felt obligated to at least walk to the cafeteria and check in with the signals boys. That and the goulash of course.

Eating alone, he pulled out a copy of the manifest to pass the time. Stinky and Cutter called him over-eager and earnest, using their own colorful vocabulary. Nevertheless, Malcolm considered himself a caretaker of the goods the B&O Railroad transported. He found it a modern miracle that people would give him all these things at point

A and entrust him with surrendering them at point B. Maybe it was all the Westerns with their road agents and moral ambiguity that got into his head. In any case, checking over the manifest gave him a window into the economy in which he was a very small cog. Eastbound legs were generally the boring bulk items, while the finished goods headed back the other way. However, one line item caught his eye: "Sherman Select – crates (144)."

The name jogged his memory of an old news article he had read in Pittsburgh years ago. It had been one of those slice-of-life curiosities they would add under the fold to spice up the front page a bit and boost sales. Malcolm didn't need any spice, but his mind retained all those vignettes, nonetheless. Some widow named Mary Sherman had been fighting with the bank over the fate of her late husband's bourbon stock. The poor man's ticker had flat given out without warning, and his one and only post-war signature batch still had five years to age. The moneymen wanted to liquidate since the whole operation was heading for failure, but the woman was having none of it. Finally, the bank gave her a choice: keep the batch or keep the house. Naturally since this made the Post-Gazette front page, she chose the batch.

Malcolm shoveled in his last bite. He folded the manifest lengthwise and secured it inside his uniform jacket. Stinky and Cutter typically didn't care to look at any documents – it was debatable if they could even read – but he understood that if they got wind of the cargo, 144 crates of bourbon would become 143 real quick-like.

Back in the cab, Malcolm checked pressures and brakes. The run out of Harpers Ferry was a notoriously slow grind. Stopping in this town killed all their momentum and was a supreme annoyance, goulash notwithstanding. At least the snow was finally gone, and the promise of Charm City at the end of the line buoyed his spirits. He kept the pressure gauge along the right edge of acceptable black. The couplings between cars tensed in the fight against gravity on the way out of the valley. Blasted bits of shale glided past with menace on his left while the springtime Potomac gushed far below on his right. He thought quite a bit about old Mary Sherman along the way. What kind of state must a woman be in to give up her homestead in exchange for a shed full of whiskey barrels? Either she was one of those Daniel Boone-loving hillbilly lunatics or her husband had been some sort of modern-day Michelangelo of whiskey. Or maybe she just missed him, and a house is not a home.

Malcolm was a caretaker. He shared in the social contract that everything gets to point B. Everything. No matter how thirsty he was, no matter how sublime the product might be. Maybe in ten years he would be kicking himself for setting arbitrary rules that only he followed. Then again, maybe not.

Chapter 9 – The Shrimp

THE PARTY OF eight sat at the table for six in the latest American fashion, meaning that couples were intentionally separated to stimulate conversation. Kalle found himself wedged into a corner between the shining star Emil and the morose unknown vacuum Gregor. Kalle was at a loss for words to start off with either of them. Fortunately, the Ambassador continued to draw attention in the American fashion, launching stories around the table as the party dug into Lani's kalua. Chatter gravitated around the games, in particular the two gold medal winners at the table. Kalle silently rehearsed the funniest possible version of the cauldron lighting incident, anticipating that either Zeke or Robert would raise the anecdote at any moment.

Kalle tried to catch Annika's eye across the table, without success. To his side, a frowning Gregor was focused on the plate in front of him, slowly separating the shrimp from pork. Kalle settled into sipping at the wine and listening to the flow around him.

"In the 5000, you were in last place in the first couple laps if I'm not mistaken. Dead last! Was that all part of your plan? Is that your *modus operandi*, jogging out and then hunting down the field in all your races?"

"Well no. In fact, I prefer to lead out from the start and set my own pace. I'm more comfortable that way. But Herbert made it clear he wanted to take the lead. There are so many unknowns in these big races that it really pays to be flexible. And if there's one thing I've learned over the years, it's how to be flexible." Emil responded with a smile. Dana choked on her food across the table.

"Well, it certainly makes a statement charging from the back. You could make it your calling card. I am not the sort to run any further than to the bar, but if I were out there against you, I would be looking backward all the time, just waiting for the inevitable. Zatopek, the Army Sniper!" Zeke took a gulp of wine to cap off his declaration.

"Zeke, the man doesn't need a calling card. He just won the double at the Olympics, for crying out loud. Not even Paavo Nurmi was able to do that." Robert came in as the voice of reason.

"Hannes did. But I bet you knew that, at least I hope you did." Annika cut in, flashing a smile up at Robert, who seemed to loom over the table even while seated.

"Yes of course, ma'am. Hannes got the double next door in Stockholm, wasn't it? No one has dominated long distance quite like you Finns. Present company excluded, naturally. It's quite startling and impressive. A country of a couple million, but you've cornered the market for distance medals. What's your secret? Are you all born this way, or is there some sort of cross-country skiing training all winter as soon as you can stand?"

"I like this question. I want in on your secret too, so I'm ready for your team next year at the European championships." Emil had edged forward on his seat, relishing a chance to talk shop even with non-runners.

"Don't be so greedy, Emil!" Annika teased. "I'm not giving away our secret weapon, especially not to a world-wide star like you. European championships? Next year? If I were you, I'd sit back and… and… bask for a moment." Annika twirled her arms and leaned back in her chair, catching the attention of a few pairs of eyes.

"Quite right, Chataway's body is probably still laying out on lane one where you left him for dead on that last lap, Emil. I, for one, respectfully refuse to turn over any of *my* running secrets," Zeke added.

"Have it your way, I'll have some more wine then in the face of all this outrageous obstruction to fair play and sportsmanship," Emil laughed as he poured.

Dana's eyes brightened at the sound of Emil's voice. The English had been washing over her in waves. She could catch most words given enough time, but the quick slurry of American-style English left her behind, drifting off in daydreams. But Emil's familiar timbre and accent reeled her back in. She could understand him perfectly in any of the languages in which he deigned to dabble. Knowing his half or third of a conversation was a beachhead to her. She hated these moments; relying on Emil, reading his face, smiling in default, holding back from issuing a stream of Czech complete with gesticulations to a group when she had something to say. That tall one, Robert, could get by in Russian. Along with Gregor and Emil, the four could at least work from common ground. However, around a cramped table of eight, English carried the day. Dana scanned further and landed on Kalle, a young friendly face – like hers. He was similarly quiet, but by choice. It seemed clear he was intent on following the conversation, whatever it was the Ambassador was prattling on about. It was a curious match, this humble conscientious-looking boy and his sparkplug of a wife or girlfriend or what have you. She was drifting off again.

·

Dinner continued amiably, with the group fueled by the propulsive energy of Emil, Zeke, and Annika. Even Gregor found occasion to chime in and break a smirk or two. Kalle took a peek at his neighbor's plate to find that the meat separation operation had concluded successfully, and the Russian was well into devouring just the pork. Kalle shot a quick glance at Annika and stood up. He made his excuses quietly to Lani and asked for the restroom.

The room was a short walk down the narrow hallway. The space itself was small and functional. Kalle did a quick check for cracks in the floorboards and cabinet, but it was obvious from the start this place was a dead end. Unwilling to make excuses in order to go exploring again later, he moved on in search of another restroom further into the bowels of the mansion.

The hallway opened to a pair of sitting rooms reborn as offices further back, followed by a staircase. If anyone came looking it would be nearly impossible to pretend that he didn't find the bathroom up front. Kalle moved with speed up the stairs. With all staff cleared out for the day, the upper floor was dark and quiet. Only the fading light from outside caromed through windows, shades, and doorways to land in splotches on the hallway flooring. Kalle pressed his way forwards, peering in open doorways as he went. He was in the private section of the house now without question. In for a pound at this point, he entered the bathroom at the end of the corridor and shut the door.

This room was much larger than the one downstairs. It was also filled with what appeared to be the Ambassador and Lani's personal effects. A second door to the room was ajar, leading to an adjoining bedroom. He closed that and set to work looking again for cracks. A large cabinet sitting flush against the wall looked particularly suspicious, so Kalle leaned obliquely into it to force a separation. The only result was the crumbling of some plaster. No hidden storeroom appeared behind a hinged cabinet façade. Kalle looked around at the jumbled collection of toothbrushes, socks, perfume, etc… "This is so stupid," he whispered to himself. As he tried to ease the cabinet back in place, he heard a knock on the door.

"Kalle, it's me." Annika's whisper came through the door.

Kalle froze for an instant, checked the mirror quickly, and opened the door. "What are you doing up here?"

"What are *you* doing up here?" Annika entered and closed the door behind her.

"What am I doing? What do you think I'm doing? This is the biggest bathroom I could find. You are supposed to be entertaining everyone as cover. Why aren't you entertaining?"

"I was, until I was interrupted by your elephant feet banging around over our heads. We could all hear you rustling about. So, I'm here to collect you and make up some excuse about how you got lost or saw a painting you liked. By the way, what possessed you to come up the stairs? What Nazi in their right mind would have lugged a ton of gold up a flight of stairs after a full night's travel to this *badezimmer*?"

"Oh, *badezimmer badezimmer* blah blah blah. This should have been a nice evening out with goddamn Olympic champions of all people. Now I'm just... we're just a farce." Kalle paused, thinking. "I'm sorry. I just saw the stairs and thought I'd find more space up here. And I did, but there's no obvious entry point." Annika moved toward the cabinet. "I already checked there. It's real. I was just about to head back down anyway. Let's go."

"It's not your fault. This was an impossible task anyway. Henrik is full of great ideas when his skin isn't on the line. Going upstairs wasn't a terrible idea. Not a good idea either, but not terrible."

"I'll take not terrible." Kalle's face softened as the confrontation ran out of steam. He avoided Annika's gaze and looked around slowly for clues. The seals on the tub and the storage under the sinks all seemed perfectly normal and boring. "A real wild hare chase – Henrik must be laughing right now. Maybe he should be deprived of the story when all is said and done."

Annika was only half-listening as her eyes roamed. "If they dragged it across the Baltic, up the hill, then up those stairs, why not a few meters more?" she asked, pointing up at the large wooden paneled ceiling. They both paused and cocked their heads at the large deep brown squares that didn't particularly fit with the rest of the bright room. From the outside, the mansion was relatively tall. With only two floors above ground there was going to be space for a rather generous attic or even an old servants' chambers somewhere above.

"Have you ever seen wood paneling on a bathroom ceiling?" Kalle asked. She shook her head. Kalle took a tentative step on to the rim of the bathtub, squeezing Annika's shoulder for support. As he found his balance and stretched up to reach the closest panel, Annika grabbed his arm and widened her eyes to say, 'be silent.' Soft footsteps were making their way up the stairs.

Kalle pulled his arm back from the ceiling. He stepped down and the pair stared at each other. Annika had been gone much longer than necessary to fetch her date from a dinnertime stroll.

"Kiss me." Annika said.

"What?"

"Christ, I have to do everything." Annika reached out for Kalle's shirt and pulled him in, planting a full kiss on his lips. It lasted just long enough for Kalle to gather his wits and begin to kiss her back, but then ended just as quickly. Annika tousled his hair and looked him in the eye, "now wipe off some of the lipstick on your lips. But not all of it, Leave a little. Here, look in the mirror."

"What?" Kalle randomly smeared in all directions, flushing red.

"Are you crazy? No don't use your hands, the towel Kalle. Use the towel. Let me."

The footsteps were closing in on the door, but Annika made no effort to whisper or cover up the chaos made by the Finns. Annika finished her clean up job just as the knock came. "Everything ok in there?" It was Lani.

Towel still in hand, Annika looked at Kalle with her deep brown eyes and said to him, "This should have happened a long time ago, you know." She turned and opened the door.

"What?"

.

"You're not nearly as interesting to look at as your brunette friend up on the hill. I mean, *our* brunette friend." Vaino was shelling shrimp at the table in one quick jerk before popping them in his mouth, juice dripping and spraying the table as he progressed through the bowl he shared with Henrik.

"I will grant you that, fine sir. But what I lack in looks I make up for in charming conversation and dirty jokes." Henrik was glad he had filled his wallet before heading out tonight, since the latest addition to the team was looking to be an investment on his part.

"Doubtful. But at least you seem in good spirits, so that's a start. You aren't feeling guilty at all, sending that lovely girl off to the wolves? Those Americans might just eat her alive if she's nosing around in the wrong spot."

Henrik considered it for a moment, as if the thought hadn't crossed his mind before. "Oh, she's not the one I'd be worried about. You saw her. She can handle herself. Kalle on the other hand…" Henrik tilted his hand back and forth in the so-so manner. "But in any case, the Ambassador is alright. He'll smooth out anything that might go sideways. He makes it look like he plays fast and loose, but in the end, he wants to be a protector. He'll find a way to cover for any fiasco Kalle might create."

"Nah, yeh can't trust those government types. They spend their whole lives telling other people what to do and suffer no consequences when they screw up. Living large up on the hill off of everyone's taxes. Their only goal is to make sure they stay up on that hill. A young Finn nobody has heard of gets caught in the wrong place, you think anyone's going to stick his neck out? I wouldn't trust your ambassador friend any further than I could push him off my boat. That goes for the whole lot of them."

"Annika works for the government." Henrik replied. "As does Kalle. As do I, now that I think about it."

Vaino wiped his hands enough to get a grip on his beer glass. "Oh yeah, well don't think for a second I'll apologize and take back what I just said. You are all still young enough. Get out while you still can. Before the vines of parliament start crawling up your legs while you're sitting at your boring desks."

"I hear you. And if our two favorite government types up there on the hill tonight can get the job done, all four of us will have enough booty to walk away without any vines latching on to us. I see you've already figured out the secret to a happy life on the water. No cares in the world, right? You'll have to teach us all your tricks."

"Tricks? There are no tricks. It's pretty simple. And I'll tell you since you seem like a decent enough fellow despite all the clever comments and that ridiculous smirk of yours. This is it. Ready? This is it. Just remember at all times that no one cares about you at all. No one. You screw up, or you do something brave? No one notices either way. And if they do happen to notice, they don't care. And if they do care, they don't remember the next day. Your skin is yours and so is everything else within that lining. Everything outside? Unimportant. Someone bumps you and curses you on the street? Unimportant. A girl walks away from your smooth talk? Un…"

"Hardly likely."

"Oh, hardly likely? Get back to me in five years Romeo. Those lines deepen on your face and the hairs gray before you know it – especially the way you're drinking."

"The way *I'm* drinking? You're the one wearing out the waiter here. And my wal…"

"Just stop, you're embarrassing yourself. Anyway, my point being… I haven't so much as thought about another person in years, because fair's fair."

Henrik was letting this string play out, and the curious part was that there was doubt written all over Vaino's face as he held forth. Posturing over drinks. A perfectly reasonable way to spend a summer evening. "I didn't make you for a nihilist, Vaino. So, if our friends up the hill get caught or if they come rolling down with a wheelbarrow full of gold bars it doesn't factor either way in the grand scheme of things? Unimportant, right?"

Vaino' eyes bulged. He waved his arms as if fending off a flock of pigeons. "Of course it matters. That barrow is one fourth mine!"

"So, capitalist then. This is even worse than I thought," Henrik straight-faced, taking a sip of beer. "If you don't care about anyone, why bother joining our merry band of gold hunters? Why give us the *badezimmer*? You could have gone up there and brought back a whole wheelbarrow for yourself."

"Wish I could, youngster. But you know as well as I do that I could never get anywhere near that place. Your oddball couple has the access and I have the code. It's one of those, what do you call it? Marriages of convenience. By the way, what exactly do you contribute to this group?" Vaino didn't wait for a response. "Anyways, all these so-called friendships are just based on circumstance – sometimes for a day, sometimes for a week. God forbid for an entire lifetime! So, circumstance brought us together today." Vaino tossed the last of the shells onto the plate, sucked the majority of the juice off his fingers, and slumped back in his seat.

The light in the courtyard was fading quickly and lamps had begun to flare up. A flashlight from the wall on the hill would be easy to see now against the gray relief of twilight. Henrik suggested that they settle up the bill and strike out on a walk in the park, to be closer to the hill just in case, but also to shake off the cobwebs from a couple hours anchored to the same spot.

"Fine. Let's grab one more drink to cap it off." Vaino said.

"Of course, have you tried the lonerko yet?" Henrik asked.

Vaino grimaced, "Christ, no. What is wrong with you, kid? Don't you dare order that tourist piss for me. Might as well dunk my head and drink straight from underneath the dock. Speaking of piss, I'll be right back." The fisherman walked away in his hurried and disgruntled manner. Henrik leaned toward a passing waiter and ordered a round of vodka, keeping an eye on the darkening hill.

Chapter 10 – Layer Cake

LED BACK INTO the dining room, Kalle couldn't help but notice an air of forced conversation in the room. The group was engaged in some sort of debate and didn't acknowledge Lani returning with her quarry of Finns. Everyone except for Dana, who didn't appear to be paying attention to the discussion and gave Kalle a polite smile as he moved back to his place at the table.

Kalle slumped back into his seat. The evening was going as badly as he had first feared. It had started as a chance to impress the Ambassador and make new contacts. Now he was just another example of the Finnish stereotype according to westerners: friendly enough, but naïve and wholly inept with manners. Annika made apologies for their absence on behalf of both of them, smoothing it over with her charm.

The table was cleared and a dessert of Russian *medovik* was laid out in the center. A warm smell of honey brightened the table. The sight animated Gregor, who praised Lani on the authentic appearance of the layer cake, creating high expectations.

Gregor nodded his satisfaction with the first bite. "Perfection. I am quite curious how a woman from the other side of the world has been able to recreate the taste and the lightness. Even in Moscow, they usually screw it up one way or another," he said.

"Thank you, but all I did was follow the recipe as it came to me. All credit is due to Robert. He suggested it yesterday and gave up his secret card."

Robert turned pink for a moment. "An acquaintance of mine at Berkeley shared it with me. It was her grandmother's recipe originally, if I remember correctly." There were murmurs of agreement with Gregor's conclusion on the cake.

"Berkeley?" Gregor asked. "Where is this?"

"California. Just across the bay from San Francisco. I was working on my post-doctorate at the university there for a while before receiving this posting."

The guests all nodded in a manner that showed they were dutifully impressed.

"What's your field? Political science or history?" Emil chimed in.

"Neither. Technically I was in the biology department, but I didn't spend much time there. I hung around the mathematicians quite a bit until they kicked me out and sent me packing to the psychology building for a while. In the end I just spent a lot of time in the library. I was a man without a country, so to speak, by the time that I left. But to answer your question, overall, I would call my field computational biology. My focus was the application of evolution to the theory of games." The table was filled with confused faces, save for Lani and Zeke, who had heard versions of this spiel a few times before.

"Well now you've done it, Mr. Zatopek," the Ambassador jumped in with a laugh. "If history is any guide, you've walked right into his trap and now we're in for an hour's dissertation."

Robert raised his hands in surrender. "Guilty as charged, but in honor of our distinguished guests I will spare you this time." A silence fell on the room, giving occasion for each to take a bite of cake thus eluding any obligation to offer up a new topic.

Annika finished her bite first and went back to the well. "But how does one compute biology exactly? Do you measure the lengths of frog's legs, one at a time for days on end? You don't seem the type to grind away in a basement lab with calipers all night long. Or maybe you are?"

With some reluctance, Robert replied, "There is some of that, yes. Especially for some colleagues who are of the documenting and categorizing sort. The descriptive taxonomy of last century is quickly being replaced with objective numerical values. But that's not for me. I've always been interested in groups at large, particularly species over time. The evolution part of the topic."

"Ah evolution. Only the strong survive, right? Like Emil and Dana here." Annika gestured.

"Well, that's actually a common misconception." Robert said gently, glancing over at Zeke, who was all smiles. Annika had a knack for pushing the right buttons. Her encouraging frown led him to continue. "What you're referring to is the classical concept of passing on a genetic heritage for the population that happens to be most efficient in procreating in a certain environment. Strength can be part of that, sure. But so can weakness – an ability to hide with camouflage for example. Other traits, we think, can be passed on as well. Instinctive strategic behaviors, in my particular field of interest."

"I'm afraid I'm even more confused now." Annika said.

"Let me give you an example. Emil, say that you're a bird."

"I'm a bird." Emil declared. He rushed to set down his wine glass, stood, and gave a quick flap of his gadget arms. Dana shook her head in false exasperation.

"Yes… a very fast bird of course. Ok, say there's a bush with green berries below your nest. You know the berries aren't ripe yet. Every bird knows that. They need a few more days. But you also know there's a neighbor bird. That stupid loud bird in the nest just down the hedge from you."

"This sounds a lot like home, huh Dana?"

"So, both you and the neighbor would be better off waiting for the berries to turn red. If you both wait, you could share and get the most nutrition out of them. Or… or instead you could sneak out tonight and eat all the unripe green berries yourself. What do you do, Mr. Bird?" Robert asked.

"Of course I want to wait. But I probably shouldn't trust my neighbor, right? I grab those terrible green berries tonight." Emil responded.

Gregor was becoming visibly uncomfortable, and interjected, "But what's to keep you from going to your neighbor and agreeing, in your bird language or whatever, and agreeing to wait for the berries to ripen? Surely you are both better off. Your simple example breaks down when parties can communicate."

Robert smiled back at Gregor, took a sip of wine, and waited for a third opinion. Annika shifted in her seat and Robert glanced her way. "So, Emil goes to the neighbor, agrees to wait for the berries to ripen, but then he double-crosses him. He goes out and eats them green anyway. Talk is cheap." Annika said.

"Quite right, even if the birds could communicate, the simple fact remains that the berries are out there. In fact, in this example, the only logical thing for either bird to do is to go out into the night. Out in the darkness they end up fighting it out over green berries. So, Emil and his neighbor hop away hungry and bloodied from the experience."

"What a terrible story. Are all Americans this cynical? I read your newspapers, and it seems like everyone's dancing and eating hamburgers. Your propaganda says that there are no worries, bounty everywhere. But here we are fighting over green berries? I will never understand you people." Gregor said with a frown.

"Not all is lost, my friend. You were right to question the simple example, and this is where my work comes in. If you wanted to test this, if you went out inspecting bushes in the real world, what would you find? Ripe red berries everywhere. The simple evidence in the field is that birds are not fighting in the night for under-ripe berries. So why not?"

By this point Kalle was no longer slumped in his seat. He remained quiet but focused on Robert's animation. Something was different about him.

Robert continued, "This is the conundrum that biologists hate talking about. When faced with overwhelming opportunities to cheat, animals of all sorts cooperate. Not always of course, but often enough that it begs the question why. Monkeys share bananas with other monkeys that they've never met before at the zoo, jackals in the wild cry out warnings of nearby predators to help the pack even though that act singles them out for attack, penguins risk freezing to death on the perimeter of a huddle during a winter storm, the list goes on and on. These actions are not in their self-interest, yet they do it over and over again. If it were simple stupidity, you'd expect evolution to press the stupid out of the gene pool. And it can't be just a learned response either. Animals in captivity apart from their mothers have the same reaction. It is instinct, an instinct that was selected by evolution."

Dana's brow furrowed, and Emil quickly summarized in Finnish for her. Kalle glanced over at Annika and saw that she was formulating a question for Robert.

"You mentioned this earlier. Why would evolution select for a weakness?" Annika asked.

"Because it seems like the weak, or at least the peace-lovers, can help each other over time. Take this example. Instead of Emil the Bird making a choice, what if he is just a mechanical gadget bird built to automatically either cooperate or cheat. Now let's put a grid of a thousand such birds in a giant field. If all gadget birds are built to cheat, nothing interesting happens and they barely subsist on green berries. Then they pass on their cynical cheating mechanics to their gadget offspring and nothing ever changes. Nothing special there. So how about if instead we drop in one gadget bird that is built to cooperate into the field? Once again, nothing interesting happens. That one bird is taken advantage of, and it dies of starvation before having any gadget baby cooperators. Are you with me so far? Now, what if, in a field filled with cheaters, what if by chance there are two cooperating birds dropped in right next to each other?" Robert dangled the question to his audience.

"The berries between them ripen, and they eat better than everyone else." Gregor jumped in, surprising Kalle next to him.

"And then?"

"And then… they produce more offspring, who in turn also cooperate." Gregor concluded.

"Exactly! And over many generations of this, they spread out across the field, dominating the cheaters. Maybe driving them out completely, or at least creating boundaries where the cooperating birds thrive. The key element is that they don't choose to cooperate this way. It is instinct. They don't know any other way to live." Robert paused for a moment. Still looking at Gregor, he added, "One more thing. They have to be next to each other to help out. Two well-meaning cooperators are each helpless if they are isolated and act on their own."

Dana listened to a quick recap in Russian from Gregor, frowning. She asked a quick question to Gregor, who passed it on to Robert in English. "Where did your two cooperating birds come from, if they didn't learn it or choose it?"

Robert responded, "That's a good question, and fortunately in this case I have a good answer. The two fundamental building blocks for natural selection are mutation and environmental pressure. Mutation happens randomly. And let's assume that any mutation to be a natural cooperator is pretty rare. So, imagine the odds of having two mutations happen to birds right next to each other. Very unlikely. Maybe a one in a million chance? Well, with a field of a thousand birds over a thousand generations, one in a million becomes likely, and eventually a certainty. One thing biologists lean on is that time is always on their side. Anything that appears inefficient in an animal at first glance needs a closer look. There's always some reason that attribute evolved. It doesn't mean it's always helpful, only that it was inevitable."

Annika then asked Robert. "If this were all true. If cooperating was inevitable, then why do we see so much cheating, so much crime and murder and misery around us? I'm very happy for your birds, but at least for humans, we are not in a field of cooperation. No matter how much we would like it."

"Well, academics have a bad habit of trying to describe the world around them by reducing everything to math on pencil and paper. And this is part of it to be sure. In reality we see a little bit of both, but certainly much more cooperation than you would expect from a naïve one-time thought experiment. One thing I was thinking about before I left was the following: what would happen if the cooperator birds were marked in a way that was externally clear to everyone? Say, they had a bright red beak instead of a brown one. Over time, the red beaks, as is their nature, cooperate and thrive near each other.

"Now, what if the same thing happens to the brown beaks? After all, if the mutation for two red beaks could occur by chance, the same could happen to the other before they are driven to extinction. Now, you have a field split in two. Two peace-loving, cooperating communities. But only cooperating amongst their own kind."

Kalle watched with interest at the lecture from a man who he had known previously only as a very large handsome heavy drinker who would trap poets in bathrooms from time to time. Kalle glanced over and saw that the Ambassador looked rather uncomfortable, as if this theory of Robert's was spinning out of his control. Were these the kinds of speculations that made up the business behind the diplomatic scenes? It all seemed too philosophical to have any real application. Too boring as well. For Kalle, the interest was no longer in what Robert was saying, but in how Zeke would respond.

"Just red beaks and brown beaks mechanically drawing lines in the sand." Gregor mused. "So how does it all end? In your model, that is."

"I don't know." Robert responded through a bite of cake. "I wrote up some calculations. I was waiting for the completion of a computer at Berkeley when this new line of … glamorous work came calling."

"Computer?" Gregor asked.

"A machine to do calculations quickly. The assumptions involve probabilities in the interactions and growth over many generations. It becomes complex very quickly. It's impossible to solve with pencil and paper, so a computer makes millions of random choices and aggregates the results. Many rolls of the dice. Like going to Monte Carlo. At least that's the idea, but the computer is still being built. In any case, maybe a stable equilibrium can form in a field with two balanced communities. That probably is better than all the costs that are incurred when one group harasses the other nearly out of existence. It would also be better than the anarchy of a field filled with cheaters. But what is better is not the same as what is likely. A lot would depend on what happens on the boundaries between groups. The action on that boundary could end up being pretty interesting.

"A psychologist at Berkeley ran a strange lab. I would stop by sometimes to see what he was cooking up. Anyways, one time he took maybe two dozen volunteers, all strangers, and dressed them randomly in white or black t-shirts. Then he sent them into a large conference room with no instructions. We just watched from outside. Within minutes, the strangers congregated into two groups based exactly on t-shirt color. I told him he should set off a fire alarm and add some smoke. He thought that was pretty funny. There is a tribalism that comes out immediately, but what is interesting to me is not just that these boundaries exist, but how robust they would be under stressed conditions."

"Well, I don't find your boundaries interesting at all. I think we'd be better off without all this separation." Annika protested.

"Like them or not, they are there… and necessary. If it weren't for some enterprising proteins creating the first cell wall, all we'd be is a giant puddle of gray goo."

Zeke made a discreet cough and Robert concluded. "In any case, the answer remains a mystery. I'll have to leave it to the next lost soul wandering the border between the biology and mathematics departments."

"Funny you should mention mysteries, Robbie." The Ambassador said, shifting gears as quickly as possible. "There seems to be one or two of those floating around this old house tonight."

"Oh, don't even start…" Lani said.

Zeke smiled at her and held her gaze for a moment, debating. Then he continued, "For example, the mystery of the disappearing Finnish lovebirds! I wonder what the story is there."

The room fell into awkward silence. Kalle looked down at the table, inspecting the very faint stains from dinners long past on the off-white tablecloth. He could not make himself small enough. Robert's dissertation had not thrown Zeke off the scent of an embarrassing story. Kalle made no effort to take the bait.

Lani feigned disapproval and stood to begin clearing the dishes. Kalle stood as well, grabbing the chance to exit the conversation even if it meant abandoning Annika. She could take care of herself against Zeke's attacks anyways.

Loaded with dessert plates and the remainder of the layer cake, the pair walked back to the kitchen. Lani put down her dirty dishes and started the faucet. Looking at the backsplash, she said, "You have to understand. He has many great qualities, but tact isn't one of them."

"So I've noticed." Kalle responded. "That's fine, it's nothing." Kalle took the top dish off of the jumbled pile. He scraped the crumbs into the trash and began restacking dishes in a second pile on the counter, aligning together better now.

"He's like a puppy. He has more energy than he knows what to do with. He sometimes makes a bit of a mess, but it is never intentional."

"It must be exhausting for you sometimes." Kalle ventured.

Lani grabbed a dish and began scrubbing.

Lani and Kalle worked their way through the pile in silence. Scraping, scrubbing, and drying. The familiar sounds and smells calmed Kalle. It was the least-foreign moment of the past few hours, which had whirled so far outside of his areas of expertise that they threatened to be meaningless. The Ambassador's sharp laugh from the other room brought Kalle out of his daze.

"You go on back in there. I'll just finish up the last of this." Lani said. "Besides, the longer you're away from the conversation, the more likely it is you're his target."

"I'll take my chances. Besides, you're away from the conversation too. It might be you he's going on about." Kalle continued drying.

Lani laughed. "Oh no, he knows better than to do that. I'm guessing he's making some observation about you and is polling the group for agreement." Lani mustered up a flat Midwestern accent with a deeper voice. "'That Kal, I don't really know him, but the way he shifts his eyes makes me think he's the sort that would kill your dog without thinking twice, don't you think so Emil?' Something like that. Or maybe, if the wine is getting to him, he might be in there accusing you of hunting for the hidden Nazi gold."

Kalle clattered a dish against the counter. He turned to look at Lani, and his expression gave him away.

Lani laughed, "Don't worry, I won't tell. I figured that was what you two were doing up there."

"How did…"

"It's a story we heard from the caretakers when we came here. They told us the tale with a perfectly straight face, but I think they're just trying to have a laugh. Watch the Americans crawl around in their bathrooms, dirtying themselves looking for a miniature El Dorado. You know, that sort of thing. I am a bit surprised to see you falling for it. You seem like a smart young man."

Kalle looked down at the floor. He had no excuse, this lark just got away from his control. It was difficult to resist the pull of both Henrik and Annika at the same time. He opened his hands out in a shrug and Lani nodded back looking at him with brown sympathetic eyes. The longer he spent in this house, the smaller Kalle became.

The two made their way back into the dining room, where all heads turned to face them. "Well, look who's back…again! We were just talking about you." The Ambassador said to Kalle with a smirk on his face.

Kalle raised his hands in the air. "Guilty as charged, whatever it is," he joked. There was a pause of silence in the room. The atmosphere gave the impression of the evening stalling out in failure and boredom. Olympic champions were in the room, and they had been treated to nothing but speculation on the evolution of birds and gossip about a middle management nobody in the Finnish export service. In addition, all of the aspirations Kalle had for the evening, personally or with the Gold Rush Four, had been wiped off the map. There was nothing left to lose. He stared intently at Annika and spoke to the group. "Lani and I were just talking about all the Nazi gold you have hidden away here. But don't worry. I'll have you know, Mr. Ambassador, she didn't give up your secret location to me."

Annika's eyes widened while Zeke let out another bark and slapped his thigh. He pointed at Kalle with a broad grin and said, "Yes! Now we're talking." The others in the room looked about in confusion. The Ambassador proceeded to roll off the legend of the hidden gold as it had been told to him, with some possible creative additions. The story varied from what Annika and Kalle heard down at the bar from Vaino. The deliveries were in small local trucks during the daytime over the course of a week and they had arrived much earlier during the war. The Ambassador also related some hijinks of porters trying to hide coins in their clothing and that sort of thing. However, one element of the story matched Vaino's identically: *badezimmer*.

All eyes were on the Ambassador as he spoke. Whatever complaints one could have about him, the man could tell a story. Everyone in the room loved the idea of panicked Germans bumbling around and rushing out of Finland without their gold. It was an image one could build a friendship on. Zeke offered a toast to the fictional proxies, Otto and Hermann, for donating their riches to the Tollefsson manor. Everyone enthusiastically responded in kind, especially Gregor. Regarding Zeke, Gregor said, "I hope that the gold is real and that your cleaning and groundkeeper staff sniffed it out years ago. It would be grand if it turned out that they were the richest people in town, working for the simple joy of it. Imagine, they feed you the story to torment you, but they sneak off on the weekends to cruise around the waters in their fancy boats." The Ambassador nodded, granting the point that this would be a perfectly acceptable scenario as far as he was concerned.

Kalle ignored Annika's "what the hell?" look and posed a question to Zeke and Lani. "So, have you seriously looked for it yet? Be honest, you must be curious after all, and you've been here three years now?"

Lani shook her head, but Zeke laughed. "Oh Lani, don't lie to these fine people. A peek here or there. Yes, of course! Well, wouldn't you? If you heard a rumor that you lived on Treasure Island, you would dig around a little bit, right? You know, just for fun of course." The group murmured in general agreement. Zeke seized on the energy in the room. With a screech from his chair the Ambassador stood. He placed his palms on the small table and leaned over the group. "Now that all eight of us are fully read in on the golden secret, I have a proposition to make."

Chapter 11 – Mass Defect

HENRIK LED OUT of the café into the twilight. Along the esplanade, the eastern horizon was already muddled in dark. He needed a brisk walk out in the fresh air – certainly a break from the smoke-laden courtyard they had camped in for too long. Vaino lit a cigarette. "How long you reckon we need to wait around for a torchlight signal?" Vaino asked as they walked. "I only mean, it could be a late night for them and if they don't find anything, it would be a late night for us too just waiting around."

"Did you have big plans this evening, Vaino? Are you saying that the heist of millions of deutsche marks' worth of gold doesn't compare to, what, drinking an entire bottle of vodka by yourself? Sitting in your boat mending nets in the dark?"

"Don't be ridiculous. I don't mend my nets in the dark."

The boardwalk was bustling with the post-dinner crowd enjoying the Helsinki summer evening. Snippets of conversation floated past the pair in Finnish, Swedish, English, and other indeterminate mushed tones.

Henrik grabbed Vaino's cigarette, took a deep drag, and commented, "Well there's no shortage of young ladies out touring the big city tonight. Pick out a pair for us to go chat up and we can kill an hour or two. Hopefully that meets your high standards for entertainment? I'll show you that I still have my youthful skills. Five years before I lose a step with my gray hairs, isn't that what you said? See those two up ahead? So tall… They must be Swedes here for the Games. Your Swedish is good, yes? I'll be Johannes and you're my crazy uncle Arvid. Come on Arvy, let's go!"

.

The dinner party returned to the drawing room to refresh their glasses. The Ambassador divided the group into four pairs, all bemused at the absurdity of it all. There was to be a hunt. A grand hunt for treasure as Zeke put it. Dana smiled broadly, standing next to Kalle, her partner for this excursion. The Ambassador had decreed that nations be split up, and he picked out Emil immediately. Robert paired with the Russian, leaving the Finns to separate with Annika heading over to chat with Lani. Dana welcomed the chance to leave the cramped table and do something, anything. Plus, it was a competition after all. No one else appeared to believe there was actual gold to find, but on the off chance they were wrong, Dana would find it.

Kalle initiated conversation with Dana in short and clear English sentences, probing how difficult the language barrier would be for their teamwork. In the background, he sighted Annika. She nodded and pointed up to the ceiling. She would lead Lani back upstairs to the bathroom to check the attic space. He turned back to Dana's open, friendly face and asked, "Where should we go?"

Dana considered it for a moment and replied, "Let's try outside somewhere. The house is a bit stuffy. It would be great to get some fresh air, yes?" Dana's English came across easily. A much simpler task for her with an audience of one. Her attitude lightened as she anticipated a nice break from the confidence game that permeated the room.

Kalle nodded and frowned. "Lani? Is there some sort of well shed or sauna outside?"

Lani replied, "Our water source is all inside. Aside from the city pipes there is some kind of seasonal spring source that comes up right here in the cellar. But sauna? Well, there is an old shack out back. I suppose that could have been a sauna at some point. I leave garden supplies there now. It might be worth a try. Take some flashlights from the kitchen if you head that way. It's getting dark now." She walked off with Annika down the hallway towards the stairs. The other men had disappeared. Only Kalle and Dana were left in a suddenly quiet drawing room, glasses still full.

Kalle led the way back through the kitchen, found a pair of flashlights, and opened the door into the settling darkness outside. The steady breeze from earlier in the day had relented. Their steps cracked in the noiseless void at the top of the hill. The weathered but well-built shed was easy to find. As they approached the heavy latched door, Kalle passed the beam of the flashlight around the edges, scouring for any joints out of place or surprising seams. It wasn't easy for Kalle to picture how any stash of gold could possibly fit into such a confined space without being found years ago. He opened the door and went in.

They propped open the door, allowing a trapezoid of gray into the small room. The shock had definitely been a sauna in a previous life. Solid cedar-planked benches contoured along the three walls. Garden tools, small pots, weed trimmings, and dirt were strewn about, aging the space.

The earthy smell reminded Dana of home. She thought of her mother's garden and the hours she had spent tending out in the sun. The days, the lifetime. Memories filtered by time came to mind as she scanned the walls with her flashlight. All of those years. Simple years before the javelin. Before Emil. These Olympics had been nothing but complications. Thrilling, yes, but littered with paths to navigate: Emil's forced delay at the airport leaving Prague, their escape from Otaniemi, their semi-abduction by Gregor, and so on. She was never one to have any patience for politics, and Helsinki was papered over with it. The only natural moment here had been running down the track and throwing. Doing her specialty felt natural in any environment. Now, twenty-four hours later, she was hunting for gold in a sauna with a stranger. Another complication, but at least it was a peaceful type of absurdity. And one without anyone looking over your shoulder.

Still flashing her light into the corners, she said, "Robert is quite an interesting fellow, what did you think of his speech in there? I had trouble understanding everything he said."

"Interesting is a good way to put it." Kalle said. "I barely understood a word he said either. To me, he's a contradiction. He's an enthusiastic cynic, if that makes any sense."

Dana nodded, forgetting the darkness around them.

Kalle continued, "I met him for the first time just a week ago and he makes me a little uneasy. I'm not sure exactly why. Probably just jealousy."

"Jealousy? Why?"

"Take your pick. He's smart, athletic, charming, tall, just so… American. I suppose I wish I had some of those qualities but hate myself for wanting them. I don't know. I don't know what I'm saying really. Forget it. To answer your question about his speech, I don't know what to think. For a while it felt like typical academia bullshit. A smart person on his own, thinking very deeply about one particular problem without reference to the world around him. It is easy to dismiss it as irrelevant. But watching the way he speaks about it makes me wonder. I don't know anything about world affairs and embassy work, but if the delivery of a message is as important as the message itself, then they have the right man for the job. He and the Ambassador are a bit of an odd couple, but it works."

Dana smiled at the term odd couple. "Why are you here tonight? If you only met Robert and Zeke once before, how did you get invited?"

Kalle hesitated and said, "Well, when you put it like that…"

Dana laughed and continued, "I didn't mean it that way. I ask because I only met them for five minutes or so yesterday myself."

Kalle looking up at the ceiling and responded, "I have no idea. What about you? Of course, you two are the most sought-after couple in Europe right now, that's a great reason for the Ambassador to invite you. But why did you accept? You could be out celebrating anywhere right now, why here?"

"The Ambassador is quite… convincing. How can you say no to the guy? Anyways, it sounded fun. Why not?"

Dana's light was shining on Kalle. He gestured around them and asked, "Well, are you having fun?"

Dana laughed again. "I am, actually."

The pair looked around haphazardly in silence for a while. Dana peeked into a box along the side. "What's this?"

Kalle walked over for a closer look. "Oh, that's the stone box. For the steam to fill the sauna, you take very hot stones and pour water over them. This box would typically be full, but it looks like the stones are long gone."

"And this metal grate at the bottom? That holds the rocks in, but lets the extra water run out I guess?" Dana asked. Kalle nodded. "So where does the water go?"

Kalle was quiet for a minute, thinking back to earlier in the evening. "Come with me. I have an idea."

·

The Ambassador took a pull from his drink, squinting at the sharp contrast to the lingering sweetness of the cake. He looked over at Emil and gestured for him to follow. He took energetic business-like strides down the darkened hallway through the office section of the embassy. Beyond the stairway, one empaneled wooden door stood out from the rest. The Ambassador led his guest into his study and closed the door behind him.

The room was small and simply appointed. A modest desk was shunted into the corner to give space for a pair of armchairs. A plain metal door stood closed on the far wall of the room. To the right, a built-in bookshelf was taken up mostly by old photos of the Ambassador and friends. A couple dozen books loomed from the top shelf; spines impossible to read from eye level. They were leftovers from the previous ambassador who must have triaged the moving boxes, leaving the boring hard-to-reach books as decoration for Zeke.

Emil wore his standard open grin, betraying no questions, eager for anything. Up close, Zeke understood the unsettling feeling his opponents must have lining up against him. He was disarmingly friendly, but the strength and determination behind his eyes was unmistakable.

Zeke knew that his natural inclination to talk in spirals wasn't always helpful. Most of the time he didn't let it bother him too much. But this was an occasion for Zeke to be efficient. Brass tacks. "You're a captain now, is that right?" Zeke said, gesturing for Emil to sit.

"Yes sir, for four years now. I'm quite fortunate. The army has been excellent in giving time for training."

"I'm sure, I'm sure. As you probably know, I spent my fair share of time in the army as well. That is to say, I'd like to speak to you frankly. One army brat to another. If that's alright with you."

"Sure, fire away." Emil replied.

"There's no gold here. There probably never was. The story circulates under its own power at this point, and it never hurts to add a little mystique to this crumbling old heap. You and I aren't here to look around for treasure. I wanted to take this opportunity to offer you something much more valuable. I would like you and Dana to come to the United States… for good. We can offer you asylum for now, and eventually citizenship." The Ambassador paused to gauge the weight of his words sinking in.

Emil cocked his head slightly, keeping his stare directly on the Ambassador. "Defect? You're asking us to defect?" Emil asked.

"Well, that's a bit of a dramatic way to put it, but yes." Silence took over the space between these two typically ebullient men.

"Listen, despite my job here, I don't particularly care for politics much. I never have. I come from a simple family. I was raised to live and let live. But what I see going on in your country and elsewhere is distressing to me. I've heard about the snooping apparatus, all the restrictions on what to say and where to go. Hell, I've seen it with my own eyes tonight with your grumpy old bag of bones 'escort.' You and Dana strike me as open-minded optimistic folk, the type of people who have little patience for that sort of thing. You are the type of people who would make a fantastic contribution to America. As Americans. I'm offering you a chance to change the direction of your lives."

The Ambassador's speech had given Emil time to formulate his reply. "I am a sworn Czech Army officer and a representative of my country at these games. I love my country and I won't abandon it. With all due respect, the answer is no."

Without missing a beat the Ambassador said, "I understand your position, but I beg you to hear me out. Let's put aside the citizenship part for now. Let me ask you one simple question: are there things you would like changed in Czechoslovakia?"

"Of course, but…"

"And, Captain, do you think you would be able to make any of those changes from within? Could you file a report to your senior officer? Meet with the state-run press and ask uncomfortable questions?" The Ambassador asked. No response. "Of course not. If you could, you already would have done so. You are the talk of these games. Your name is on the lips of every Finn who watched you run. But do you know who *isn't* talking about you? Everyone else in the western world who wasn't there yesterday. People want to know more about you, but you are nowhere to be found. You are shunted away from cameras and people, locked away in a camp during the height of your career. In the States you would be a star. You would have the full attention of a free press. You could shine a light on the problems of your country from a better vantage point, so the world at large could see. The way I see it, the only way to help your country in its current state, is from the outside."

"But I haven't done anything wrong. I won't be an exile." Emil protested. It was a weak response that landed flat. Emil regrouped and tried again. "I have family and friends. They would be forced to denounce me. Anything I say from the comfort of a New York apartment would just be called propaganda from the West by a traitor."

Zeke considered this for a minute. "So, your family denounces you out loud. What does that matter? They wouldn't denounce you for real though, would they? It's just another empty statement and everyone would know it. I'm glad you bring up family. That's an important point. How about your family?" Emil didn't follow. "Dana. And the kids I'm sure you two plan to have someday. Do you want to see them go through school the way you did? Reciting whatever the propaganda is for that week? Attending 'voluntary' Party meetings for hours on end before scrounging for food? I've spoken to some of your people. I know what's going on. At school in the States, children think for themselves. It isn't always pretty of course, but still. Listen, I'm trying to paint a picture for you but I'm a terrible artist. I'll stop talking, but I'm sure you know that I'm right."

Emil was no longer looking at the Ambassador. One of the frames on the repurposed bookshelf glinted back the light from the ceiling. Enclosed was a grainy black and white photo. Even from a distance, Emil could immediately identify the casual shapes of soldiers hamming it up for an impromptu photo. Young army men always telegraphed confidence in photos like these. Emil's photos were in better focus and in color, but they were the same. He took a couple steps toward the photo, now curious how the Ambassador looked as a young Captain. Staring at the image of Zeke smiling with two fellow soldiers, he said, "What would you say if you were in my shoes? If I asked you to leave your post, leave your country?"

The Ambassador moved towards Emil's sightline. "I would probably tell you to get lost. I'd tell you that you didn't understand the first thing about my country, or my love for it despite all the problems. But it isn't a fair comparison. I'm not you. You are stronger, more open-minded, more capable, more… everything. I'll say it again. You know everything I say about the States is true. You know a move would be best for you and Dana. If you stay, your sensibilities will only diverge further and further from the path of your country. The gap will widen, and you will be alone. By then, well… by then the opportunity to jump across will be gone."

"What happened to the man I met a few hours ago at the gate? I didn't expect such a serious side." Emil said, deflecting.

"I'm only serious when I see bad things happen to good people." Zeke replied.

"The Czech people, we have been through quite a bit just in my lifetime. I cannot express to you how tough and resilient we are. We can achieve anything we want. We will be able to make our own way, I can assure you of that. In all sincerity, I appreciate your concern and the seriousness of your offer. And I thank you for the invitation tonight. It has been very pleasant and interesting. But my answer remains the same. No." Emil returned to scrutinizing the photo.

Zeke hid another disappointment behind another smile. Emil was spending so much time on the photo that Zeke had no choice but to address it one way or another. "Great War days. People think I display that photo because there is a President on it." Zeke said as he pointed out Truman. "Maybe that's a little bit true, but in reality, I keep it out because of Augie, over here on the left. In the first week of boot camp, he told us to call him Augustus. You know, like the Caesar? So naturally we called him Augie. He pretended to hate that, but I had my doubts. He was the card, the mischief-maker in the group. He always had a joke ready. He would play tricks on anyone, no matter the rank. Did impressions like you wouldn't believe. He could impersonate anyone in the battalion. He spoke God knows how many languages. Sometimes he would call out orders in German with a perfect Bavarian accent. It would scare the pants off the trenchies out in front of us, thinking they had been encircled. Ha! He had a flair for the dramatic, you could say. He once even organized a drag burlesque show when we were rotated back for a week."

"Do you two still keep in touch?" Emil asked.

"No. He's dead. We were artillery, so pretty far back of the line, you know. And Augie, see, he refused to use the latrine holes we'd set up behind the equipment. Augie got it in his head that he needed to do his business '*au naturel*' as he would say. Every night, with a lit cigarette mind you, he would trudge off along the ridge take a dump right out in the open. Of course, we'd tell him just one lucky sniper is all it would take to end him. But he would wave us off and say something like they were so far away that they didn't exist. Or that if any of them were that lucky, we'd all be dead by now.

"And for the longest time, he was right. Until the night that he wasn't. He went off as usual but didn't come back. We sent out a search party but didn't find him until dawn. He was shot clear through the neck with his pants down, ass pointed east toward the enemy. We figure after he was shot, he had just enough time to turn himself around and give them one last salute. Anyways. He always said that today would be ok because yesterday was."

"A good man." Emil offered in condolence.

"Naïve is what he was." Zeke took a sip of his drink. There was a faint banging and scraping of furniture coming from above, evidence that the gold hunt was still on elsewhere in the house. He fished out a small keychain out of his pocket and turned toward the steel door in the back of the study. "I have one more thing to show you."

Zeke opened the door to expose the room within the room. It was a narrow corridor bricked up at the other end. Lining the walls were shelves filled with cardboard banker's boxes. He muttered to himself scanning the labels, stopping halfway down the path. "You can read Russian, I presume?" The Ambassador asked.

Emil nodded side to side in the "more-or-less" fashion.

"Well, you can read this for yourself then." Zeke handed him a thin folder red stamped "Secret" with a series of codes at the top and Cyrillic lettering underneath. As Emil hesitated to open the folder, Zeke introduced the contents. "Minutes from the Central Strategic Committee meeting last fall. You'll see there was substantial time devoted to "Czech development." We don't have the full report, but a summary of steps is on the back page. There's another dozen files or so just like it. Same thing for Hungary. But you'll get the general idea from this one."

Emil looked at the Ambassador and opened the folder. As the stone-faced Olympic champion read, Zeke scanned the shelves. Parts of this job he would not miss. Even though Ike would be recalling him soon, he would retain these files in his head. Not the details of course, but the labels at least, knowing that behind each ambiguous label were sheaves of information. News, uniformly bad news. The good news always found a way out into the light, the rest landed here. When not sufficiently distracted, he thought of the brotherhood. The dozens (hundreds?) of other diplomats with their own labels swimming around in their heads. A semi-secret cadre bearing the weight on behalf of their countrymen.

Emil had scanned ahead to the back page, taking time to reason out the concluding language. His angular face had taken on an inscrutable intensity. Zeke interrupted his review. "It's not a theory, not an idle rumor. It's going to happen, Emil. I'm not supposed to show this to anyone. Jail time for me if this were to leak out!" He shrugged. "But if you leave here tonight to return to your barracks, you can do what you want with what you've seen. Tell your commander or keep it to yourself, I don't care. But you can't say I didn't warn you: the gap will widen, and you will be alone. Or… or instead you and Dana can stay here with Lani and me for a day or two while we arrange a flight to the States."

"What about Gregor? He won't leave here without us tonight." Emil layered on another objection.

"Don't concern yourself with Gregor. You let me deal with him. It's a big decision, I know. But it's one that has to be made tonight."

.

Dana and Kalle walked shoulder to shoulder across the property, the jerking cones of light from their torches delineating the seen and unseen in the night. They moved ahead silently. Dana asked no questions about where they were going or why, but the spring in her step betrayed her curiosity. The pair were heading past the summit of the hill down towards the back. Ahead was the garden and the site of the kalua that Kalle dug up hours earlier. The thick summer grass yielded temporarily to their footfalls, soundlessly springing back in place. The depression on the backside of the hill gave a wider variety of vegetation a chance during the peak season. It was the natural choice of location for the garden.

Dana's torchlight careened up to make an oval on the waist-high flagstone wall. The pointless wall. Dana broke the silence and asked, "What's behind this wall?"

"Nothing."

"You think the gold is *inside* the wall?" Dana asked.

"Not exactly. As far as anyone knows, this wall has been here forever. We call it the pointless wall. In fact, Annika and I were talking about it earlier today. It certainly wasn't built by the Germans. I was out here earlier with Lani, and I happened to see a grate at the base of the wall. That's the part I'm interested in. It should be around here somewhere."

Without any warning, Dana hopped up to sit on top of the wall and wove her torch around in wide circles on both sides, shining her light indiscriminately. Dana did what people of all ages and all stations have done forever when sitting on a wall. She began swinging her legs back and forth. Her voice was light. "Your girlfriend's very pretty. How long have you two been together?" Dana asked, peering over the opposite edge of the wall at nothing.

Kalle didn't respond right away. The careening rays from the torch and the sway of Dana's legs had destabilized him for a moment. In a flash he recalled the agreed-upon sign to Henrik down below, but it was too late now. "We're just work colleagues." Kalle said. It sounded ridiculous, and it was.

"Good." Dana replied.

Kalle found the shovel he had set aside earlier, still perched over the grate. He gripped the shovel tightly and began to probe around the edges of the grate. "Good?" he asked, smiling.

Dana shone her light down over the grate, covering a wider and slightly dimmer circle from her vantage point. "You don't seem all that happy around her, that's all. Better to be an unhappy work colleague than an unhappy lover I guess."

Kalle was wedging the blade between grate and grass, working his way around the perimeter hoping for a weak or rusted spot from which to pry the rectangle loose from the underlying stone. Making matters worse, the metal itself was in good condition – certainly much younger than the wall itself. He made it to the end of the first side with no success and turned to face the light above. "Maybe it appears that I'm unhappy because I'm just awkward next to her. Not knowing what to say, how to act around her? Just trying not to screw up?" Kalle spoke freely up to Dana's outline on the wall. He couldn't make out her face with the saturation of light coming down, but her head appeared to be leaning forward in close attention.

"Maybe." Dana said.

Kalle went back to work along the second edge in the ensuing silence. The metal was encased into the rock here as well, but the rock itself wobbled under the pressure of Kalle's shovel. He probed away from the grate, and the blade slipped easily between two cobblestones partially covered in grass. Leveraging the tool, Kalle exposed a clear, straight-edged opening. Judging from the bulging grass and stone, the opening was at least triple the size of the grate itself. Large enough for a man to drop down. Large enough for a small crate to drop down.

Dana hopped down next to Kalle, grabbing his shoulder for stability. She uttered something in Czech. The context and intonation meant the only reasonable translation was "holy shit."

The cover was hinged and heavy, made of a combination of metal, stone, and cemented rock aggregate. Kalle set the cover back down to remove as much soil and grass on the edges as possible to manage the weight. The two worked silently, with Kalle forcing the opening with the shovel and Dana jamming the resulting angle with flagstones until the cover was high enough to topple with a thud. Kalle shone his light into the void below to find a floor of cobblestones a few feet below. A metal ladder was bolted to the edge of the opening connected to the hinges. Dana inspected a metal stamp along the hinge. She read out *"Baumeister GmbH – Bremen."* They exchanged smiles and raced each other to the ladder.

The subterranean space was dark and cool. The pair of flashlights hunted out the borders: about five feet high and about the same in width. It amounted to a long corridor that trailed off into the darkness. The damp atmosphere was confirmed by a slippery floor with occasional puddles. Kalle had never seen a dungeon before, but his imagination as a child reading Dumas was very close to this. The purpose of this place was opaque to Kalle. His only initial impression was that it was old – much older than the German occupation of the past decade. "Shall we?" Kalle said, pointing with his torch into the emptiness ahead.

Any residual light from the opening above faded as they walked, leaving only the torches to reflect the slimy walls and floors. Their footsteps reverberated in the tight space. Kalle had to walk crouched over and the pair kept close to each other in the middle of the pathway, uneager to brush up against the walls.

Ahead on the right, the stone walls became rough and discolored. A large hole had been knocked out on the side. A crawlspace in the upper half of the wall extended back for at least fifteen feet. The interior of this space was laid in with a mix of stone and scrap lumber. It seemed to post-date the main chamber by generations. Kalle pressed himself onto the ledge in order to crawl in a bit and peek further into the room. He shone the light into each of the corners in turn. He described to Dana what he saw. The room was empty and featureless, save for some scraps of plywood sheeting strewn about and scratch marks along the walls and reinforcing studs. This place had not always been empty.

Kalle backed out of the hole, and they set off down the corridor. The floor sloped gently down, and the puddles merged into a more persistent lake. Shortly they came to the end of the dark hall. In the far wall, just above the shallow waterline was a pipe opening, about six inches across. Kalle crouched low and shone the light into the pipe, but there was nothing to be seen. It was time to brainstorm some ideas with his partner, but talking in the enveloping blackness would have felt like a broadcast. It was impossible to know for sure that they were alone. He pointed the light into the water at their feet. Diffuse light scattered across the cramped area at the end of the tunnel.

The light dappled with the small wave perturbations in the clear water. Small hemispheres skipped across Dana's face, demarking the curves of her nose, chin, and neck. She was grinning from ear to ear. "It was here! The gold was in that side room, right? We should go back in. I'll go in this time and dig around in the corners." Dana blurted. She was fully absorbed in the thrill of the chase.

Kalle had been turning the dimensions of the hall over in his mind, crouched down inspecting the mostly waterproof floor and wall. "A cistern." He said. Dana's sparkling face registered no recognition. "A cistern. The wall above probably holds up a snowbank in the winter, all the snowmelt comes here in the spring. This pipe heads... I don't know. But the pointless wall has a point. A cistern. A literal water-room. *Badezimmer.*"

Dana spoke over him, "If they were in a hurry and broke open cases, some coins could have fallen out. Or maybe they couldn't take it all in one trip, so they just covered up the rest. You didn't check under the plywood, did you?"

"I can't tell, but I think we've walked closer to the house, meaning this pipe heads into the house. Meaning the cistern stores spring runoff as a summer water supply. Or at least it used to."

"The cases would be too heavy to lift out, so they had to break them open and get bars or coins out a handful at a time. Maybe it wasn't organized, just each man for himself. We should check on the floor and in the puddles too."

"Lani said there was a spring, but there can't be a spring on the top of a hill like…" an eerie grating sound cut off both monologues. Dana and Kalle looked at each other, keeping their lights pointed down into the water. Reverberations shot back and forth in the small space, gifting a handful of decibels into the stone on each trip. Neither moved in the silence that followed. Kalle had cocked his head to locate the source, but the original sound was too short, and the echoes came from all directions. Dana shone her light back up the tunnel, but no movement could be seen.

After an interval, a low mumbling came to them. It was a voice, a man's voice – deep and warped. The voice continued, and it became clear that the source was the pipe. In the shimmering light, Kalle mouthed to Dana, "who's that?" She shrugged back.

A second voice joined, louder and more insistent than the first, but just as garbled. The tortured path of the pipe left no distinct words. It was impossible to determine the people or even the language at the other end.

The two voices grumbled back and forth at each other for a while like a pair of wet beasts deep in the African night. Kalle and Dana smirked as they listened in. It wasn't eavesdropping if you didn't understand a word of it, Kalle reasoned. However, the cadence contextualized the conversation. As the exchange went on, the louder voice picked up the rhythm and increased the total number of incoherent words. The quieter voice remained subdued, always waiting a beat before responding.

"Fro juuurb waas zzzst zeonon piskah."

"… bwofam."

"Kiirsch djen im djeen wahwahsoto klsh zzt um frunfrun!"

"...oos bokudh, soun warlon."

"Paner ooof! Soun lao toto boushkin fitbin boushkin fitbin tahto warrkk warro kaoly. Seerw you! Seerw you moussah piskah! Ourn ooak boozah? Woarn ooak boozah? Kiirsch weerenotow bearno frunfrun! Frunfrun."

"..."

· The silence seemed to signal a truce, until a pair of words from the louder voice cut through crystal clear.

"NO! NO!"

They heard brief spasms of gurgling sounds over indistinct scraping and shuffling. The shuffling stopped. A sickening thud rang out, followed by silence. As the echo drove into oblivion, Dana's eyes widened at Kalle. "Emil!" She yelped and rushed toward the ladder.

Kalle followed on her heels, loping along hunched over like an animal. He grabbed a rung with his flashlight hand. The wall behind was briefly illuminated. Faint graffiti flashed in the light. *Die kasse.* He scrambled to the surface, greeted by darkness cut with the light from the back windows of the manor. Dana was rushing through the garden toward the back door. He called out for her to wait. He walked methodically toward her to mask his uncertainty over what to do.

They stood between rows of thin leaves. Carrots with only sparse green straws poking through to sip sunlight. A faint smell of charcoal lingered in the air. Unsure what else to say, Kalle repeated his question from below. "Who was that? Did it sound like Emil to you?"

"No." She replied. After a quick breath she amended it. "I don't think so. I don't know."

"It didn't sound like Emil to me." He said to reassure her without any justification.

"Did we hear somebody falling? Did we hear someone being …? What else could it have been?" Dana asked.

"I don't know."

Dana looked toward the lights of the kitchen window, only a handful of steps away. Answers were only a handful of steps away. She turned back to Kalle, her face seeking agreement to go in.

He raised a finger in response. He was thinking.

"We can't go in there blasting questions. If someone was … if something bad did just happen, who can we trust? Right now, we don't know anything. We should just walk in and say nothing. We heard nothing, saw nothing. We only looked around the sauna and that's it. We smile and walk around to find everyone else as quickly as possible without raising suspicion. And then we'll see who's missing. Hopefully no one. Hopefully it's just a misunderstanding. But if someone is missing, we'll take a close look at their partner in this gold search. Bruises, torn clothes, acting strange. I don't know. Something like that. But no matter what, we'll figure this out together."

Dana narrowed her eyes at him. "Ok." She hooked her arm through his and they walked to the kitchen entrance.

Interlude – Atlantic

Spring 1952 – The Atlantic

HNLMS VAN SPEIJK was not impressive. Not by beauty, size, or any other measure. She began her life as a simple short-haul merchant vessel, plying the wicked North Sea routes, with an occasional foray into the Baltic. The gregarious first owner was also her chief designer, adding some atypical specifications. By all accounts he was an idiot. A rich idiot though, at least temporarily. He installed four additional boilers below, outrageously overpowering the vessel for her size or expected duties. It isn't clear what the plan was exactly, but it was likely something along the lines of speeding up transit times to both move more freight in a year and extract some premium for the express service. The reality was that the only thing that sped up was the rate of fuel consumption. The Van Speijk was a thirsty boat, refueling bunker oil at every port of call and killing whatever lead she had on the competition.

When the war came, she was pressed into service for the crown. The hull was reinforced with steel cladding, the fuel tanks were expanded, and she was fitted with some basic light arms. She became an ad hoc frigate, carrying loads and running protection on the Atlantic resupply route between America and Britain. For once, the extra boilers came in handy, making good time even in the foulest of weather. While some of the crew would later claim she outran many a German U-Boat, the truth is that she was too small to be bothered with.

Post-war needs for serviceable vessels continued, as the supply of bombs brought over earlier turned into demand for reconstruction supplies of all sorts. Unscratched, the Van Speijk continued churning out laps in the north Atlantic. Burn oil, make steam, turn prop, cleave water, repeat. Day after day, month after month. Waves sprayed onto the deck at a regular beat, creating a fine mist that traveled through the galleys. Salt caked in everywhere: inside the wiring, underneath chipped paint, into the threads of unseated bolts threatening to snap. In those hard first few post-war years a tradition developed in that each crew left the boat in a slightly worse condition than they found her. The sailor's code of spotless upkeep disappeared with the sails, if it ever existed at all. She never fired all boilers at once anymore. Instead, the extra four steam machines allowed the mechanics to only deal with fixing up the fifth-worst unit below deck, leaving the balance to gather dust and grime.

So now in 1952 the smallish heavy ex-frigate bobbed forward through massive swells, making the Baltimore – Antwerp run in pedestrian time. She would miss her call by a day or so, but no one minded too much. The cargo was no longer so vital. She carried a variety of items for Europe: pig iron, corn meal, spare parts, paper stock, and on this occasion Kentucky bourbon whiskey. The crew called her the slop bucket, carrying an agglomeration of odds and ends. There was a sputter here and there in those cold waters, but she would make it to Belgium… eventually.

Chapter 12 – Radiate

REGULARLY SPACED LANTERNS lit the esplanade in the cooling evening air. Kinetic shadows tilted, shrank, and dissolved as tourists and locals walked off their dinners. "Johannes" and "Arvid" strode up to a striking pair of obviously Swedish girls. Henrik launched into an introduction with his best schoolboy Swedish and the closest thing to a flat accent he could muster. The prettier of the two smirked behind a raised hand and glanced over to her friend, who was tasked with a response.

"Darling, I have no idea what you just said but it sounded absolutely lovely. Could you repeat that in English, please? Pathetically, that's all we know." The girl with frizzy dark hair spoke with a radiant open smile and engaging eyes.

Henrik was only able to catch every third word, as the girl spoke fast and with an accent he couldn't place. Flustered, he looked over to Vaino for help. Vaino only shrugged. Henrik understood enough to know she didn't understand him. He scrambled to gather an armload of English words to string together a reasonable response. Mismatching verb tense and omitted words aside, the gist of the reply was that his English was not all that great but maybe he could have a lovely teacher like her to help him. He also welcomed them to his waffle and hoped that they were enjoying the hanging.

"Well, that's quite an interesting collection of words there. Let's try this again. Hello. My name is Margie, and this is Winnie. What were you speaking before? Was that Finnish?" Margie asked slowly.

Henrik responded that it was Swedish, not Finnish.

"Oh, so you're Swedish?"

"No. Finnish."

Margie paused a moment, looking back and forth at the two men. "But if you're Finnish, why were you speaking in Swedish?"

"Good question." Vaino muttered softly to Henrik in Finnish. Henrik raised an eyebrow back at him, wondering how much of this he was following.

The conversation looped around over and over, making slight progress by the sheer willpower of Henrik and Margie to remain near each other. An improvised blend of English and sign language became the *lingua franca* for the pair.

The group strolled slowly along the pathway as the great struggle rambled on. Winnie was conspicuous in her silence, watching her friend ahead of her. Vaino was oblivious to Winnie's uneasiness in walking next to a haggard fisherman at least twice her age. He leaned closer to her in his part friendly/part creepy way. "Your friend is quite the chatterbox. She already has my nephew all wrapped up in a bow. No small feat, mind you. Most days that I see him, he's brushing off girls left and right. Just like I used to, back in the day!" Vaino wiped his nose with a sleeve.

"Your English is much better that your nephew's. Don't you want to help translate for him?"

"Not really."

Winnie cocked her head and gave a confused smile.

"I like watching him struggle. An old fart like me needs some entertainment. His confidence could use a knock down every once in a while. Like how dough left alone just rises and rises. You have to punch it down every so often or you'll just get a big bubble you know?"

Winnie shook her head. The group of four non-Swedes moved slowly north into a thicker band of restaurants and bars. Behind them a faint white light flickered on the hill.

.

Dana pushed through the back door into the kitchen. Unlinking arms from Kalle, she veered off to the block of knives. They were shiny, standing at attention in their slots patiently awaiting orders. Dana pulled a small one out to inspect the edge. Kalle coughed. She knew the expression he was wearing before she turned around. She gave a thin smile and a shrug before replacing the steel.

Weapon or not, Dana knew that if Emil was in any sort of trouble, she would plow through and destroy any of these pathetic people who stood in her way. She had a pop in her step as they made their way back toward the drawing room – the adrenaline of crisis.

Kalle was speaking in a tone suggestive of something banal – part of his cover. Dana wasn't listening. She rocked her head minutely, trying to pick up other sounds: shuffling feet or muffled voices being proof of life elsewhere. Nothing.

Emil would be dead, victim of some disagreement that escalated out of proportion. Dana would corner the murderer and detain him until the police arrived. Word would leak out that the others had to hold Dana back from tearing him limb from limb. The home press would paint the story of a national hero lost too soon, the grieving widow a collateral victim of the senseless horror. But Dana would be the hero of the story, not the victim. Those around her would see her resilience, her self-reliance. She would move, she would train, and she would coach others to follow behind her. TACK tack tack tack, launch through the narrow tunnel. The new narrative crept forward. Eventually the public would see her for her, without the asphyxiating honorific "widow of the late Emil Zatopek."

Kalle was tapping her shoulder with a question on his face. She looked down, flushing slightly. "I'm sorry, could you repeat that?" She asked.

"I was just asking if you remember which way Emil went before we left? I think Annika and Lani went upstairs, but… well…" Kalle trailed off.

Dana noticed his sympathetic eyes and understood his goal was to find Emil first as well. Before she could respond, footsteps rang out from the ceiling. The two followed the sound with their eyes, down the hall toward the stairs Kalle had climbed an hour earlier. The women were coming down. Emil would have to wait, dead or alive.

Lani and Annika came back energized. Their faces broadcasted that they had been on an adventure. Years were stripped off Lani's face as she relayed the story in her light rapid rhythm. There was in fact an attic! Above the bathroom! Who knew? And we clambered up there! And so forth. Dana forced a smile and nodded, even as she was catching every second or third word. Whatever this story was, it was going nowhere. She kept her ears tuned for the lower frequency of footsteps or men's voices. At some point Annika had cut in to add to the story, with her stupid pretty eyes and her stupid pretty mouth laughing at her own anecdote. She was laying a casual hand on Kalle's shoulder. Kalle nodded along to the attic adventures. He tried to catch Dana's eye, but she was looking right past him. To nothing, nowhere.

The wall behind wasn't blank, but it may as well have been. Prohibited from immediately searching for her husband and disinterested in attic story time, Dana stared at the mottled colors of the wall. Whether it was wallpaper, paint, paintings, war trophies, or framed certificates of commendation, Dana didn't know or care. These minutes of inaction stretched near the breaking point. Who would want to kill Emil anyway? The Russian? No, too old. Also, why wait until here when he could have done the job in the car? The big charming American? Maybe. Strong enough to take Emil in a fair fight in any case. Certainly not the Ambassador. Too important and again, too old. The guard out front? A young fighter, so maybe. But again, why? Who would hurt Emil? Even Schade loved Emil, despite being ground into the track by him. Dana thought about Emil and his countless hours of training. His ability to outwork everyone everywhere. A smile flitted across her face. No, Emil wasn't the one to worry about.

Dana turned to Lani and asked, "Our husbands are together, yes? Did they go down to some sort of lower level? If we don't find them, they may just keep talking forever."

Lani laughed. "Yes, we should save them from themselves. I think I know where they are." Lani led the group toward the business section of the house with Dana close on her heels. Down the dim hallway, the Ambassador's office door was shut and there was no sound coming from within. A thin line of light shone along the base of the door, free of any shadow breaks. The group of four hushed as they approached. Lani raised an eyebrow to the others and knocked gently.

Nothing.

Dana was done with waiting. She stepped up to turn the knob. The door was locked.

The women took turns knocking and trying the handle again, calling out names. In the ensuing hubbub, Kalle backed away from the group and retreated down the hallway.

.

"And the Yankees are back in business here with two away in the sixth. A chorus of boos for Berra as he trots around for his 21st of the season. This kid is really seeing the ball like a grapefruit this year. The Cleveland crowd is settling down now in nervous anticipation as Mick strides up to the plate. I would feel a bit of dread too if I was them. Mantle 0 for 2 so far today, looking to get in on the action. Here's the pitch… outside ball one."

The tinny radio voice pinged off the walls of the guardhouse. Charlie Gibbons listened to the game only in an abstract sense, keeping his attention focused on the intersecting twenty-yard circles of light around the gate. Baseball games were listened to intently only with your feet on a table and a beer in your hand. But tonight, Charlie was on duty, and it wasn't a real game anyway. The crunch of gravel ran over the announcer's dialogue. A silhouette approached from the house side. It appeared to be that quiet Finnish fella.

"What is that sound? Baseball?" Kalle asked. Charlie nodded while turning down the volume. Kalle paused, trying to work out the logistics of such a thing.

Charlie saw the confusion on his face and offered the details. "It isn't the game, not the real game at least. That's old Chester Whitfield you hear there on AFR out of Denmark. I guess their signal can radiate all the way through the Baltics – beats me really. Anyways, he gets the box scores wired to him right after the game back home. Then he makes up the play-by-play in the studio. Right on the spot. He has a lackey sit next to him to do the sound effects and everything. The crack of the bat, crowds cheering, the organ. All that. I don't know, next best thing to being there I guess."

Kalle frowned slightly and asked, "So he gets a slip of paper and just makes up the game from that?"

"Well, I would say he just fills in the details. Adds color, you know?"

Kalle pressed on. "He adds color. But what's to keep him from making up everything, winners and losers included?"

Charlie gave the bewildered look of a man on the street unaccustomed to being interviewed. "Nothing I suppose. What's to keep any man from making up everything?"

Kalle thought on that for a moment, looking at the ceiling of the guardhouse. "Well, the truth lingers out there, just bouncing around. Maybe sometimes it comes back to haunt you. Sometimes not."

"If you say so… what can I do you for?"

Kalle gave his best attempt at a conspiratorial smile and replied, "Oh I just had to get the hell out of there. The atmosphere is quite… stuffy inside. If you know what I mean."

Charlie played it straight with a polite smile and no response. Kalle pressed on. "A lot of very important achievements being discussed inside, but I can't for the life of me think of one interesting thing to say. And… and if, God forbid, I ask a follow-up question it just sets off another avalanche of stories. I'm getting buried in there. Do you have a cigarette?"

The two stood at the threshold of the guardhouse door, smoking and listening to the game (Mantle grounded out to end the inning). Kalle waited a bit before casually asking his question. "So has anyone else come out for a breather?"

"I'm sorry?" Charlie asked.

"I mean, have you seen anyone else come out here tonight? Just wondering if I'm the only one. I guess… I mean… I haven't seen your boss for a while. I thought the Ambassador may have made a run for it or something." Kalle made a small laugh. He found himself in the unusual position of carrying the conversation. "The Ambassador usually seems to be the one with the greatest number of stories. And greatest quality too. Quantity and quality… yep. So, imagine my surprise when among all this chatter, he's missing."

"The Ambassador is missing?" Charlie cut in, concerned. He moved toward the intercom inside the guardhouse.

"Oh, no no. Not missing really. Just missing out on the stories. That's all."

Charlie looked past Kalle with a smirk and said, "That's not the Ambassador I know." The two smoked through the commercial break. The stupidity of the silence between them was amplified by the happy insistent voice selling gum and whatnot. Kalle wondered why there was a commercial break if the game was over and was just being read off of a sheet of paper. Asking Charlie would only expose further ignorance.

Instead, Kalle screwed up the courage for one more ingratiating rally. "I think you and I are cut from the same cloth, eh? I'm definitely a fish out of water at these fancy dinners. It makes a simple man want to tear his hair out. I was wondering; if I wanted to just sneak out of here, would you still record me in your book there?" Kalle asked and gestured to the open logbook.

"Sorry, but rules are rules. Date and time, every time." Charlie responded.

"Yeah, but… you know… to help a friend out? Maybe just add an extra couple hours on the 'out' time so I don't look like a prick?"

Charlie shook his head.

Kalle edged closer to the logbook. The dim light showed columns of writing, with the far-right column blank for each of the last few entries. How many exactly, he couldn't tell. He shrugged and made a joke. "That's fine. Instead, I suppose I'll have to sneak out the back. You know over that low wall behind the garden and just walk down to the bars on the esplanade."

"Then I suppose I'll go ahead and call for an ambulance now." Satisfied with Kalle's narrowed eyes, Charlie continued. "The back cliffs out. The edges are always slippery, and the fall has to be at least 50 feet straight down. Then there are fences everywhere else, my friend. Anyone who leaves here in one piece leaves past me."

The answer wasn't fully convincing to Kalle, but it was the best he was going to get. He spread his arms in surrender. "That's a fair warning, much obliged. I guess I'll have to go take my chances back inside with the wolves." Kalle noticed that Charlie's face had set into a posture of grimly polite patience. "One small favor to ask though. If anyone else does decide to sign out, can you buzz it through on the intercom? I don't want to be the first to leave of course, but I would love to be the second, you know what I mean? Just use a code word on the intercom. Who was the player, Mantle? Just say Mantle check in, or something. Yes? I would much appreciate it, friend."

Charlie gave a small noncommittal nod. "Good luck back inside, *friend*."

Kalle's English was good enough to hear the sharper emphasis on the word friend, but not good enough to understand the meaning of it. He nodded and walked back up the path toward the mansion.

The gravel crunched under his worn dress shoes. Nothing of this evening made sense. Was he certain that he and Dana heard what they thought they heard? With all the muffling it could have been anything. Friends fooling around? A radio left on by the staff? A script read off for a radio show, just like the baseball game. It was at least as likely an explanation as murder.

As he approached the house, on impulse he veered off the path to the right. At the sudden change to a soft and quiet surface, Kalle heard a rustling in the dark brush. He paused and held his breath for a moment but heard nothing else. He continued to encircle the house, deciding to reenter through the back door by the garden.

The east side of the house was mostly black, framing a soft yellow bay window. Dana was standing at the window staring out. Kalle stopped in the shadows and watched his formidable partner. Her stance was determined and confident, despite the worry written on her face. Kalle considered this woman: friendly but independent, compassionate but fierce. The light from the room glowed around her short wavy hair and simple dress. In a heartbeat, she turned her head and looked straight at Kalle. He quickly cast his eyes down, looking intently at the pattern of pine needles at his feet. Kalle didn't dare look back up. If he was made, he would preserve at least some plausible deniability. He crouched to look at the needles more closely to buy himself some time. The rustling in the trees returned. It was time to move on.

Kalle made his way past a copse of fir trees and came out near the garden. The window to the kitchen was covered in blinds. Two figures in shadow displayed on the screen. The outlines were generic and Kalle couldn't make out who they were. The heads leaned toward each other – close enough to be whispering.

Without hesitation, Kalle approached the back door. Three quick steps through the mudroom and another four through the pantry brought him to the kitchen. The sound of gently running water washed out the sharpness of his footfalls. Ambassador Williamson was at the sink, scrubbing. Alone.

.

Dana tempered her relief when the office door was finally opened by the Ambassador. He and Emil gave lame excuses for ignoring the pounding and knob rattling for minutes before finally unlocking. Dana's instinct had been to rush to Emil, but she instead hung to the doorframe and pretended indifference. It was a curious thing, locking yourself in an office with a nearly complete stranger. Emil's wan smile at her didn't help.

Back in the drawing room, Dana stared out the window. Most of the pane was blanched out by the electric candelabra backlighting, creating a mirror out of the glass. The shadow cast by her body on the window carved out a photonegative fragment of the world outside. A tunnel into the void shaped like her head and shoulders. There was nothing to see: black trees in even blacker shadows. There wasn't even any sway to the trees, so the wind must have died down. Dana stood and luxuriated in the dead stillness through the tunnel. The complete absence of life. The end, just on the other side of the pane. She caught a flicker of movement on the periphery, but it was probably Lani behind her reflected in the backlight.

Dana turned back to the interior of the drawing room and gave her eyes a moment to adjust. Aside from the obvious relief, the reappearance of her husband and Zeke had simplified matters. Now only Gregor and Robert were unaccounted for. If only Kalle were around to discuss the next steps. Where did he go, and why didn't he mention anything to her? If he wanted to act on his own, so could she. It was time to find a basement or cellar in this house. It was obvious that an underground pipe would connect there, somewhere below her.

Zeke's jolly voice rose up an octave and twenty decibels behind her somewhere. She turned and joined Emil and Lani in wandering toward the sound. The Ambassador was holding court in the kitchen, a mélange of rapid thick words and barking laughs as he was relating some story. Kalle had returned from the void with Annika closely at his side. Dana made no attempt to follow the English. She let her eyes wander the kitchen, now filled to the brim with people: Lani listened with a rigid smile, Zeke shifted his weight as he spoke and dried his hands on the front of his pants, Kalle kept firm eye contact with only Zeke, Annika laughed along, and Emil stood blankly with his natural light a shade dimmer than usual. No sign of Gregor or Robert here either. Every moment that passed without those two showing their faces increased Dana's conviction that someone was dead.

Eventually, Zeke's tone signaled the end of a story. A vacuum of quiet came in after a few helpful laughs from the group. As if prearranged, everyone began filing out of the crowded kitchen to find greater space and refills up near the front of the house. Dana grabbed Kalle's arm at the bend of the hallway and led him to the side. She kept it quiet and brief. "Cellar. How do we get to the cellar?"

"Right. I have an idea. Follow me." Kalle responded. He had noticed a door underneath the stairs he took up earlier in the evening to the second floor. They reached it quickly without drawing any attention. Kalle yanked on the knob. The door opened into a downward spiraling stairwell. The stone-encased cavity was already well lit, with bare bulbs shining through the metal slatted stairs at regular intervals. The chasm smelled of iron and decay. To Dana, the scent of cemetery.

Kalle led the way down. Dana shut the door softly behind her and began her descent. Looking down through the slats, Dana found Kalle already a full rotation below her. Another dive into the caverns with this quiet pale northerner. She smiled despite herself at the familiarity of the moment.

The arrhythmic clanking of shoes on the gridded metal reduced to only Dana's steady footfalls. Kalle had reached the stone floor and stood at the threshold of a room below, peering in. His stillness caught Dana off-guard, and she stopped as well. A quiet moment passed. Dana held her breath above and waited for a sign.

Kalle raised a hand to the side of his face and rubbed his temple. He looked up to Dana and made to speak. Nothing came out but a slow sigh. Dana rushed down the last circle of stairs to reach Kalle. She saw the scene and replied, "Yeah."

Chapter 13 – Tamper

BLOOMS OF SMOKE spread through the dance hall, obscuring the details of the flowing figures on the floor. Tall dark-clad gentlemen led around their pastel dates with enthusiastic angular elbows, knees, and chins. The equally upbeat band cut through the smoke with a bright big band mix of fifteen-year-old American swing covers and spiced-up 100-year-old local folk favorites. The band came fully prepared to peddle nostalgia to a willing audience.

The small dance floor was demarcated by the band stage on one end and a tight collection of tables and booths the rest of the way around.

Vaino sat at a small table on the perimeter, tapping his foot while a forgotten cigar hung lamely from his hand. He gazed nowhere in particular, appreciating the sound of musicians past their prime making up for it with honest effort. Winnie sat opposite him, scanning the dance floor. Margie's wild black hair was easy to spot, even in the smoke. It was her speed that made her hard to track. One glance away and she could be lost halfway across the floor in the thicket of limbs. The table pair had settled into a quiet truce, having run out of things to say while Henrik and Margie tore up the dance floor. Winnie resolved to keep a close eye out, if only because tomorrow was a big day. She would drag her teammate out of there if she had to, regardless of how charming this Finn was. Another half hour and she would step in. It wouldn't be the first time.

The young crowd of dancers on the tight floor demanded up-tempo, and the band obliged. Boards squeaked, but without enough volume to carry against the horns. A musky summer air fought a slow losing battle against the varied whirling perfumes and pomades. Smiles masked the heavy breathing of the less fit in the crowd. Henrik and Margie moved effortlessly, jutting and spinning with frequent glances at each other.

Henrik felt a flap on his foot. He excused himself for a second and went to the edge of the action to tie his shoe. Margie careened around faster as if to cover for the temporary fifty per cent loss of energy in the couple. Her sharp elbow swung around and clipped another woman coming the other way. The smallish woman tumbled down. Margie laughed off the accident and reached over to help her back to her feet. Her offer was met with an abusive collection of Swedish words. Margie knew none of these words but understood everything. Taken aback, Margie glowered, arms folded.

Henrik had successfully double-knotted both laces. Satisfied that all of his problems were now solved, he looked up to find Margie. The music played over the top, but he could see that Margie was involved in some kind of shouting match with another girl. The frenzy of the other dancers slid around them unimpeded. He covered the distance in a few quick steps. The girl saw him come over, so she directed her assault on him, with a long list of creative names for Margie and she did this and she did that and so on. Margie, not one to take it, gave a stream of English vitriol back the other way. Both added gesticulations to make sure their point got across with the racket of all the horns and breathing and board squeaking around them. Henrik looked briefly from one to the other. He sighed and began to unbutton his cuff links. The women paused. While calmly rolling up his shirtsleeves, Henrik looked at the short woman and said in Swedish, "Just go get your boyfriend."

Vaino saw Winnie flinch out of the corner of his eye. He followed her line of sight to a small stationary group on the dance floor, showing all the markings of an impending tussle. Vaino stood on instinct and moved his chair to make a clear path to the aisle between the nearby booths. The band played on, and dancers continued to circle, oblivious to the small core of non-dancers brewing in their midst.

Standing on the perimeter between booths, Vaino tapped his foot in anticipation. He waited for the first punch. He begged for the first punch. White flashed as arms extended from jackets. The stationary core erupted with bodies flying in all directions. No more insults or complaints, just action. The melee began to pulse, with an inward press of bodies quickly replaced by haphazard recoil outward every few seconds. Each successive round of violence rippled out to nick a new layer of bystanders. The response of the peripheral bystanders varied, but the general theme was immediate and arbitrary retribution. It wasn't clear who the antagonist was, but fists must fly. The band took notice after a few generations of expansion and ceded the soundtrack to the scuffling crowd.

A short young woman made her way out of the crowd and ran toward the aisle where Vaino stood. He blocked off her escape route. "No way missy, you started this. Now go back in there and finish it!" he shouted over the din. With that, Vaino turned her around by the shoulders and gave her a firm kick to the backside. He scanned quickly in order to target others fleeing the scene. He pushed one dapper boy back into the maw of the crowd, but it was less satisfying than the first time. Uncertain what to do next, he looked at the now-empty booths next to him. He grabbed half-full glasses of wine and bottles of beer and began lobbing them indiscriminately onto the dance floor. Muffled thuds and shattering reported back. He grabbed more and more. The chaos had become total, as all fought all. Bodies were on the ground and others tripped over them. Do-gooders went in to mediate but were immediately attacked and consumed by the many-headed beast.

Vaino's armory of glasses and bottles quickly ran out. He returned to his table to retrieve chairs for launch. Winnie had disappeared by this point of course. He reached for the closest chair, but instead found himself falling face-first to the floor with a meaty weight on his back.

.

The body just laid there. Prone on the concrete, with one arm pinned underneath. The first instinct was to think it was an extremely uncomfortable position to be in before being reminded that dead men are not uncomfortable, at least as far as anyone new. And this was without doubt a dead hunk of flesh. Dead flesh, dead bones, dead eyes, looking nowhere.

The quiet and the bright pair of lights above gave the room a ghastly museum feeling. Kalle and Dana approached with caution, avoiding contamination of the scene.

Due to the position of the body, there was no visible stab or gunshot wound. But the trauma from where the head had hit the floor was obvious enough. If whatever felled him didn't kill him, the floor had finished the job. It was difficult to tell without moving the head, but there was at least a broken nose, a fractured skull, a shattered orbital bone, and a concussion. Not that any of that mattered. Blood had escaped through the fissures in the face, but it didn't make it too far. Instead of flowing in a rivulet across the room, blood had congealed everywhere along the skin and shirt, The surface tension had proven irresistible, staying with the body after the end. Tiny fragments of bone nestled in the morass like boulders caught at low tide. A pinkish foam had oozed out of the exposed ear, dribbling partway down the cheek. All the components remained in proper measure, but the rearrangement of order rendered the animate frozen, the future past, something nothing.

Neither Kalle nor Dana spoke for a few minutes. Each moved about the body slowly, ersatz detectives assessing the condition of the victim, shallowly hoping that he would gasp and wake up, obviating the need to raise the highest of alarms and the greatest level of complications. Eventually, they moved a respectful distance away and whispered their plans together. No sense in bothering the corpse over the details, after all.

They conducted an abbreviated search of the cellar. They opened a chest filled with a variety of heavy tools, each one looking guiltier than the last. There was an empty sump well in the corner, with a circular pipe opening in the wall near the bottom. Apparently, the connection to the cistern.

The clock was ticking, and they had settled on their plan, so they gave the body a wide berth and ascended the stairs. Kalle opened the door at the top of the stairs a crack, to check if the coast was clear. Annika was staring right at him with a frown. He took a breath, opened the door wide, and came up with Dana right behind.

"What were you doing?" Annika asked in Finnish as casually as she could muster.

"Looking for Robert and Gregor, of course." Kalle made sure to announce both names clearly. Gesturing to Dana, he continued, "Gregor is her escort back, and he's been gone for a while. Plus, between us, I'm beginning to wonder if those two found what we came here for. Wouldn't that be something? An American and a Soviet splitting the gold…"

Silence and the shifting of weight.

"I'm going to check in on Emil." Dana said, giving Kalle a quick glance before heading up the hallway.

Annika's stare remained fixed. Kalle returned to the issue. "Seriously, have you seen either of them?"

"No."

"Ok, well we need to keep each other in the loop. We've seen no sign of the *badzimmer*. I know the attic was a dead-end, but did you and Lani find anything else?"

"No Kalle. I don't think there's any loop to stay in at this point. I'm tired of this game. It's late, let's just go." Annika said.

Kalle stood still and thought for a moment. "Yeah, let's go."

The corridor was quiet and cold. Kalle strained to hear voices as they walked toward the common areas, but only their steps reported back. Kalle suggested that they should say their goodbyes and Annika nodded, pointing ahead to the threshold of the jungle room. The Ambassador and Lani were speaking quietly there, as if waiting for guests' departures. A broad smile came back to Zeke's face as he tracked their approach. Kalle gave a weird grin and dip of the head in the international symbol for it was a great time, but we have to get going.

"So good of you to come – both of you." Zeke said. "It ended up a bit chaotic there at the end, didn't it? All in good fun though, yes, yes. We'll walk you out." The foursome made their way through the ferns and waterways to the front door and out to the stillness of the midsummer night.

Kalle measured his pace as slowly as he could get away with, buying time before arriving at the guardhouse and the exit. Zeke was charging ahead, chatting aimlessly with Annika. Lani lingered with Kalle and said, "He's taken a shine to you, you know that, right? I mean, with all his bluster and rapid-fire comments, it's easy to think he doesn't pay attention to anyone. A man in love with his own voice. But he does listen… sometimes. I can tell that he listens to you. That is, when you do finally pipe up."

Not knowing how to respond, Kalle took the twisted compliment with a smile and plodded on ever closer to the front gate. The pathway lights cast shadows that outpaced their living counterparts only to fade and come back for another lap, and another, and another.

Just before the gate, Kalle turned and said, "I was hoping to catch Robert before heading out. Please say my goodbyes." Lani nodded. "I couldn't seem to find him. Have you seen him recently?"

"No," Lani replied. "But he has a way of popping up when you least expect it."

"I can imagine."

The foursome had reached Charlie at the gate. Kalle gave him a questioning stare, trying to elicit a clue about any early departures. Charlie's eyes were shaded by his brow against the harsh overhead light. His return stare was plain and inscrutable.

Kalle had let the string play out as far as he could, and he had nothing to show for it. There was nothing left to do but pipe up. He turned to Charlie and asked, "Do you have a phone line here in this guardhouse? An outside connection?" Charlie glanced at the Ambassador and nodded. "May I use it for a moment?"

Charlie ushered Kalle into the small shack and pointed to the receiver and cradle on the desk. Kalle glanced at the far wall, with the service rifle secured in what appeared to be its standard location. He reached for the phone, ran his hand along the wire to the base in the wall, and yanked. He bundled up the frayed cord with the phone and walked past a confused Charlie.

"I'm afraid this estate is a crime scene." Kalle blurted out.

Zeke laughed, looking at the equipment in the Finn's arms. "I would say so, seeing how you've mangled a perfectly good piece of American property there." He pointed his finger gun and said with a sarcastic western growl, "yuuuur under arrest!"

Kalle didn't return the smile. The mood deflated to match the still air. All eyes were on him. The floor was his.

·

Dana found Emil sitting alone in the Ambassador's office. It was a comfortable-looking leather chair, but Emil was perched on the edge of it as if ready to bolt from a starter's gun at any moment. Relieved to switch back to Czech, she said, "I don't think I've ever seen you hide out from a party before. You seem tired. I know it isn't the race catching up with your legs, you looked fine on the track earlier today."

Emil was hunched over looking at Dana's shoes as she spoke. He snapped out of it and looked up. "No, the legs are fine. Just sitting here thinking a bit."

"Thinking." Dana sounded doubtful.

"Yeah, thinking. Don't give me that look! Listen, we need to talk through something. We may need to stay here at the Tollefsson house for a while."

Dana paused a moment before responding. "How did you know?"

"The Ambassador had a chat with me. He had it all planned out. Wait, how did *you* know? Did Lani mention it to you too?" The look of confusion on Emil's face mirrored Dana's.

"Lani didn't say anything to me. I found him all by myself. Well, with that Finn, Kalle. It's horrible… What do you mean the Ambassador had it planned out??? Oh god."

"Well, his speech. I mean it was a convincing speech for us to stay. I don't know what you think. It feels like so much to change on such short notice. We would be criminals. But what fun, what a challenge! Even if we did… let's say we did do it. We'll have to get around Gregor tonight. We'd have to contact our family…" Emil had begun tracing out the circles of arguments that had been in his head for the better part of an hour.

Through the scattershot, Dana had no idea what her husband was talking about, but at least she knew they weren't talking about the same thing. "Emil, stop. Emil. I don't think you'll have to worry about Gregor tonight." From the look on her face, Emil knew to shut up and listen.

Dana pulled up a chair of her own and laid out the events that she and Kalle had witnessed. Emil's naturally bright face had already turned bland and uncertain thanks to the Ambassador's recruitment. Now, Dana's story darkened his eyes and mouth in a way she'd never seen before.

They sat in silence briefly, Emil processing and Dana wondering what it was that Emil thought would be fun but would make them criminals. Not that it mattered at this point. The sounds of heated debate broke through as a door was opened elsewhere in the house.

"All I'm saying is, I'm saying, well you say 'there's been a crime' and I say 'fine' and then you say 'shut the gates' and I say 'fine' and then you say you're in charge now and that's where I say 'hold your horses.'" The Ambassador was animated and projected his voice through the first floor of the house as the group came in through the din of the jungle room.

Emil and Dana rose to join the rest. They had made it no farther than the entrance hall. Kalle was struggling to get in a word edgewise with the Ambassador at full speed.

"I'm saying 'hold your horses' because you are on American soil here, and if there is a crime here as you say, it is an American crime. I'm happy to embargo the house if there is due cause, but only because I choose to, not because you order it so. Is that clear?" Zeke didn't wait for a response. "You know, I was beginning to like you. Robbie was too. So, if it isn't too much trouble, Inspector Poirot, kindly inform us as to what the hell is going on."

It appeared for the moment at least that he had gotten it out of his system.

Kalle turned and saw Dana approach. He replied quietly to the Ambassador, "Please follow us." Kalle and Dana led the group to the cellar stairs.

Dana had no interest in clanking down these spiral stairs again, particularly with a full party in tow, yet here she was. The plan had not called for a spectacle, but it was unavoidable at this point given the Ambassador's agitation. All these people were about to be crammed in the cellar around a large familiar corpse with the blood and the bits of bone and the vacuum of personality... agitation wouldn't begin to describe the situation only two rotations away. One rotation. There was still time to stop it. Clank clank, time's up.

Kalle reached the floor and stood behind the body. Dana followed suit. The two waited with hands folded in front like a pair of funeral directors ushering in the family for a last viewing. Gasps came in sequence from Emil, Annika, and Lani as they came into view. Dana watched closely for the Ambassador's reaction. Zeke rushed up to the body on instinct and reached for the head and shoulders, giving a small shake. "Jesus Christ, why didn't you say anything earlier? Did you call a doctor yet? Did you? Why didn't you call a doctor?" Zeke looked up at Kalle, who shook his head.

"He's dead Ambassador. I'm very sorry. Robert's dead."

Chapter 14 – Strong Force

"TWO PRETTY FINNISH girls decide to treat themselves to a day at the spa. There are three saunas, so they wrap up in towels and head to the first one. They step in and see three fat hairy men half-naked speaking in Russian. The blond clutches her towel tight, turns, and walks back out the door, with her brunette friend right behind. 'No way am I going to risk our innocence being violated by those brutes!' she says, and her friend nods in agreement." Vaino stared out into the still blackness of the sea as he spoke the lines he'd delivered countless times before. Henrik rested his bruised arms on the gunwale and with bleary eyes gestured for the old man to continue.

"So, the girls move on to the second sauna, expecting better luck, you see. They walk in and see three skinny beady-eyed men speaking German. The girls again grab their towels tight and run out, fearing the worst from those cold-hearted krauts.

"Finally, they walk slowly to the last sauna. Afraid to even open the door, you see. So, they walk in and find three tall men speaking Swedish. The blonde sighs in relief, tears off her towel revealing her gorgeous curvy body, and sits down on the bench. Her friend stares at her in disbelief. She shuffles over the bench with her towel still wrapped tight and whispers something like, I dunno. 'Aren't you afraid these big men will attack us and violate our innocence?' The blonde replies, "of course not. That's Hans, Aarvik, and Mathis. They're my cousins.' 'Oh, what a relief,' says the brunette. Then the blonde says. Listen, she says, 'yes you have nothing to worry about. They must be exhausted. I fucked their brains out this morning.'"

Henrik snorted easily at that one despite the pain shooting through his ribs. He offered up a response. "How do you stop a Swedish invasion? Post a sign at the border saying, 'Please shoot yourself in the head.'"

"What's the difference between a shark and a Swedish grandmother? One is an enormous slimy smelly bloodthirsty beast that will rip your head off. The other is a fish."

"A Swede, a liar, and a thief walk into a bar. The bartender says, 'Hi Rolf, what'll you have?'"

Vaino leaned in toward Henrik in a serious regard and asked. "Honestly now. Did you really say, 'just go get your boyfriend'?"

Henrik smiled and gave a shrug.

Vaino cackled and absent-mindedly rearranged his nets at the bottom of the boat, struggling to suppress a creeping feeling of respect for this stupid handsome man. After their escape from the chaos of the dance hall, Vaino had the sense to retreat to his fishing boat and cast off a modest distance. It was unlikely anyone would be able to point them out as the instigators, but at this hour of the night it was better to keep some distance from everyone. The boat lazily bobbed in place. There was no need to drop anchor on a night like this.

Vaino made himself comfortable, the weight of the long day bearing down on him. A nap on the boat for old times' sake. His thoughts were interrupted by Henrik. "Annika and Kalle. I wonder how they made out tonight. I have a feeling that we'll have the better story to tell when we catch up with them. I feel bad for them, up in that stuffy old house filled with rich old Americans no doubt. I can imagine Kalle tonight. Just sitting there dead silent with his innocent wide eyes. I put him up to all of this, you know? I told him what a great opportunity it was. I thought the gold story would spice it up for him a bit. Who knows, but my money is on Annika causing some kind of minor fiasco with the other guests, and Kalle will be there to smooth it all out in his vanilla fashion."

"Gold story? It's no story my young blockhead friend. I think you underestimate both of them. First of all, Annika seems capable of a *major* fiasco, and Kalle, well I think he'll find the gold." Vaino said. Henrik looked skeptical. "I'm serious."

Vaino reached back to haul over the long oars. He whistled as he reattached them to the oarlocks. Henrik's unchanged skeptical face reflected in the faint light of the distant esplanade lamps. Vaino stared back at him in defiance. "What? Let's go find out for ourselves." He gave a few expert short pulls to gain momentum south. "I'll show you the mooring where I spied the Germans. Maybe we can load the cargo back on from the same spot. Wouldn't that be something?" Vaino's fatigue evaporated in the promise of a newly constructed adventure. It was a way of living, daisy chaining small goals day after day after day, bouncing in disparate directions, disregarding any bearings on the horizon.

The Vaino-generated breeze was enough to clear the buzz from Henrik's head. As they progressed around the southern tip of the peninsula, Henrik recalled the glint in Margie's eyes when it became obvious that violence was going to be the solution. All night the two of them had struggled to keep up the basic back and forth of modern flirting with his stupid lower grammar school English. Coming across like a goddamn child. But when the argument with the Swedes began tipping over to a fight, her half-second look toward him was pure animal bloodlust. A mutual understanding that communicated volumes, to be broken immediately by the pressing concern of fists and knees and elbows. He lost track of her in the scrum, but her look was frozen in place in his mind.

Henrik spotted a dock ahead which acted as terminus to the Tollefsson manor service road. He nodded to Vaino, who laid off his pulls. It was darker around this corner. No traffic and no streetlights. "What a nice empty dock, Vaino." Henrik said in deadpan. "It's so nice of you to show off this important piece of your fake history. If only I had a camera on me to capture the moment."

"Ha ha."

"So, what is the plan exactly? We just stay here and wait for the wheelbarrows of gold to arrive? Or should we storm the gates?" Henrik laced his curiosity with enough sarcasm to deny his renewed interest.

Vaino looked absently at the darkened hill along the shoreline.

"I got in a couple good swings early, you know. On the dance floor that is. That poor kid probably had never been in a real fight before. But then the glass started shattering. The strangest thing – these bottles started dropping out of the sky. Surely you saw them? Everyone panicked and started trampling over us. They were kicking and stomping on the guy I was supposed to be stomping on. Who on earth would toss bottles indiscriminately like that I have no idea. What would be the point? Anyways…"

Vaino shifted on the bench. After a short while he replied, "I don't know what's got you all worked up. You had a bit of fun with the Aussie girl, didn't ya? It's been an entertaining night, yes? Now we can relax and tell stories about how we're such interesting people. Maybe take a nap and head back at first light. No?"

"But what was the point? Everyone was all dressed up, having a good time with that old band and their old tunes. Someone took the time to schedule the band, reserve the room, clean the tables, and order the wine. Many people for that matter. The whole evening was built up in good faith. All that work to build up just gets knocked down by one miscreant with terrible aim and worse common sense."

"If I remember correctly, you threw the first punch." Vaino replied.

Henrik waved his arm at the void to dissipate the argument. "Oh, that was a private matter. Just a local dust-up. People should just mind their own business."

"Yes, yes. And your business was what? Defending a girl that you barely knew by assaulting a boy you didn't know at all?"

"It's none of your business either."

The water was so still that the boat only rocked to the gesticulations of the men on board – sharp erratic movements that attenuated by half after each cycle. Vaino let the point drop, keeping his eyes on the hill.

Despite knowing each other for only a few hours, they retreated to their own thoughts like a bitter old couple. Henrik sat in the stern facing out into the sea, whose presence was only known by the sudden occulting of stars along the horizon. In the bow, Vaino continued to gaze back at the hill, the outline of which was determined in the same fashion.

A star along the silhouette of the hill began to move. It juddered down to earth with a varied intensity. Vaino sat up straight, rocking the boat again. Convinced that his small hour eyes were not playing tricks on him, he grabbed hold of the oars and began turning in for the dock.

Henrik refused on principle to ask what was going on, but Vaino couldn't help but crow a little. "I see a torch. They're coming this way."

.

"Come on, we can't stay down here. It won't do you any good." Lani spoke to her husband but kept a fixed stare on Kalle. The only progress Zeke had made since first seeing the body was to skootch back a few feet to sit with his back to the wall.

Kalle remained in his funeral director's pose. Lani was right of course. Herding the group down into this cramped macabre setting served no purpose other than to increase everyone's anxiety. He scanned the room slowly and sensed a wave of hatred pointed in his direction. Lani looked darts at him for withholding news of Robert's murder earlier. Annika had been left in the dark too and appeared more than ready to leave, by herself. Dana must have been confused why he would scuttle their plans almost from the beginning. Maybe she didn't hate him, but she was at least very disappointed. He didn't dare glance her way. The Ambassador wasn't speaking at all at this point, a bad sign. He probably thought Kalle killed his friend. The last person across from the body was Emil. There was no specific reason for the three-time Olympic champion to hate Kalle at this point, but there was still time.

As far as he knew, there wasn't an established rule on the proper length of time granted for deferential silence during an active investigation, but Kalle figured on erring to the long side. Aside from Lani's brief words for her husband, the room bore a heavy quiet. Dana finally broke it by leaning into Kalle and murmuring a reminder. "Gregor." Kalle had the impression that she was only being held back by her English. In Czech, she would have dispatched with this case all by herself by now.

Kalle laid out for the group the obvious: Gregor's disappearance and the presumption of guilt. No one offered any alternative explanations. Instead, a nervous chatter bubbled up over the immediate practical question of Gregor's whereabouts.

"It's been so long, he could be halfway to Leningrad by now, right?" Annika asked.

Kalle shook his head. "As far as I've been told, this property is pretty well sealed off. We would know if he had tried to leave. Right, Ambassador?" He looked over at Zeke, who nodded.

"So, we're dealing with a killer trapped in the house? What kind of weapon does he have? A gun? A knife?" Emil asked.

Dana and Kalle looked at each other. Kalle responded, "We don't know."

"It has to be a gun. There's no way that old man could have taken down Robert any other way. I mean, just look at him." Annika gestured to the fallen mass, still an imposing figure prone and lifeless.

"He's not that old." Lani said. After everyone turned her direction she continued, "I mean… he's no older than Zeke. Probably."

Emil considered that for a moment. "He is stronger than you'd think. With the element of surprise... maybe."

"Surprise? Like, 'hey let's look around for some gold' then blammo?" Annika gave an enthusiastic thrust in the air. "Ok maybe, but wouldn't there have been a struggle, with blood sprayed everywhere?"

"But if it was a gunshot, we all would have heard it." Emil countered.

"Not at close range. But you're the army expert, you tell me."

Emil took a step toward the body. "Let's just roll him over and find out."

Kalle broke into the sparring. "No no no, we can't touch the body. This is evidence and the authorities will want it like this. You know, preserved."

"Oh, for Christ's sake!" The Ambassador had come out of his catatonic state. "One minute you're the grand inspector, ordering us around. Now, you want to wait and defer to 'authorities?' What authorities? Finnish police? American marines? Bah! You can't abdicate your responsibility – the responsibility you grabbed all by yourself I might add – just because you have no goddamn idea what to do. My colleague and friend is dead. His killer for all we know is just up the stairs and around the corner, yet here you are staring down at your stupid little hands and mumbling about process and authorities. Jesus, grow a pair of balls and take action!"

Kalle knew every word the Ambassador said was true, and he hated him for it. He turned back to Emil and said, "Fine, let's roll him over and see what we're dealing with."

Robert's corpse was limp and heavy. His massive shoulders made for a wide base to overcome. Emil crouched low to push against his bloodied right shoulder while Kalle bent over from the other side and pulled on the right bicep to try to bring torque. Kalle yanked hard, but instead of bringing the whole torso around, Robert's right arm sped backwards in an unnatural angle, making a crunching sound at the rotator cuff. Robert's dead hand slapped

Kalle's leg as added insult. The angle change in the corpse's arm caused Emil to lose balance. His knees fell into the congealing pool of blood and bits of bone.

Both men paused to regroup. Kalle walked the long way around to join on the right side of the body, Emil still working the shoulder but Kalle taking position at the hip. Kalle mimicked Emil's crouch, not all that different from a sprinter's pose at the starting line. On the count of three they both pushed.

Then the sliding began.

Lubricated by the unseen miasma of blood underneath, Robert's corpse slid nearly two feet on the efforts of the two men. A bright red streak was exposed, pocked with bare concrete ridges and deeper brownish red pools. The slurping sound of the wet body was partially masked by the gasp of the onlookers, but the worst part couldn't be obscured. While the rest of the body slid more or less uniformly, the head rotated counterclockwise. The chin and smashed facial bones had caught on the floor and rotated to face Emil directly. Robert's misshapen face was a mask of clotted blood. The red was set off only by the white and blue eyes, staring through Emil, nowhere.

Kalle and Emil both stumbled this time, with knees and hands taking on more blood. Lani couldn't stand to watch anymore and moved to a far corner of the tight room with Zeke accompanying her.

Kalle looked up to Dana. He said, "You have to help us. Can you find a broomstick or a brick or something? We need something on the other side as a brace to stop the sliding."

Dana walked over to the body and simply planted her right foot just next to the side of Robert's chest. "Ok, go."

Emil and Kalle crouched once more and pushed. This time the body rotated on the foot-fulcrum. Dana skipped out of the way just before the back flopped down on fresh floor. The degree of freedom at the neck allowed the head to remain stationary as the rest of the body turned. Emil looked down in surprise to see Robert's crushed face still pointed at him in a solemn, unblinking regard.

The three of them plus Annika peered over the body. It took a few moments to sort out what they were looking for in the mess displayed before them.

The gash wasn't very long, only an inch or two, and very narrow. Clearly the work of a knife, not a bullet or an improvised weapon like a claw hammer or shears. The location was deadly and expert. Just above the collarbone, angled in toward the base of the throat. It was hard to think of one stab wound felling such a large strong man, but if there was a blow that could do it, it would look a lot like this. Possibly a lucky hit. Possibly something more than just luck.

Emil and Kalle stood, looking at their red-stained hands and ruined clothes. "So, it's one man with just a knife. Let's get up there and find him before he decides to give the cliff jump a try." Kalle said. The gory physical effort brought his pulse up.

Emil was still hounded by the risk of gunplay. "One man with *at least* a knife. How long has he been out there?" Emil gestured broadly. "Ambassador. Ambassador. Is there anything dangerous laying around upstairs he could get his hands on?"

Zeke wasted no time responding. Without a word he broke away from Lani and charged up the spiral stairs two at a time, yanking on the interior railing every other step.

The Ambassador's urgency caught the rest of the group off-guard. Dana looked to see if the two remaining men were going to give chase, but they only fiddled with their clothes. Emil and Kalle lingered, wiping their hands and sleeves in vain on their pants, making things worse. Dana led the way to catch up with the Ambassador. Lani and Annika followed with more caution.

Emil and Kalle were left standing over the corpse. The men took a moment to stare in silence at each other's gore-spattered clothes. Kalle considered the scene and pointed at the Czech's stomach. He deadpanned, "Your... your shirt's untucked."

Emil looked down and rearranged his shirt. He gave a thin smile and opened his arms wide. "How's that?"

"Ah yes, much better." Kalle led the way to the stairs to join the rest of the group – safety in numbers and all that. Emil was last out, stopping briefly at the base of the stairs to sneak a look back at the body.

.

Dana reached the hallway at the top of the stairs and looked each way. There was no sign of the Ambassador, who had gained a sufficient lead. She marched toward the front door, the house silent save for the clambering of the other women well behind her. Dana decided to start at the front and work her way back. She would take a quick peek out to the front pathway in case Zeke had snapped and went into flight.

Dana slowed down in the dark winding path of the jungle room. The dark burbling sounds of waterfalls and pumps covered her own breathing in this humid foyer. Oversized leaves and fronds leaned into the pathway, obscuring the most direct way to the front door. Black nooks and crannies seemed to multiply in what would otherwise be a smallish simple room. Dana stopped abruptly as if to catch the sound of a footstep from anyone following her. Only the burbles reported back.

On approach to the front door, the color from a nearby window briefly flickered between medium gray and black. Dana stopped again and squinted at the window, waiting to see if the flickering returned. A scraping noise came from the other side of the door. The sound of feet scuffling on gravel. Dana hustled to the nearest corner and wedged herself low between walls, pumps, and unrecognizable vegetation. Dana calmed her breath, straining to pick up sounds. Her breathing was accompanied by the low thrumming of an impeller turning somewhere underwater. A never-ending spinner, filtering and shoving water around this man-made circuit day after day.

Hemmed in, Dana waited for the door to open. Being small helped, but the space was tight. It would be impossible to defend herself from this position, even if she had grabbed a knife from the block. She made her profile as small and dark as she could in the shadows. It would be an odd way to die; stabbed far away from home, crouched in a Polynesian terrarium inside a political powerhouse enclave in the northern hinterlands. Her scenario list was growing longer and weirder by the day.

The door opened abruptly, bringing in the hubbub of jostling, shifting, and grunting. With her face hidden, Dana could only make out the feet emerging from the propped open door. And the feet kept coming. She hadn't prepared to count, but there could have been six, eight, nine feet passing by. Nine? That would be unlikely. As the shoe parade passed through her line of sight, disembodied voices rang out. Finnish most likely. Dana couldn't understand a word, but the tone and volume were serious. As rapidly as they had arrived, the voices and their owners were gone, hustling into the house proper.

The thrumming of the impeller returned. Dana reached up to the sill and levered out of her corner. She was intent to follow the loud and numerous Finnish authorities. The retreating sound of their footsteps came from a corridor to the left of the entrance, opposite the reception and dining area. Dana moved quickly to keep up. The Finnish speakers had turned a corner at the end of the hall. Approaching the corner, she heard a yelp then the sound of urgency padding toward her. Step… step… step step stepstepstep.

There was no doorway to duck into and no time to turn around. Dana crouched and planted her feet. A body careened around the corner and was immediately on top of her. Gregor's wide-eyed face flashed in front of her. She braced and lunged her shoulder into the knees of a man who could not stop his momentum. He went tumbling over her and crashed headfirst into the worn floorboards.

A tall young man edged past her to gather up the slumped and bruised Gregor, slamming his head into the wall while standing him back up. The man said something to Gregor in Finnish, which sounded like something along the lines of, *"Nice try, asshole."*

Two more men came around the corner appearing as bewildered as Dana. The older one was another stranger, but the kid she knew. The Marine out front at the guardhouse.

The two strangers exchanged words briefly in Finnish while Dana and the guard looked on impatiently. The older one was the more animated of the two. Eventually he turned to Dana and switched to English. "Much obliged, miss. You're one tough cookie to drop him on the spot like that. I wish that it didn't have to go that way, but this moron soldier couldn't keep a grip on a man three times…"

"Marine. I'm a Marine."

The older man turns to Charlie, dumbfounded for a moment and turns back to Dana. "Ha! You see there? Americans. You aren't American, are you? Because no offense, but you see there? He corrects me on the soldier part, but the moron part? He's fine with that! Well, fair's fair. Mr. Moron Marine, I stand corrected. In any case, as I was saying, we surely appreciate your help trapping this rascal here. You won't believe the trouble he's put us through. I dunno all he's been up to tonight, but it sure as shit can't be good by the looks of him." The man gestured to Gregor's bloodstained shirt. He wiped his nose on his sleeve, shot out his hand, and said, "All the same, my name's Vaino, pleased to make your acquaintance."

Dana caught enough of the Finnish accented fast English talker. She shook hands and smiled back due to her adrenaline and pride in the clean rugby tackle she had never practiced before in her life. Emil will like this story.

Interlude – Belgium

July 16, 1952 – Antwerp

THE BELL JANGLED and Caroline let out a sigh. Customers before noon were never a good sign. She was just going to start opening after lunch and do away with the hassle. Dealing with the stock in the back wasn't difficult but bouncing back and forth between the counter and here just created confusion. She often had to start over on the inventory. Not to mention that blasted door. She was beginning to annoy herself with all the slamming. She was just going to install those swinging half-door things like in those American westerns. That's what she was going to do. Saloon doors they were called, right? Oh, the customer... If this was Hermes again, she would give him a piece of her mind. He can't come in every day buying a bottle at 10:00 am and expect her to just not bat an eye about it. She would take his money, of course. But she would be stern and judgmental about the whole thing. *Spiritueux Desrocher* had developed a bit of a reputation after all. It wouldn't do to have the Hermeses of the world hanging about every morning, despite any affection she had for the old man.

 Caroline passed into the front side (slam!) toward the counter. A young woman with sunglasses stood there scanning the shelves. "Good morning, how can I help you?" Caroline asked, first in Dutch then French.

The woman responded in Dutch, "I'm looking for something different. Something surprising." She then repeated the phrase quickly in French as well.

At her age, Caroline didn't bother to suppress her eye roll. It was too early in the day to play the language game. The customer's Dutch was very good, but not perfect. Caroline swooped in for the kill by responding only in French for the duration. To help her client, naturally. "Did you have a price range in mind so we can narrow that down just a little bit?"

"Price? Oh, that's no concern. Something surprising, as I said."

The response was so curt that Caroline actually believed this woman. "I do have a couple different bottles of champagne that are quite difficult to come by. Rare domain, rare vint…"

"I'm tired of champagne." The woman cut her off and removed her sunglasses. "It's a bit old-fashioned and boring don't you think? I'm begging you. Find me something I would never think of myself."

Caroline got a better look at the customer's face and straightened. "Yes of course, Your Highness."

"Just Jo. Please call me Jo. All my friends do. My ship is leaving for Helsinki shortly. I have a thing to do at the Olympics. Dreadfully boring stuff of course. I'm to visit with my grandparents while I'm there and I want to surprise them with something different. I understand that this is the place to come for that sort of thing. Unless I've been misinformed."

Caroline turned to the shelves behind her, seeking. A squat amber bottle stood out and she grabbed it without hesitation. "Sherman Select. You may have had whisky before, Your Highness, but I guarantee you haven't had bourbon."

The princess read the label. "What's a Kentucky?"

"It's a place in America. Out in the desert near Montana. The Wild West basically. I have a connection who was able to bring me this bottle. It's supposed to be the best. They smoke it with switch grass and bury it underground, the way cowboys used to do it. It's a taste of the American frontier. Now, is that surprising enough for you? Unfortunately, I have only the one bottle…"

Caroline named a price and Jo agreed immediately. Princess Josephine returned her sunglasses to their accustomed spot and walked out to a waiting car.

Caroline counted the francs quickly. She was surprised the princess even carried cash to begin with. Maybe she just asked her driver for a handful of bills. She returned to the backroom (slam!) and retrieved another bottle of Sherman Select out of one of the many cases on the ground. "What's a Kentucky?" She laughed to herself. The bell jangled again.

Bottle in hand, she came back to the counter to find Hermes waiting, slowly adding his unique smell to the room.

"Hermes, my pal. You're late. You'll never guess who beat you in this morning."

Hermes had the look of someone who, indeed, would never guess.

"Princess Jo. Daughter of that Nazi pig fucker himself." Caroline spit and smiled.

"Alleged." Hermes mumbled to the floor.

"Huh?"

"Alleged Nazi pig fucker."

"If you say so." She reached for the ouzo. "Anyway, on to more important things. The usual today?"

Chapter 15 – The Super

KALLE AND EMIL found the Ambassador in his office with Lani and Annika. He was pacing and checking drawers, muttering to himself. The simple act of movement delivered him out of his funk. Zeke didn't register their appearance at the office threshold.

Kalle swept the room with his eyes and turned to Emil. "Where's Dana?"

He figured on the response even as he posed it. No one knew. Without another word, Kalle and Emil turned back into the hallway. The two young men marched through the labyrinth at speed, leaving a faint trail of bloody footprints, each step a shade lighter than the last.

They heard a clattering in the distance and rushed toward that general direction as best they could. They turned a corner and came upon the source of the commotion. It took Kalle a moment to reconcile the scene in front of him. Henrik held Gregor firmly in his grasp while Vaino was recounting to Dana how he and Henrik had dragged the Russian out of his stalled car. The young marine stood mute in the background. Kalle and Emil pulled up short.

Henrik's initial smile at Kalle's arrival faded as he looked down at the pair's reddish-brown hands and clothes. He turned to Gregor, then back again to Kalle. In Finnish he said, "Jesus Christ! What the hell are you all doing around here?" Kalle stared back, noncommittal.

"Please tell me you've been slaughtering a giant animal as some sort of weird American ritual. Or maybe fighting off a bear. I mean, Vaino and I caught this guy sneaking around down by the shore with blood on his shirt. Obviously, we're thinking he's up to no good. But look at you! It's worse. You're covered in it. Look at your friend here. Wait, is that Emil Zatopek?" Henrik exhaled. "I just… do I even want to know?"

"Not really, no."

"Does it have to do with, you know. Our thing?"

Kalle stared at him, not comprehending for a moment. "Oh, that. No, we've moved on to bigger problems."

"Yeah, I would say so. Say, do any of these guys speak Finnish?" Henrik asked quietly. Kalle frowned uncertainly, tipping his head slightly toward Emil. Henrik took on a Laplander thickness. "Is the cod bin up past your hips here, Kalle? Do I need to ring up the barrel heads?"

"No no. Nothing like that. It's better to keep this low-key for now. I'm making progress and bringing in this guy here will break it wide open. Thanks for that." Kalle paused a moment, looking at the floor.

Henrik took the cue. "Well, I for one would be happy to avoid adding any more paperwork to my life. If it's ok with you, as far as anyone else is concerned Vaino and I just went for a late-night stroll and helped a drunk stranger find his way back to a party. What do you say, Vaino? Wanna go find another dance floor to obliterate?" Switching to his hesitant English he said, "I wish you a good night all. Kalle is good for helping you. More good than me and friend." With that he shoved Gregor over to Kalle and Emil, who each grabbed an arm. Gregor had yet to say a word and didn't protest any of the rough handling since his tumble onto the floor.

Vaino gave a quick wink to Dana and turned with Henrik toward the exit. The volume of his chatter diminished on the way out. "Any chance we can take a quick peek around for the you-know-what? No? Fine, be that way. Truth be told I'm happy to get out of this stuffy old Swedish monstrosity. I never liked it from the outside, and it's even worse walking through the innards. Good riddance. That girl was something else though, eh? Solid as iron, she was. Cute as a button too. An iron button. Damn."

Kalle turned back to the marine and said, "Come on Charlie, we're going to need your muscle with this guy. You didn't bring your rifle from the gatehouse? No matter. Let's get this Russian to the Ambassador. We can secure him in the office."

Gregor offered no resistance as Kalle and Emil walked their catch down the hall. No one asked Kalle for a translation of his conversation with Henrik, and he didn't offer one. He kept his focus on the tension of the Russian's forearm, waiting for an early warning of another flight attempt. None came. They marched together in silence.

.

Dana was at the back of the group when crossing into the office. Between the various taller bodies in front of her, she could only make out Lani's face and her look of alarm. They were, after all, dragging her friend's killer into a tight room with her without warning. The adrenaline of the moment had drained away. Dana posted her suddenly tired self at the doorway to observe.

There was a minute of hesitation as Kalle and Emil were physically in charge of the "prisoner," but the Ambassador loomed large and took command of the room with his eyes.

"Have a seat, Gregor." The Ambassador said.

Gregor skulked over to one of the armchairs in the center of the room. He still had not spoken a word since being sent airborne by Dana. On display, he avoided eye contact with the room. He slumped in the chair. A defeated man tired of the chase. Silence. Seconds rolled into minutes. No one dared speak up, acknowledging that at least for the moment this was between Zeke and Gregor. The room was tense, but Dana figured that if Zeke was going to attack the man, he would have already done so.

Finally, Zeke spoke up. "Of course I'm curious as to why you did it, but we can get to that later. First off, I think it's better if we clear the air. If you plan on denying everything or playing the strong silent type, that's fine. My friend Kal here will be happy to escort you to the Finnish police station house. Or Charlie can get on the horn with the Marine constable. But instead, I propose we talk about it, own up to what happened. Like men. Like the doddering old men that we are. What do you say to that?" He paused, probably more for effect than anything else as he didn't wait long enough to grant space for a response. He continued, "Here, I'll go first. Robbie was a colleague and a friend. A good friend, as much as anyone can be in a short period of time. But it almost goes without saying that he could rub people the wrong way, what with his intelligence and that odd lecturing manner of speaking. I'm sure more than a few people around the office would have wanted to take a swing at him at one time or another were it not for his size. But the thing is, the part I don't get is this: you just met the man. What could he have done or said to you? Come on, out with it. And don't give me any of that self-defense bullshit either. He knew better than to start a fight with a Russian of all people right here at the Embassy. So why? Was there any rationale, or are you going to pretend you're just a garden-variety Russian madman? Out with it."

Gregor looked up at Zeke as he spoke but didn't immediately respond. Dana glanced around the room, Lani and Annika looked uncomfortable and ready to leave the room altogether. Kalle and Emil were focused, still flanking the Russian. Charlie the Marine seemed to be in over his head, fidgeting with his hands and trying to find a natural way to stand in the corner.

With no response forthcoming, the Ambassador looked up to Kalle and Charlie in turn and said, "Just get him out of here, boys. I don't care about the jurisdiction. You two sort out who gets him and let me know where I should go to give my deposition in the morning. I'll leave the doors unlocked and the lights on for the *real* inspectors."

Kalle reached down to grab Gregor's arm but was shrugged off.

"It doesn't matter," said Gregor.

Zeke and Lani exchanged glances. Zeke spoke up. "What doesn't matter?"

"Finnish. American. Whoever you try to take me to, it doesn't matter. I'm already a dead man."

"Well, that's very dramatic. I have a happy surprise for you then. You'll find the justice system here is not quite as harsh as Uncle Joe's. You'll get a lawyer and everything. A real lawyer, not some fake stooge. I bet you'll end up with a large number of years that you can plead down due to your advanced age and the inevitable onset of senility. It's all very civilized."

"Oh, shut up already. All you talk about is yourselves. You Americans and your perfect systems. Your systems won't even get the chance. I'm already a dead man thanks to the perfect Soviet system."

"I don't understand."

"Imagine my surprise. Of course you don't." With that, the Russian folded his arms and signaled no intention to move an inch.

Sensing an opening, Kalle jumped on it. He turned to Zeke and said, "Dead man or not, I certainly don't hear him denying the murder. Do you, Mr. Ambassador?"

"No, I don't."

"I have enough to go on. I don't really have an opinion on why he did it or why he thinks he's a dead man. We'll take our chances with a couple burly Helsinki beat cops. Let's go."

Gregor turned up to face Kalle from his chair. "Isn't that so very Finnish of you to say? 'I don't have an opinion.' You don't have an opinion on anything, do you? Always sitting on the fence, with your arse getting sore. But you don't dare complain about it, do you? No no no. That would attract attention. Don't want that. Christ, at least with the Americans you know what you get. Assholes. But you Finns are nothing but quiet cowards. No one trusts you or likes you. You just serve as… as buffer. Just a little padding along the borders. A no man's land in the fight of ideas. What a waste. Pick a side. Make a decision! Oh but no. Instead, just run me out to the nearest police precinct for everyone to see. Just follow protocol and don't ruffle any feathers. Pass off the responsibility elsewhere. My compatriots will get to me and end me. Fine, let's go then." Gregor stood up.

"Hold on." Zeke shot back. "Hold on, how could your compatriots end you? And why? What's the point of that? What aren't you telling us?"

Gregor surveyed the room before responding. "Maybe the two of us should talk in private?"

Everyone in the room instinctively shook their heads. Zeke barked in the quick laugh of his. "Is that what you said to Robbie before you stabbed him in the neck? No, I don't think you get to talk to me in private, ever. Anything you have to say can be said to all of us."

Gregor shrugged and reached into his trouser pocket. Kalle and Emil tensed up and stepped closer until Gregor slowly pulled out a small, folded scrap of paper. He held it between index and middle finger and extended it toward Kalle with the sad smile of the smartest kid in the class waiting for everyone else to catch up. Kalle took the paper, unfolded it, and looked at the paltry contents: a few simple diagrams of circles, curves, and arrows, three or four numbers and a couple symbols he couldn't recognize. Maybe Greek? "What is this?" Kalle asked.

Gregor ignored the question. "Mr. Ambassador, would you be able to tell Robert's handwriting, even from only a few letters and numbers?" Gregor asked.

Zeke reached for the paper. While looking at it, he repeated Kalle's question. "What is this?"

"The Super."

Dana had been keeping up with the English, but with this response she was lost. She polled the room with her eyes and noted that she wasn't alone. Every face had remained dull, with the clear exception of The Ambassador, whose eyes bulged. He appeared as if he was going to be sick. She didn't dare pipe up to ask him to repeat, but she didn't need to.

"What's the Super?" Kalle asked.

Zeke responded quietly. "A super bomb."

"You mean an atomic bomb?"

"No. Bigger."

Kalle remained confused. "What can be bigger than an atomic bomb?"

Gregor gestured with an 'if I may' hand to the Ambassador. "The atomic bomb you speak of – that we all speak of – is a fission device, yes? From what I understand, I don't know anything really mind you… From what I understand, you gather up a bunch of uranium or … what is it you call it in English?"

"Plutonium." Zeke offered.

"Plutonium, yes. You have to make that in some reactor, right? Anyways, you gather this up and just slam it together. And hey presto, a Japanese city disappears."

"It's amazing how talkative he becomes when death and destruction is the topic for discussion." Zeke said to no one in particular.

"Do you want to hear this or not? But, even from the early days of exploring a path for a fission bomb, Russian scientists had also explored a path to create a fusion bomb as well. You Americans too. Our comrade Fuchs told us that your boy Oppenheimer had a fusion path going the whole time out in that desert hole of his. But time was short of course. Everyone wanted to cram these bombs down Hitler's throat as fast as possible. Fission or fusion, it didn't matter. So, fission got the money and the brainpower back then. Nice job on that, by the way. But now there's time to return to this other path, fusion.

"Many say that it's a dead end, this fusion. Some in my department swear that the whole thing is an elaborate ruse set up by you Americans to waste our time, our resources."

"And what do you think?" Zeke had settled into the armchair opposite, the scene taking on a more congenial hue.

Dana couldn't help but marvel at the way the Ambassador could draw people into a conversation under any circumstance. The technical English rapid speech of Gregor washed over her again in a way not dissimilar to Robert earlier at dinner. She focused on the eyes of Gregor and Zeke. There was a connection between them, and it was the willpower of Zeke who created that connection out of thin air.

"What do I think? Who cares what I think? I have no idea. No one asks the messenger boy about physics. Although since you ask. I have to say that if Teller, Bethe, *and* von Neumann have really been working on an impossible fusion project for years just to get us off on a wild goose chase, it would be one very expensive ruse. And now, if that slip of paper you're holding is to be believed, your boys have cracked the code. Again. Robert said the first test will be this year, but that it's a formality. It's going to work."

Zeke looked down at the paper.

"I know what you're thinking," Gregor continued. "It's barely anything. A couple numbers, a couple arrows. It could still be a ruse. But Robert mentioned Kurchatov by name."

"Who?" Kalle interrupted.

"Igor Kurchatov. You could call him our Oppenheimer. Everything in atomic development goes through him. Anyway, Robert said 'show this to Kurchatov. He'll understand immediately.' Then he went on about some technical, how do you call it? Mumba jumba?"

"Mumbo jumbo." Zeke answered. "What kind of technical mumbo jumbo, exactly?"

"Really? You want me to go into detail?"

"Yes please." Zeke's eyes had a shine to them.

"I don't remember all of it of course. But he said something about how the key was the separation of the primary ignition source from the deuterium fuel, and something about channeling. He said if the primary was inside the secondary it would be blown to bits before criticality, that the separation was crucial in order to focus the radiation. How one goes about focusing radiation is beyond me. It seems contrary to the very definition of radiation. I don't know; we were two non-physicists speaking to each other about physics. Like two monkeys trying to play Shakespeare. All down in your filthy basement." He gave a small shrug of resignation.

Kalle had been shifting his weight for a while and broke in with another question. "Ok, let's take Robert at his word. And you too for that matter. Let's say this scrap of doodles holds the key to The Super."

"Yes."

"So now the Americans and soon the Russians can have atomic bombs with either fission or fusion?"

"Yes."

"So… who cares?" Kalle launched this question to the room.

Gregor narrowed his eyes and hesitated to respond.

"Seriously. The bomb is the bomb. Why get all twisted up in knots over the technology? The end result is the same."

The Ambassador cleared his throat and leaned forward in his chair, towards both Gregor and Kalle. "I'm afraid there are two answers to that question. Neither is good news. The first is fuel availability. There is only so much uranium in the world, and the isotope of uranium necessary is less than one percent of the naturally occurring uranium to begin with. Add to that the issue that plutonium doesn't even exist naturally, and you have yourself a classic supply chain problem. Rifles and tanks are one thing, but a plutonium production plant is probably a bit of a fickle beast. But with fusion, the fuel is hydrogen. It's in the water all around this house right now. Not exactly a supply problem. And then there's the second answer." Here the Ambassador hesitated. No one else moved an inch, waiting. "The second answer is scale. I believe I read in the papers, maybe some of you have too, that these fission bombs can only get so powerful. After a certain size, they lose efficiency and eventually fizzle out under their own weight. But with fusion, there is no size limit. Just add more hydrogen, more or less."

"But surely there is some limit." Kalle again.

The Ambassador shook his head.

"How do you know?"

"Look at the sun."

Annika had been half-sitting on the desk in the corner, but at this statement she rose and straightened her skirt. "Hold on, hold on. Who on earth would want to build such a thing? What is the point?"

Gregor turned to her in all seriousness and replied, "My dear, that is simultaneously the most reasonable and the most naïve question possible. The answer is that it will be built because it *can* be built. No one wants to build it, but even the remote chance that the other guy does it requires you to do so."

"You sound a lot like Robert, with his green berries. I thought that we had elevated ourselves beyond that simple cynical result." Annika said.

Kalle nodded at Annika's question and followed up. "Quite right. Speaking of Robert… You are saying that he brought you this invaluable information about the U.S. fusion work, yes? And you are Soviet, yes? Then why did you kill him? I'm not a spy, but it would seem to me, if someone brought me valuable information, I would be grateful and ask him to bring me more. Isn't that cultivating a source? According to you, you had a traitor fall into your lap, begging to be brought into the fold. Yet, you didn't." Kalle trailed off momentarily then continued, "Let me put this plainly. Are you just the world's shittiest spy? Or are you a double agent for the Americans? I don't get it."

Gregor gave the smirk of a man with nothing to lose. "You can draw your own conclusions on whether I am, as you say, 'the shittiest' or not. Frankly it is typically in my best interest if you underestimate me and my abilities. However, it is necessary for you to understand that I am a proud Russian. My loyalty is, and always has been with the motherland. I defy any implication otherwise. Double agent! You have been reading too many dime store books, Finn. It is no surprise that only the basest "literature" is ever bothered to be translated to your gibberish tongue. Even worse, you might be reading your own homegrown talents in an act of desperation. Personally, I gave up on the Kalevala about halfway through and moved on with my life. I would suggest the same for all of you. I will send you a copy of Chekhov's plays if I ever make it out of here alive." Gregor paused to gain some composure and surveyed the room. "In any case, my intuition tells me that Robert was no traitor either. I think he was a simple man with a big brain and no common sense. At root he only wanted peace. While I agree with the sentiment, I disagree with his conclusions. Mother Russia is better off if this scrap of paper remains out of her hands. Even more, it is better that the very existence of this paper is not known to Mother Russia. An informed Kurchatov is a dangerous thing."

"Why?"

Gregor shifted in his seat. "An informed Kurchatov is an enabled Stalin. If we are behind in the technology race, he will pour his resources into catching up. It gives him something to do, you see? But if we are on an even footing with technology, he would get all sorts of ideas on how to create an advantage. And you don't need much creativity to realize that all of those ideas do nothing more than push us all toward the cliff of nuclear annihilation. To be perfectly frank, it is better for everyone that America has a head start when it comes to weapons with this kind of power – unlimited destructive power. Just imagine. I don't trust my guy with it. Do you?"

"But it will only be a matter of time, right?" The Ambassador countered. "You know as well as I do that the atomic secret was never really a secret. If this paper is the real deal, your scientists will get there soon enough on their own."

"Of course you're right. Scientific truths don't remain hidden forever, but we can buy ourselves a couple years… there is talk that Stalin is slower walking around the office these days. Shaking a bit. Say a five or ten-year head start can open up a different type of relationship between our countries." Gregor raised his eyebrows by a fraction and allowed a smirk. "I happen to believe that you Americans won't press your advantage of this weapon by wiping us out with a prophylactic fleet of bombers. Virtually everyone I work with would disagree with me on this. Which is what brings me here tonight. Your colleague Robert has been… what's the word… *insistent* with us for the past few weeks about his so-called very important information. We see guys like this all the time. They always claim it's very important, you see. An urgent meeting, time is of the essence, that sort of thing. But we knew he was from Berkeley, so there was a good chance he was bringing something atomic. My bosses can't help themselves on that subject."

"So why didn't you just tell him to pound sand and walk away? Or even better, take the paper, thank him, and say you'll be in touch. Then burn the paper and never follow up. Why kill the poor kid?"

"The way he spoke. You know what I mean, Mr. Ambassador. He was very passionate and committed to what he believed. He would have made his own follow-up. If I withheld anything from my bosses, Robert would have eventually ensured that I'd be discovered. Now he can't. I intended to walk right out your gate tonight and report back that his information was useless, or that he had been uncovered by your side before we met and has disappeared. I don't know, anything would have worked as long as he couldn't come back to refute it. And now, if I'm brought up on charges for his murder, it will be as if Robert is coming back to refute it anyway."

The Ambassador sat hunched over, stroking his clean-shaven chin in thought. Kalle glanced over at Annika, who appeared equal parts scared and disgusted. After a minute, Zeke stood up and turned to Marine Charlie. "Watch this guy for a couple minutes for me, will you? Emil, you too please just make sure he stays put. Kal, you come with me." And with that, the Ambassador and Kalle walked out of the office and down the hallway a dozen steps or so to be out of earshot.

"So, what do you make of this?" The Ambassador asked.

Kalle frowned a bit while considering the question, attempting an academic pose. He pointed to Zeke's hand, still holding the scrap of paper. "The first principle for me is the authenticity of that note. Is it gibberish? Is it real? There's no way to tell. Even if it is legitimate physics, it still might not amount to anything. Are you sure that the handwriting is his?"

Zeke nodded with regret. "Sharp angles, tiny, nearly aggressive. Unfortunately, there is no doubt. It's him. I hate to say it, but it seems pretty clear now that he was a Soviet source from the day he came here. Or at least he was attempting to be one. I like to fancy myself a good judge of character, but…" Zeke waived the paper as counterargument.

"Have your Marines take him into custody. Let your CIA figure it all out. I don't want a territory fight on this and I'm pretty sure I speak for all my country when I say that the less we are involved, the better."

"Understood. But between you and me, kid, they are going to bury me over this. A Soviet source right under my nose? My right-hand man with access to… oh god. Even worse, he was only uncovered because of a Soviet agent I let in for dinner? That will all come out too. I will be run out of this business altogether. I'll be lucky to avoid prison for negligence." Zeke looked absently at paint flaking on the wainscoting, nearly talking to himself instead of Kalle. "I have half a mind to just turn the other way and let him walk right out the front door."

"If he's telling the truth, it's not a bad idea."

"Um hmm."

"But there's no way to know if he's telling the truth."

"Um hmm."

"There's no history with him, no credibility. It would be better for everyone if we could be certain he was telling the truth, but..." Kalle saw that Zeke was losing the thread, his thoughts elsewhere. Kalle tried to joke him back into the conversation. "Oh, blast it all. Just flip a coin and be done with it."

The Ambassador smiled thinly and made to reply, but he was interrupted.

A sharp grunt caromed around the hall, coming from the office. There was a clattering of furniture and the piercing shout of Annika in Finnish, "Oh shit oh shit! Help! Help! Kalle!"

Kalle and Zeke raced back to the room to see a scrum on the ground. Gregor, Emil, Charlie, and Dana were wrestling in a desperate bundle. Zeke moved in to separate everyone. After a moment, the four sat back on the floor, heaving. Before Zeke could get any words out demanding an explanation, Charlie gave it to him.

The Marine held up his fist to Zeke and slowly opened it to produce a small handful of white pills. "He dug these out of his pocket. He tried to hide it, but I saw him bringing them up to his mouth. So, I tackled him." Charlie looked over to Emil and Dana. "And I got some help."

The Ambassador passed his gaze down to Gregor, still on the floor. "What is this?"

The Russian stood up and straightened his mangled shirt. He replied matter of fact, "Cyanide."

The Ambassador shoveled the pills into his breast pocket and brushed off his palm on his pants. "Yeah right, good one."

"Believe what you want. These are standard issue to every comrade in this profession. Surely you know this."

"Alright, enough of this horsing around. Charlie? Call up your CO and ask to bring some MPs over ASAP."

"Yes sir." The Marine brushed off his hands in the same manner as the Ambassador and marched briskly out of the office.

The Ambassador turned his attention back to the Russian, now awkwardly standing next to a toppled end table. "Do me a favor,

Gregor. Can you put that table back up, have yourself a seat again, and try not to kill yourself for the next hour or so?"

Gregor was defiant, nostrils blazing. "No. Give me those pills back. That or let me go. I won't leave here in the spotlight of your pathetic Military Police."

"Sorry, but that's exactly what is going to happen."

"You still don't understand, do you? What time is it now, 3:00? 4:00? I've missed my rendezvous and the backup one already. My chance for an alibi that Robert didn't show to dinner or whatever has passed. They know something is wrong and are waiting to blame it on me. Your MPs will be overpowered. My own staff will kill me. But they will be sure to torture me beforehand. They will pull out my fingernails first, then my toenails. They will use electric shock, they will flay my skin, burn my skin, dip my body parts in acid. I cannot un-see Robert's scribbles, and eventually I will break just like everyone else. I will recreate those scribbles with my remaining good fingers, and I will tell them everything I heard. And only then will they finally have mercy and kill me. I'll end up in an unmarked grave in the middle of nowhere. And you... you will be responsible for the contents of Robert's paper landing on Kurchatov's desk."

The Ambassador studied the man in front of him. "Our MPs aren't pushovers. You are being paranoid."

"Your MPs? Right. Let me guess. A group of three or four boys – half asleep. They'll arrive from the northeast along the main road driving two Willys – ten years old and beaten up from the war. Each man with a single bolt-action rifle, also war surplus issue, and virtually no ammunition. It's summer, so no hardtops on the jeeps. First overseas assignment for all of them, no practical experience, little training, bright white visible bands on their uniforms, and white felt caps. Am I close?"

The Ambassador didn't respond. Lani stepped into the vacuum, "Wouldn't you have the same problem if we just let you go?"

"Maybe, but one trained man alone in the woods stands a much better chance. This is what I ask of you. Let me go. Or if you cannot trust me, give me the pills and let me die here on my own terms. In either case, the fusion secret stays in this room. With the MP parade, you are rolling the dice on a global conflagration. Fire raining down and down without end, everywhere. I am not being paranoid. Ambassador, I believe that you saw enough of war to understand that."

The Ambassador mumbled to himself, "Roll the dice. Flip a coin…" He walked over to Lani over by the desk and whispered in her ear. The look of alarm remained on her face, but she reluctantly nodded her head and whispered back to Zeke. Kalle stood frozen, straining to pick up a word but was ultimately unsuccessful. After a brief exchange, Lani left the room.

"Gregor, I don't wish you a gruesome death, or even a peaceful one for that matter. On the other hand, as executive of this station and representative of my government I obviously cannot allow a Soviet spy to walk out my front door after killing a citizen. You have put me in a corner."

"You and your corner. You Americans are always spoiled for choice and refuse to admit it. Mr. Ambassador, the Marines are coming shortly, presuming they can find four of them sober enough. And despite all your talk, you haven't argued against my logic that this information must stay out of Soviet hands. Time is running out. I am a ticking time bomb for you. You must kill me or let me go."

Zeke turned to Emil and Dana and said, "I'm afraid I must ask my Olympic champions one more small favor. Could you please hold our Russian guest here in this room for a few moments? Trained or not, I hope that this old man won't pose a problem for the two of you. Kal, you're with me again. Let's grab a drink."

The pop had returned to the Ambassador's step as they cruised the windowless hallways back toward the front of the house. Lani was waiting for them in the drawing room, hands cupped together as if in offering. She was holding a dozen or so deep red berries. Zeke nodded quickly and moved past her to the bar. He reached up for a half-full bottle on the shelf. Sherman Select – straight bourbon whiskey. As he made himself busy collecting three small glasses, he said to Kalle, "Rob's bourbon. You had some earlier tonight. He said it's the best he's ever tried, and I believe him. I have no clue how he was able to secure this bottle. It seems the man had more than a few secrets."

The Ambassador read the quizzical look on Kalle's face. He motioned to the glasses and continued, "Oh, this isn't for you. I've decided to take your suggestion."

"I'm afraid I have no idea what you're talking about."

"We're going to flip a coin, so to speak." On a small serving tray Zeke poured out three neat tumblers of bourbon. Healthy two-finger-plus pours. He gestured to Lani, who poured the handful of berries into a small unused ashtray. As he spoke, Zeke used the muddling pestle to squeeze a clear liquid from the berries. "These are pupula berries. I'm pronouncing that right, Lani? Typically Polynesian, the plant seems to thrive here indoors as long as it is in the humidity and gets enough sun. We've seemed to luck out with it. A vibrant plant. Smells great. But its berries happen to be terribly poisonous." Zeke raised a pair of mischievous eyebrows.

Kalle forced a mild chuckle to show he wasn't going to bite on whatever this weird joke was.

"I'm quite serious I'm afraid. What you see here in this ashtray is probably enough to kill five, ten men within 24 hours. Seriously, don't even touch it."

Lani added in her incongruous calm voice, "There are neurotoxins in these berries that are found nowhere else on earth except the Amazon. There are no effects right away, but people will begin to feel slow and numb a few hours later. A few hours after that, the fever comes, and breathing becomes constricted. Fortunately, the victim will usually pass out before the end when they choke on their saliva or simply stop breathing."

Kalle didn't chuckle now. "I don't understand. Are you going to kill Gregor with this?"

"Maybe." Zeke replied. "As you said, a coin toss. He's right, I can't turn him over to the MPs. That much I know for sure. That's priority number one. There is too much for all of us to lose if he's being honest. But I can't let him go without knowing he's telling the truth. You said that yourself. That's priority number two. And finally, priority number three. If possible, I'd rather not let him die. Oh, and don't forget that we don't even know what these things are." He pointed to his breast pocket. "Is this really cyanide or just aspirin he's using to bluff us? How could we possibly know? I'm sure as shit not going to taste test it. Are you? So, Kal, I propose a game of chance. Three glasses of bourbon, one with 'cyanide', one with popolo, and one straight bourbon. We explain the contents to Gregor. He picks a tumbler, drinks it, and leaves. If he refuses, the jig is up, and the MPs can come in take the lying murdering Russian away. Agreed?"

Kalle's head was spinning. "Yesssss… agreed."

"Now, Lani, could you please step outside for a moment."

Lani walked out into the hallway. Zeke said, "We'll do this double-blind. You are my witness that this is on the level." He slowly poured the popolo juice into one glass, crushed the pills to a fine white power and mixed them into a second glass, and left the third untouched. "You agree that I've done as discussed?"

"Yes."

"Good. Lani! Come switch with me. When I'm out of the room, rearrange these glasses so that I don't know which is which." The Ambassador walked out, and the glasses were carefully shuffled. Zeke came back. "Satisfied?" Kalle nodded. "Great, let's go. We're racing against my felt-hatted MPs after all."

Zeke carefully carried the tray down the hall, slowly rotating it so that Kalle could no longer be sure which was which.

The office atmosphere was quiet and tense when they arrived. Gregor had returned to his armchair, exhausting himself in his earlier appeal to the Ambassador and resigned to his fate. Zeke spoke quickly and precisely. "Ok Gregor, we're gonna give you a chance here. This is how it's going to work." He explained the contents of the glasses and the conditions of his release, which he summarized as, "Drink and walk. That's it."

The recently righted end table held the tray of bourbon in front of the Russian. Kalle imagined for a moment that the old Russian might flip over the tray and use the commotion to make a break for it. He'd be taking his chances with Dana guarding the door, though. He was already 0-1 on that score. Kalle tried to make out differences in the glasses, flecks of white substance or a small difference in refraction. Nothing. He held his breath along with the rest of the room.

"Drink and walk?" asked Gregor.

"Drink and walk."

Gregor looked around the room at each of his captors. He reached down and grabbed a tumbler. "I accept. To your health." With that, he raised it a fraction toward Zeke then drank it down in one gulp.

After a quick tight grimace he said, "Woody. A bit sweet. It's… it's not bad." The room stood quiet. All eyes observing, waiting for a sign of something going horribly wrong with Gregor. He continued, "I don't mean to be rude, but I suppose I should be going, yes?"

"A deal's a deal. I'll walk you to the gate."

.

The sky was already a light gray even at this early hour, the Finnish summer sun threatening an early return. The two older men walked up the path to the gate. From a distance they could be mistaken for two grumpy old friends telling tall tales and complaining of aches, pains, and wives. Out of earshot, what they discussed was anyone's guess. More likely than not, Zeke was filling the silence with any random words that popped into his head. *I hope you don't asphyxiate? Good luck avoiding the torture? What else can one say in this circumstance?*

Kalle stood watching from the threshold with the humid jungle room at his back. A breeze had picked up overhead which was sliced, subdivided, and dampened by the bristling needles of the surrounding firs. There was just enough remaining momentum to usher away most of the weak fog that had tried to settle in overnight. The sun would finish the job shortly. The earliest birds had begun to stir, twittering in the background blissfully unaware of the human drama around them or the stakes involved.

"Well, that's that." Zeke returned buoyed by sending off the Russian.

"So, it's all true then?" Kalle asked.

"What is?"

"The Super. The concept of The Super is real?"

"Yes."

"And you're going to build one? Build thousands?"

The Ambassador pulled the scrap of paper from his pocket and brandished it. "Sure seems that way, kid. Just our bad luck that it was possible after all."

"What happens now?"

"Well, this," he nodded to the paper, "goes up in flames on my first cigarette break this morning. Everything else goes back to normal. More or less."

"What about Stalin? Is it true he's ill?"

"Probably, but who's to say the next guy won't be worse? Best case, we have a few years of a head start with the Super, no more."

"And what will America do with those few years?"

"Press our advantage to the absolute maximum, in a reckless fashion most likely. It's not my department. Listen, kid. You did well tonight. You proved yourself. Gregor, and you, and Dana gifted the world a brief peace. Brief. That's more than any individual could ever hope to accomplish, but it isn't forever. Us old guys are marching off into the fog like poor Gregor there. We need you and Dana, the younger generation. The smarter generation living on the borders, the margins between us so-called superpowers. It'll be up to you to keep the peace. Over and over again." Zeke looked over Kalle's shoulder and nodded at Lani inside. "Alright, we have one last bit of work to sort out before the night's done."

Interlude – Finland

July 18, 1952 – Helsinki

JO'S HEELS MADE a reassuring clack on the mosaic tiles as she strode her way into the Hotel Kämp lobby. Her eyes flashed quickly around the open space: heavy drapes, gold leaf, mahogany furniture with brass fittings. It would do. The hotel exuded the same desperation she had experienced ever since disembarking this morning. There was an eagerness to please above and beyond the usual up here in the hinterlands. Nervous stares lasted a fraction of a second too long, searching for a hint of disappointment from her. 'You will simply love Hotel Kämp, Your Highness. Oh yes, the Kämp is the only suitable place. Excellent choice for you and the delegation! It is without doubt the finest place north of Copenhagen. The décor is authentic. Each ancient door is a work of art in itself. Not to mention the cuisine. You must try their caviar…' Choice. Delegation. Décor. Ugh. It was time to find a drink. Jo turned to her butler. "Regis, please attend to the bags. I'll be in the bar, don't wait up for me."

The Kämp pub was cozy yet refined. The styling was rustic, approximating a hunting lodge but without the fetid carcass smell or the humid peat she recalled from that one miserable trip to Balmoral. Jo warmed to the place immediately. Gauzy shades had been drawn to attenuate the early evening sun. Jo took a moment at the threshold to let her eyes adjust. She smiled as she took in the familiar sounds of clonking glasses, whispers, and the odd cackle. Her eyes were drawn to a table near one of the filtered windows. A handsome young man sat alone, slowly turning his tumbler. Too tall to be French, too handsome to be Russian, too confident to be Scandinavian, but not arrogant enough to be British. Must be American.

"You don't mind, do you?" Jo asked in English as she was already pulling out the chair opposite.

The man rushed to stand and replied, "I beg your pardon, I am actually waiting for a friend…"

Jo had already seated herself. "Perfect, I can actually keep you company until she arrives."

The man smiled. "Until he arrives. It's more of a business meeting you could say, but I'm afraid he is already dreadfully late. It may be just the two of us from here on out." He reached out a hand. "Robert Silverton, pleasure to meet you."

"Jo… just Jo." They shook.

"Well Just Jo, you thirsty?"

The drinks flowed and the words tumbled out. Jo would have been content to stay here for the rest of the trip if such a thing were possible. The dim agreeable room was a chapel of anonymity, with this rugged man the oblivious centerpiece. There was no princess here, Just Jo and her keen American.

"You work at the embassy? So, stamping passports all day or something?" Jo teased.

"Something like that, yeah. More paperwork than I'd care to admit. But the bottom line is we help Americans who find themselves way out here. One way or another. That and we try to improve relationships."

"Improve relationships. With whom?"

"Everyone, I suppose."

"Well, if you are going around one person at a time, it's working." Jo took a long sip of her champagne to give herself time to watch him blush. "Everyone, huh? I won't spoil the evening with politics, but I would venture to wager that there is a certain group of people with whom you are decidedly not improving your relationship. After all, I heard a rumor there's a war going on somewhere or other."

"Well, war is not a great look for anyone right about now. Just don't quote me on that."

"What is it about Americans that made you pick a fight in Korea? You didn't get enough of the action the last time around?"

"We have a short memory, and our average citizen didn't suffer like you did. Not that you are an average citizen, of course. You know what I mean. Anyway, I can't imagine how the devastation in Belgium affected your … I don't know. Everything. You must have seen it, smelled it, lived it. Us young Americans just watched it in the movie theater of all places. Newsreels before every matinee. It was literally a movie to me and my school friends. We don't yet have the sensibility of real life."

"It must be nice."

"What is?"

"Having those two giant oceans to protect you from all these European homicidal maniacs. You're wrapped up in a big security blanket."

"In the past, that's absolutely true. But…" Robert hesitated and looked down at the napkin he had been twisting with his fingers.

"But?" Jo prodded.

"Nothing. It's all true. As you said, there's no need to have politics ruin such a lovely evening."

As night fell, the room filled up with enthusiastic patrons. Jo and Robert edged closer to each other to be heard over the din without resorting to half-shouting. Why raise the intensity when one can simply reduce the distance?

"So, no Mrs. Silverton?"

Robert shook his head. "I'm much too young for all that. I'm having too much fun now." He parried.

"Well one day you'll wake up and you'll be forty. Then fifty. And before you know it, you'll be dead."

"I'll take my chances. How about you? No Mr. Jo? I'm certain you've had your opportunities."

"Suitors? Oh yes, I've had my share. I have a rather serious one right now in fact."

Robert made a show of looking nervously over his shoulder and Jo obliged with an easy laugh.

"Take it easy, he's in Luxembourg. As far as I know that is. It's hard to keep track of him, actually. A bit like a stray cat that pops in for food then is gone for days."

"Well, he sounds delightful. I am exceedingly happy for you both. Do you think it's going to stick?"

Jo played with her empty glass. "Probably. He's a good man. He's a good match for us."

"Us?"

"For my family. He's close with my father and his… business. It helps everyone."

"An arranged marriage… how modern and progressive of you." Robert chided.

"You don't understand the family business."

"Ah, so the family business comes first?"

"The family comes first. Anyways, what does it matter? In a few years we'll have kids, and they will be the center of my life. It would be the same with anyone else as the father so why not him? I have aunts who wanted to wait for the perfect man. Naturally they are still waiting, spinsters just sitting by the fire rubbing cream into their wrinkled hands and pulling their shawls tighter. I won't be like that. And you shouldn't either for that matter. A tall, charming, handsome man like you. Strike while the iron is hot, if you want my advice. Find a nice little porcelain doll in your office and gently scoop her up."

"Porcelain doll… no thanks. When I do find someone, she won't be fragile. She'll be able to handle herself. A couple should push each other; challenge each other to do better. You know what they say in my country? 'Wives obey thy husbands…' what hogwash! A woman who simply wants to follow my lead is doomed for disappointment. One day I'll find someone who thinks like me, who wants to be equal and is up to the challenge. But all things will happen at the right time. With all due respect, I won't wake up forty years old tomorrow. I have all the time in the world."

Jo cocked her head at this weird, intriguing man. She had refilled her glass. "Here's to the man with all the time in the world. May he find ways to make the absolute most of it."

Robert clinked his glass and took another sip. He winced. "This champagne is so dry I think my lips are shriveling up into nothing."

"I can fix that for you." Jo rose and walked toward the hotel lobby, giving the waiter a quick nod on the way out. A bellhop subtly passed her a set of keys without hesitation as if this had been his one job all evening. Along the way to her room she said, "I have a bottle you should try. Bourbon actually. A taste of home for the weary expatriate functionary."

"Sounds perfect."

"It's from Montana. Authentic cowboy whisky buried in the desert. You'll love it."

Robert hid his confusion behind a smile.

Jo and Robert reached the end of the hall. Jo fumbled a moment with the lock, and they entered. The ancient door creaked shut behind them.

Chapter 16 – Accretion

ROBERT LAID THERE, waiting. Without enthusiasm, the gang returned to the basement to deal with the body. Charlie stayed up at the guardhouse to turn away the MPs that still had not arrived. 'Be creative, call it a test or something, I don't care.' Zeke had suggested.

The Ambassador checked his watch. "We only have two hours before the staff starts arriving. Ok, the plan is… the plan is we get him up the stairs and out the door. Kalle and Annika, you came on foot, right? No car? Ok, you can take our car. You take the body to the docks somewhere, borrow a boat and, you know, take him out into the sea somewhere. Then just find something heavy to tie on him, an anchor, you know?"

Kalle and Annika exchanged snickers. "Borrow a boat? Sorry, but no one borrows a boat around here. Everyone uses their own. Taking someone else's boat would attract a lot of attention. The questions we would get coming back ashore would never end. Well, questions or beatings, depending on whose it is."

"Take your own boat then."

"Well, I don't have one. Anyway, driving a dead body around in a car with diplomatic plates seems like a bad idea."

"Well, he can't stay here, Kal. It would be an absolute shitstorm. Not just for me, for all of us. He's gotta go somewhere he won't ever be found, and quickly."

The room fell silent as eyes slowly focused on Kalle. He avoided the stares, looking down at his clothes. His shirt and pants were soiled beyond recovery with a mix of blood and dirt. Dirt… "Mr. Ambassador, do you remember Aanders Järvinen? The voice of the new Finland. Recall where he ended up? I think I have just the *badezimmer* for the task."

.

Breathe two three four, brace two three four, PUSH. Dana had encircled the meaty thighs with her arms. The knees were pinned just under her ears at the base of her skull for leverage. With each PUSH, she tried to lever up and forward to take as much weight off for Emil as possible.

At first, everyone was skittish about touching the dead body again; it was disgusting enough the first time around and now that they had put some distance on the event there was no enthusiasm to relive the experience. But once they had dragged Robert's corpse to the base of the metal spiral staircase, practical matters took over. The stairs looked much steeper once a 200-pound 6' 6" lump of flesh was introduced into the equation. Furthermore, the staircase was so narrow that only one person could possibly fit at a time. Despite being six able-bodied adults, there was no space to employ their combined forces. Two people above pulling one arm each just dug Robert's back into the metal stairs. Two people below trying to lift from the belt jostled into each other and lost purchase for any lifting. After numerous failed configurations, the trio of Dana, Emil, and Kalle stumbled into the workable process that Dana found herself in part way up the stairs. Kalle was positioned above the body, pulling on both armpits. Dana was below with her shoulders in the crook of his knees. Then there was Emil, the lynchpin. Emil sat on the stairs facing downward, with dead Robert sitting in his lap. On the count of four, he would press up with his iron quads and in one swift motion advance uphill by one stair. Breathe, brace, PUSH, repeat.

Zeke, Lani, and Annika promised they would take over whenever they needed a break. But the unspoken agreement from the working trio was that they were in it for the long haul. It was a mindless, exhausting, degrading, and laughable task, but it was their task. After a few stairs, the body was no longer the friendly well-spoken American she had met on the infield just after her gold medal performance. Now it was just a load.

Lost in the rhythm of their slow advance, Dana thought back to the simple question Annika had asked earlier. 'Who on earth would want to build such a thing?' And Gregor's response. 'It will be built because it *can* be built." Decades of scientific refinement and progress. Centuries, millennia of discoveries painstakingly accumulated. Leaps ahead and small contributions alike fanned out in all possible directions in order to later coalesce into fundamental truths. The topography of the physical universe was always there, mostly hidden. Only with meltwater and gravity could the contours become clear. And now, after enough time, they could view the sea.

Unlimited destructive power. Scoop up a bit of the most abundant element in the universe and destroy everything ever known to humankind. It should be an elaborate fiction with the falsehood uncovered in the third act. But Dana knew that this scrap of paper was the truth. Now she knew. Fusion wasn't a dead-end choice. It was the inevitable. This was the sea, and there would be no more speculating or worrying about what the end would be. It was just the way the topography had been all along. The map was written in the hard angular Greek scribbling made by this lump of flesh, this collection of carbon, iron, and zinc. Arranged slowly over years in pattern for no godly purpose, just for the random event of bumping into this group on this day.

A scoop of hydrogen. The celebrity cities would go first, DC, Moscow, London. Gone in a flash, the inhabitants would never even know what happened. The first world would get the VIP treatment, no pain or worry. Another scoop. The far corners of the superpowers and countries guilty by association would be next.

Wyoming, Kamchatka, Canada, Czechoslovakia. Nearby secondary attacks by any remaining bombers would create firestorms, earthquakes, and acute radiation poisoning. These deaths would be slower and more painful, but equally certain. And then the waiting would begin. No remaining bombers, no remaining scientists to scoop any more fuel. Even in Armageddon the third world would get the thick end of the stick. No one would bother to bomb the African plains, but columns of smoke hundreds of miles in diameter would eject the charred microscopic remains of houses, factories, quarterly reports, books, museums, trees, parents, and children from elsewhere high into the stratosphere. A global communion above would decimate crop yields below year after year after year. A dimmer sun, poisonous rain, and poor pH in the fields would slowly freeze and starve the rest of the world. But it would take time, and some would maintain hope… at least for a while. The hope would be the cruelest part.

She watched her husband at work. Brow furrowed, he pressed, slid, and repositioned on repeat without complaint or break. Dana and Kalle did take some weight off, but there was no question that Emil bore the lion's share. The Gadget was ratcheting upward, accomplishing what no one else could possibly do. She pitied him for his excellence. 5000 meters, 10,000 meters, learning languages, making friends, he topped the world in any direction he pointed himself. Even his pies came out perfect the one time he tried. His sheer capability shrouded him from the life of everyone else. He didn't understand the world because he didn't struggle in it. At least it didn't appear that way to her. Tonight, for the first time she saw a break in his manner. His eyes didn't have the usual sparkle she knew so intimately. It wasn't clear when it happened, but it was before finding Robert. It was another thing to discuss in private once they had a chance to be just the two of them again. In the meantime, breathe, brace, PUSH. With legs around her neck, she couldn't look up. Maybe they were halfway, she had lost track.

The gang of six hoisted the body on their shoulders and passed through the kitchen on the way out the back door. They kept the blood off the carpet and saved their backs in the process. The bright morning sun cast long shadows across the garden as the procession shuffled toward the pointless wall. Against the daylight, this rag-tag scene of blood-smeared pallbearers would have been a visual scream to any casual onlookers. But this was summer in Finland. Bright sun like this came out well before 6:00 am, and no one casual was up yet.

Kalle levered open the grate and descended the ladder into the black of the cistern. The loose plan was for the others to lower Robert down while Kalle propped him from below. Kalle had not been expecting him to come in headfirst. In in the limited light below the opening, Kalle tried to bear hug the corpse to steady him, but the body was very heavy and awkward. Above, hands slipped off holds on the belt and pockets. Robert went into a brief freefall, stunning Kalle and knocking him onto the cobbles.

Emil, Dana, and Zeke clambered down with flashlights in hand. Dana led the way to the crawlspace in the side chamber. Dragging was the only option for the body in this dark cramped path. It was slow going over the slimy stone floor. The number of injustices imposed on this body compounded over time.

With a last effort, Robert was lifted up into the crawl space and laid out in as natural a pose as was possible. A bloodied body left untended down here would attract all sorts of bugs and worms. The following months of decay would be rapid and disgusting. Kalle took a few even measured breaths and focused his flashlight on the carving marks in the stones making up the wall. Zeke stayed behind in the crawlspace for a moment while the rest returned to the summer surface.

The four guests stood idly on the front path, waiting for their hosts to see them out. The women wore simple flowered print blouses with overalls while the men struggled in ill-fitting slacks and musty long-sleeved polo shirts. Like a group of country cousins arriving late at the wedding. But at least they were clean. No one wanted to leave the property looking and smelling like a crime scene.

"So, you fly back next week? Do you have to make a connection in Vienna or something, or is it a straight shot to Prague?" Kalle asked.

"It's chartered. So, straight shot." Emil responded a little flatter than usual.

"Mmmm." Kalle nodded in understanding. "So, are you going to give the marathon a go after all?"

"Not sure. We'll see I guess."

"Yeah."

Annika looked west along the tree line, waiting for the sound of footsteps from the house. Her wish was soon granted.

The Ambassador burst through the front door with Lani at his side. "My apologies, I'd rather offer you at least some coffee and toast on your way out. But the staff… you know." He looked at his watch. "Anyway, shall we?"

At the front gate, Charlie gave raised eyebrows and a half smile as a good-bye. According to the logs, they had all signed out around midnight.

Before Zeke could launch into a parting speech, Annika said, "Thanks for the change of clothes. We'll be sure to get these back to you."

"Oh, no trouble at all. Please don't worry about bringing them back. It helps reduce our luggage. It was a pleasure meeting you and I hope to bump into you again before we head back in January. Perhaps drinks in town with you and Kalle. Something a bit less dramatic, let's say?" He turned to Emil and Dana and shook hands vigorously. "Think about what I said earlier, Emil. Don't hesitate to call if you need anything. I mean it. In the meantime, best of luck to you both. The sky is the limit, as they say."

With that, the four guests walked downhill toward the water and the main road. The couples paused at the junction with another round of good-byes, handshakes, and shoulder pats.

Before splitting, Kalle squared up with Dana and said, "Our first murder case, solved and cleared up in just a few hours. Not bad for a couple of rookies, eh?"

"I guess so." After a moment, Dana raised her eyes up to meet his. "Take care of yourself."

.

Kalle and Annika walked along the esplanade, each lost in their own thoughts. The row of bars and restaurants stood in silence, taking a breather. They passed the terrace where the Gold Rush Four had met just hours before, the blue and yellow awning fully retracted overnight. An old lady hosed down the alleyway, arcing the stream back and forth to coax the grime toward the street where it would no longer be her problem.

"We gifted the world a brief peace." Kalle said out of nowhere.

"Sorry?"

"That's what he said. The Ambassador. He said we gifted the world a brief peace tonight. Do you believe it?"

"I don't know. I'm just tired, Kalle."

"Yeah. I mean, if true it's better than finding gold anyway. Speaking of that, I think it's best if we don't talk about any of this to Henrik or Vaino. Don't you think?"

"Kalle, I would be fine never talking about this to anyone, ever."

"Yes, of course. Right."

Kalle and Annika continued walking northeast to face the gauzy insignificance of day-to-day life at the export and trade office and the idle happy hour chatter with people they barely knew.

Dana and Emil walked northwest along the coastline to embark on the changed life reserved for Eastern Bloc gold medalists; days filled with ceremonial meetings and PR events accompanied by the cheers of adoring fans echoing off of the iron curtain.

Dana was straining to tell Emil her parts of the story, but he was withdrawn on their walk back up to their boat. Most of the town was still rousing itself, so the traffic was light. But there was a buzz of activity along the dock by the market. Boats teeming with herring and cod were already being unloaded and fishmongers at the stalls were sorting and packing the catch on ice to keep for the full day ahead.

Their skiff was easy to spot along the pier. The slender boat was dangling two-thirds out of the water, the fore mooring line taut to the bollard. Nearly vertical, the boat twisted haphazardly like a fish on a line. The ebb tide had claimed another greenhorn vessel. Emil went to the bollard, trying to undo a loop, but the line wouldn't budge.

An old woman shouted out to them from the shore. Her voice carried the incomprehensible Finnish syllables they had become accustomed to in the past week. Emil and Dana shook their heads in response. The woman tried again by swinging her arms in an exaggerated digging or swimming motion. It was even less helpful than the Finnish. The Czechs raised their hands in defeat. The woman was not so easily deterred. She marched her way out to the pier, muttering the whole way. Brushing Emil aside, she grabbed the mooring line, hooked one foot around a piling, and pitched herself off the pier. She slid headfirst down the line to the boat and quickly detached the thimble eye clip. She clambered back up to the pier, brushed off their thanks in Czech and English, and marched away.

The skiff now liberated; they pulled it to a lower section of the pier. Dana boarded first and took the seat with the oars. Emil made no objection.

A stiff breeze had picked up, creating some chop on the water on the way back to Otaniemi. More nuisance than anything. Dana decided to take the long route and set a course out into the open sea. There was no hurry back to the barbed wire camp and the sharp eyes and the schedules and the speeches.

Emil was still lost in his thoughts. It was just as well, as Dana gave herself up to the rhythm of the oars. She planted her feet and let her body sort through the trial-and-error search for efficiency. Nothing was rushed but everything was fast. Above the eastern horizon the sun glinted off the multitude of miniature peaked waves. She rowed her way through a field of diamonds. Right now, she was the captain of the Czech navy. Right now, she controlled the speed, the heading, everything. Right now, she flew.

·

Ezekiel Williamson stood in the reception area on the business side of the Embassy. He made sure to greet the staff as they came in by twos and threes. He attempted to tune his chatter to the same level of friendliness as usual. But it was impossible to know for sure. One colleague asked about Robert. Without hesitation, the Ambassador shrugged that he hadn't seen him yet today. This part of the plan would need a bit of work, but at least for the first few days, ignorance was the name of the game. Who knows what Rob's gotten himself up to after all? No idea! Look at all the work he's saddled the rest of us with. Part of his plan, no doubt. Ha ha. In any case, the Puzzle Palace in Virginia would send instructions eventually. Until then, he would just play dumb. The role he was born to play. Ha ha.

His welcoming duties complete, Zeke made his way back to the office. Lani was inside, sitting in one of the chairs. He flopped down next to her and sighed. "What a night. I hate to say it, but I think we're getting too old for this."

"*You're* getting too old for this. Your retirement can't come too soon. Then we can start going to bed together at a reasonable hour."

"That sounds fine by me." Zeke looked around the office absently for a while before changing the subject. "I really screwed the pooch with the Emil thing tonight."

"Not really your fault, though. He simply didn't go for it. Any idea why not?"

"They haven't beaten all of the optimism out of him yet. He thinks he can turn things around there at home. You can't really blame him, though. After the week he's had, he probably feels like he can do anything. I should have approached the girl instead."

"The girl. You mean his wife? The *woman* who won a gold medal and nearly put you in a corner tonight with her sleuthing?" Lani chided.

"Yes yes. His wife. She's the more pragmatic of the two. It could have worked if I started with her. Appealed to her wisdom or woman's intuition or whatever you call it these days. But it was a complicated night, all said and done. Getting all the pieces to fit just right would have been a miracle."

"Charlie held up well though, don't you think?"

Zeke chuckled. "Yeah. For a moment I thought he might actually go off and ring the MPs to come storming in. Can you imagine the scene that would have been? The paperwork? Yeesh. I had a good chat with him beforehand, about letting Augie … whoops I mean 'Gregor' pass and all that. But you never know for sure with those youngsters when they have to think on their feet. He's a good kid."

Lani let the silence build for a moment as the corners of her mouth flattened down. She leaned toward Zeke and said, "I'm very sorry about Robert. I truly am. I know you liked him. People grow on you quickly, and vice versa. There's nothing wrong with that. I just… want you to know that I know it feels horrible right now."

Zeke let out a breath and rubbed his forehead. "Thank you. I tried to find a way to help him, but he was already lost by the time he set foot here in Finland. Too clever for his own good, I suppose. We were left with no other choice."

The side table next to Lani still held three glasses, two of which were still full. She had also brought over a picture frame. Harry, Zeke, and Augie. She picked up the frame and smiled. "Look at that. You were all so young and handsome. And so full of … I don't know … confidence, I guess. You three were world-beaters out to make your mark."

"Hmmm. And look at us now."

"Exactly my point." She laid the frame down in her lap and leaned closer to Zeke. "It was good to see Augie again. He hasn't changed a bit. It was good to see you with him again. Two peas in a pod, reading each other's minds as you made up those scenes on the fly."

"I have to admit, Augie was in rare form tonight. I was just along for the ride. We didn't plan to do so much improvisation. But he was always the consummate thespian, never missing a beat even under pressure." Zeke snorted a quick laugh. He continued in an indecipherable accent. "'At least with Americans you know what you get. Assholes.' My god. What a performance. And you weren't so bad yourself, dear." Zeke paused for a moment, absently rubbing his knuckles. "I do hate mixing Augie up in this miserable business. It's too much to ask of a friend."

"Oh, this isn't his first rodeo. Besides, I think a friend is exactly who you ask for in these things. Anyways… after this, you deserve a few days of R and R. Let's get away."

"Not on your life. There's more to do than ever, even as a short timer. And I'll have suspicions to tamp down for while I suppose."

"Suit yourself old man." Lani reached for the two full glasses of bourbon and passed one over. "We'll settle for a whiskey breakfast. To Augie."

"Augie… and Rob."

They clanked glasses and let the sweet, fiery, woody liquid drain down their dry throats. After setting the tumblers down, only a thin sheen remained on the glass walls, coalescing into narrow rivulets on the way to the bottom.

The couple walked back through the hallway.

"Which one did you get?" Zeke jerked his thumb back towards the office.

"Me? The crushed aspirin, I think. A little on the gritty side. Not too bad though. You?"

"Nothing but pure delicious bourbon."

"Lucky."

"Every day with you, babe. I guess that means Augie was stuck with the berries. Bleh, that must have been nice and sour. Ha!" Zeke's bark was coming back to him.

"Now that you mention berries. *Pupula* berries? What on earth are those? How deep into your twisted mind did you go to invent that nonsense?"

"I got that one from your mother. Years ago. She told me about them in one of her long boring stories of back in the day on the island."

"That's *popolo* berries you numbskull. And no, her stories are not boring or long. You're thinking of your own back in the day stories."

"Let's agree to disagree on that. Popolo… yeah that sounds right now that you mention it. Oh well, close enough. And what about you? Neurotoxins? Nowhere else but the Amazon? That was a nice touch. I had to cover my mouth on that one. Where did that come from?"

"I read."

"You read?"

"I do. More than you, professor."

"You're setting the bar quite low for yourself there."

"That's the story of my life."

"Ouch."

Epilogue – Winsome Cripps

May 7, 1984 – Melbourne
ABC Television, Aussie Today 7/5/84 0830, target-only transcript:

Are you sure I can't interest you in some more? Well, let me know, you can always change your mind with me. Are we ready to, oh its already rolling? Fine. I understand you came here to talk about Helsinki? Well, that was a while ago, and I don't really remember it all that well. I can't imagine how interesting I would be for your viewers.

Yes, well with the build up to Los Angeles…

Yes, yes, all very exciting.

Well, I have a fondness for my time in Helsinki. I mean, just taking the plane to get there was a new adventure for me. I had never been on a plane, had never travelled outside of the country. Back then it wasn't a common thing to do, you see. We were all so young.

Margie, Shirley, and I were inseparable on that trip. We arrived early; I remember. We had a few days to train on the surface and also do some sightseeing with the delegation. A beautiful town, wonderful people. The weather was gorgeous, and everyone was full of energy. I guess the summer is pretty short up there so everyone makes the best of it before everything goes drab and cold.

I recall that we attracted quite a bit of attention from the boys! Yes, well Margie was the leader of the pack, as she always is you know. She said that I was the bait, and she was the hook. My hair was blonder then, so she said she would use me to draw boys in. Local boys, UK press boys, those fencers from France, was it? Whoever. Winnie the Bait, she'd say. Ha! Anyway, once they were within shouting distance, Margie would take over with her charm and that motor mouth. Her crazy nest of brown hair and the wide smile. It was really something to watch. We got into all kinds of trouble. All kinds. Margie even started a huge fight that almost tore down a dance hall. [inaudible] No, I'm not joking! I had to pull her out before she sprained an ankle or something. Don't use that part though, ok? We laughed so hard. All harmless fun. Margie and I were 21 then, so you know how it is. You must be about that age yourself? [inaudible, laughter]

The opening ceremonies? I don't really recall. I remember mud. They issued us fancy new white shoes for the parade uniform. That was a bit of a cock-up of course. Can I say that? Oh, I don't care anyway. A cock-up. Yes, I remember a lot of standing and a lot of mud. That's it. I was getting nervous by that point. We had the 100 heats just two days later and that was all I was thinking about. Margie though, she was joking around as if it was another weekend out. She always had so much confidence, I never understood… She never said it of course but you had the impression that she had already won the gold, and we were just waiting for the gun to go off to make it official.

And she proved it too, of course. In the 100 heats she was untouchable. I was 12.0 with a bunch of other girls. In fact, I was very close to missing the final because so many of us were bunched up at 12.0. But Margie was yards in front of everyone. Did she set a world record in the heats? She did, didn't she?

The final was quite something. So many people were in the stands. Margie was lined up just to my left in the block. From the gun I just watched as she floated away from me. All I remember is her shoulders just pulling away from the rest of us and then seeing the soles of her feet blinking at me. Left right left right. Shirley and

I came across together. I was so happy for her. She got the bronze and really deserved it. I was proud of my fourth place. I still am.

I was always better in the 200 meters, because my lousy starts didn't matter so much. Margie told me she thought I would win gold. Of course she was full of malarkey, because she was so fast right then it was obvious that it would be really just a race for silver. But I took her to mean I could win silver, and I was grateful to her for saying that.

In the meantime, Shirley won the hurdles, and we were screaming our heads off in the stands watching. The press was starting to come in asking for interviews and photos of the three of us at this point. There was a lot of hoopla, at least from my experience at the time. Nothing like it is today, of course. All I had to show at that point was a fourth place, but the photographers liked the three of us together: Margie, Shirley, and Winnie. Called us the holy trinity or some rubbish like that. You know how the press is – no offence.

I had a bad draw for the first heat of the 200. I remember that clearly. That South African girl who got silver in the 100 and the American who was also in the 100 final. Both in my first heat. We were nearly the last heat to run, and I noticed most of the times were 25 low which made me feel better. I could do 25 low in practice with a stiff wind. In any case, I made it through qualifying ok and started to feel like I was going to hold up my end of the bargain for the trinity, you know?

The 200 final was a bit of a blur. I had an outside lane, which always put me off. I liked to be the hunter you see, to know that the curve was my advantage, and I would pull them all in. Instead, with my bad start as usual I could hear the footsteps coming right away. The sound of being chased. Ugh.

Of course, Margie won, but then three of us leaned together at the line in a tie for second. I could feel the Russian girl next to me lean, but I didn't feel her jersey was in front of me at all. Well, some official lined us up right after and just put me fourth in line while they waited for that fancy finish photo to develop. Yes, back then you had to wait for it to develop with the chemicals and all that. What a bother. I wanted to go hug Margie and congratulate her, but we stood like horses in our line. I remember watching the head judge when the photo finally came out. I couldn't hear him talking to the other officials, but I saw him literally shrug his shoulders! You know that French pout and shrug? Yes, exactly! The final result just happened to be the order we were standing in. No one will admit it, but I believe that it was the random placement after the race by a race volunteer that determined silver, bronze, and nothing for the 200. You know, why mess with the order everyone already sees in front of their eyes? Don't stir the pot. Bah!

But enough of the 200, I bet you really want to talk about the relay, don't you? No, don't be shy about it. I'm happy to do it.

There was one race left for us. The 4x1. At this point, we were the favorites. The Russians looked pretty good and the Americans too. But they didn't have Margie. She was our secret weapon. Well, not a secret of course. She was our weapon. I would always run third leg and Margie would anchor. I knew if I gave her the baton anywhere near the lead, it was over.

The qualifying heat was a blast. Shirley got a great start and Verna did well to keep the lead in the second leg. Everything was clockwork. We had done nothing but practice exchanges the day before. We cruised around the track. Not only did we win the heat, we set a world record. It was really exciting! I think Shirley and Margie were happier for me than anything. We stood ten feet tall. We owned the stadium on that last day. No girls in the world have ever been faster. Ever.

Then the finals came. There wasn't much rest after the heats. Maybe an hour and a half at most? Well, no matter, we were ready. Holding that baton together before the race, I'll never forget that. We looked at each other and knew this was ours to take. Being third leg, I had a full jog across the infield to get into position. My legs were snapping across the grass. I remember the feeling, like I was spring loaded, you know? I even thought to myself, this must be how Margie feels all the time! Full energy, focused into one fiery ball.

Everything went right in that race. I mean everything. Until… I don't know. I got the baton in first and I extended the lead. We had planned beforehand that if we had a clear lead, Margie would hesitate a half-stride on her break into the exchange. We didn't want her to sprint away from me in all the excitement and make any mistakes. Of course, instead I barreled up on her right away. I can see it even now in slow motion. Despite how quickly I caught up with her, I somehow got the baton into her hands. But she pumped her arm back as she accelerated and slammed into my knee. Or, really, my knee slammed into her. The baton just shot right out of her hand…

The Americans. They won, and they re-broke the world record. Our record. Margie found the baton and tried to recover, but there wasn't enough space. We were fifth.

I came home with two fourths and a fifth. And I had been a world record holder for 90 minutes.

What's that? Oh, I won't lie. There were some tears shed that evening. It was a tough, tough way to end the trip. I think what got me through that disappointment on the flight back was the thought that we would host the Olympics in four years. Margie and I would still only be 25. We would be in our prime! We had all the time in the world to get me on the podium. That's how Margie said it: 'Get the Bait up there on that podium!' Yes, fond memories. It really was the time of our lives. Time has a funny way of honing down sharp edges. I said to you earlier that I don't really remember it all that well. As you can see that's not really the case. I remember everything.

Any regrets? Oh, no. Well… Well, it probably helped at the time to think about Melbourne in 1956 as a second chance. But of course, I didn't know there was a little fourteen-year-old girl by the name of Betty Cuthbert out there who would take Australian track and field by storm. I got faster, but my prime was just not good enough to make the team in Melbourne. I was a 1952 athlete competing in a 1956 world. What I guess I mean to say is, back then I didn't know my abilities were really only of my time. If someone on the streets of Helsinki had walked right up and told me that 1952 was it for me, that was my only window of opportunity, maybe I would have focused more. A lean at the finish, a lower knee in the relay, fewer nights out destroying dance halls. A million little things. Maybe. But I like to think I would have just laughed in their face and shot back that I was indestructible, I owned that stadium, and that the best was yet to come.

ABOUT THE AUTHOR

Nathan Hebel grew up in Indiana watching the likes of Edwin Moses and Mary Decker circling the track, feeding his early fascination with the Olympics. He received degrees from The Johns Hopkins University and Cornell University, sadly not in creative writing. His understanding of elite athletic performance comes from personal experience (gold in the 1996 Plastic Disc/Foam Football Decathlon in Gaithersburg, Maryland and silver in the 2001 Donut Run 5k in Ames, Iowa). He now lives in Montreal with his family. *Helsinki Gold* is his first novel.

Printed in Great Britain
by Amazon